Su of

Seventeen

Jane Harvey-Berrick

HARVEY
BERRICK
PUBLISHING

First published in Great Britain in 2014
ISBN 9780992924614

Harvey Berrick Publishing

Copyright © Jane A. C. Harvey-Berrick 2014

Cover design by Nicky Stott
Cover model: Harry Llewelyn
Cover photograph by Sophie Callahan Photography
Additional model: Rob MacGregor

Summer of Seventeen

Jane Harvey-Berrick

DEDICATION

To Mark, Steve, Rob, Anoki and Delano—the guys from Stones Reef Surf Shop and really nice people, despite having to beat off women with sticks. And Wanda, their den mother.

To Ana Alfaro from Panama, who would be happy that her name has been taken in vain, but moved on to the next great adventure before this story could be finished. RIP.

ACKNOWLEDGEMENTS
AND HUGE THANKS

To Kirsten Olsen, editor, Beta reader, de-Britisher, friend, partner-in-(imagined)-crime, whose patience in talking me down from the ledge knows no bounds.

To Nate Tria, my 16-year-old Beta reader. Does your mom know you read this?!

To Trina Marie for being the smile in our team, the gal who knows all the hot gossip, and hotter male models, the go-to gal for just about everything.

To Aime MetznerG for all things Panamanian and for helping me with the colloquial Spanish.

To Ena Burnette for her support and marketing expertise.

To Sheena Lumsden, for being a PA without pay, friend and staunch support through thick and thin.

To Hang Le for her stunning cover work and never-ending creativity. And she's just so lovely.

Audrey Thunder, Dorota Wrobel, Dina Eidinger, Bella Bookaholic (Mary Rose Bergundo), Lelyana Taufik for never-failing support.

For photos of hot cowboys and for legal advice, Tonya Bass Allen.

To Rosie and Steve, owners of the real Sandbar (although not in Cocoa Beach).

For lovely messages that make me smile, Ana Kristina Rabacca, Marie Mason, Clare Norton, Abril Lerma and Dano, Jenny Angell, Celia Ottway, Lisa Ashmore, Lisa Matheson Sylva, Gitte Doherty and Jenny Aspinall.

A. Meredith Walters, Roger Hurn, Monica Robinson, Devon Hartford, Gillian Griffin, Sawyer Bennett, Kirsty Moseley, LH Cosworth, Kirsty-Ann Still, Bethan Cooper, Penny Reid, Karina Halle and the wonderful Ker Dukey, friends who share the writer's lonely path!

The Stalking Angels: Sheena, Aud, Dina, Bella, Shirley Wilkinson, Cori Pitts, Dorota Wróbel, Barbara Murray, Emma Darch-Harris, Sophie Callahan, Kandace Milostan, Kelsey Burns, Lelyana Taufik, MJ Fryer, Hang (MJ), Gwen Jacobs, Kirsten Papi, Trina, Sarah Bookhooked, Sasha Cameron, Rosarita Reader, Jacqueline Showdog, Remy Grey, Ashley Snaith, Kandace Lovesbooks, Jo Webb, Ky-Bree Loves-Books, Jen Berg, Carol Sales, Meagan Burgad, Andrea Lopez, Paola Cortes, Kelly O'Connor, Gabri Canova, Whairigail Adam, Julie Redpath, Jade Donaldson, Sharon Mills.

The Red Red Red Devotees—who were there from the start.

Other Titles by Jane Harvey-Berrick

Series
An epic love story spanning the years, through war zones

The Education of Sebastian (Education series #1)
The Education of Caroline (Education series #2)
The Education of Sebastian & Caroline (combined edition, books 1 & 2)
Semper Fi: The Education of Caroline (Education series #3)

All the fun of the fair … and two worlds collide

The Traveling Man (Traveling series #1)
The Traveling Woman (Traveling series #2)
Roustabout (Traveling series #3)
The Traveling Series (Boxed Set)

Blood, sweat, tears and dance

Slave to the Rhythm (Rhythm series #1)
Luka (Rhythm series #2)

Standalone Titles
Dangerous to Know & Love
Lifers
At Your Beck & Call
Dazzled
Summer of Seventeen
The New Samurai
Exposure
The Dark Detective
Playing in the Rain (*novella*)
Behind the Wall (*novella*)

Audio Books
One Careful Owner

www.janeharveyberrick.com

"How would you like to stand like a god before the crest of a monster billow, always rushing to the bottom of a hill and never reaching its base, and to come rushing in for a half a mile at express speed, in graceful attitude, of course, until you reach the beach and step easily from the wave to the strand?"

Duke Kahanamoku (1890-1968)
Hawaiian surfer

 Prologue

You know that experiment we all have to do in sixth grade? The one where you put a drop of black ink on wet blotting paper and the colors all separate out? What if it's the other way around, where black soaks up every color and holds them hostage? Like today.

My shoes are black and my pants are black and it's so weird. But even among the sea of black, there are colors. My hand is golden-brown, tan from the first days of summer. My fingers are white and they're beginning to tingle.

It's strange. Shouldn't they be numb? Shouldn't I be *not* feeling?

Then I realize it's because Yansi is holding my hand so tight she's cutting off the blood. Her hand is darker than mine: brown, like rain-forest wood.

Her palms are soft. Not like mine. Mine are rough, calloused. I don't know if it's from the sand, or the elective I did in shop this semester.

The cuffs of my shirt are white.

And then a bald guy I've never seen before shakes my hand.

"Sorry for your loss," he says.

Chapter 1

Everything and everyone pissed me off: school, my sister, my friends. Even my mom made me angry, and she was dead.

I was all twisted up inside, like if I had to feel one more emotion or think one more thought, my head would explode.

I was looking for something.

Julia was waiting for me when I got home from school. That's when she dropped a bomb.

"I've put an ad on Craigslist. We're renting out the den."

We'd never called it 'the den' before. It had been mom's room.

"We are?"

"Don't start," she said.

"Start what? I'm asking: since when are *we* renting out the den."

"Since *we* need the money."

I probably sounded like a whiny bitch and looked like a deer caught in headlights, but to say that I was shocked is a huge fucking understatement. I had no clue she was thinking of doing that—the whole idea came out of left field.

She was always moaning about money, how much things cost. Did I know how much a gallon of milk cost? I guess I was supposed to think about things like that now. I guess it meant we were poor.

Maybe my sister figured with people arriving in town looking for summer jobs, she could find someone to rent the den quickly.

I decided I was over this conversation and headed to my bedroom—assuming it was still mine and she wasn't going to rent that out, too—and I looked up the listing.

*Seeking professional working male
or female roommate
$590 a month, utilities included.
Cocoa Beach, FL.*

Not $600, but $590. Like it was going to look way cheaper if you shaved off ten bucks. Do people still fall for shit like that? Like you go into a store and see something for five bucks and think, *Oh this is way too much*, but then the clerk says, *Oh that's not $5.00 it's only $4.99*, and all of the sudden it's so much more affordable.

Yeah, I don't think so.

We could buy three gallons of milk with that ten bucks. I checked.

I wasn't happy, but it wasn't like she listened to me anyway.

Julia was probably hoping for a long-term rental but I was pretty sure she'd take what she could get. I didn't care, I just didn't want some douche.

That was yesterday. Today, it was officially the start of summer break and vacationers were flooding into town ready to spend their money. I'd been looking forward to it. *Had been.*

I heard the front door slam and knew that she'd gone out. She hadn't spoken to me again, although last night I'd heard her yelling about me to her boyfriend Ben. Maybe she went grocery shopping. Maybe she couldn't stand looking at me anymore. She said that one time. Because I had blond hair and blue eyes and I looked like Mom. And Julia had brown hair and brown eyes and she looked like her dad. Not my dad. Nobody knew what he looked like. Except Mom, I guess.

Julia had sold a load of our stuff—Mom's stuff— because she said we needed the money. I hid my iPod just in case she decided to go completely crazy, and I still had my Tony Hawk Huckjam 401 skateboard which was pretty cool and cost nearly a hundred bucks. It was a good one, not great, not like a Plan B for pro skaters, but it wasn't a twenty dollar piece of shit with Moshi Monsters on it either.

I hadn't ridden it since Mom was sick in the hospital, and it was wedged under my bed behind a stack of porn mags that Sean had given me. I think he got them from one of his brothers. I felt weird about putting them out for recycling and, you know, I might want to look at them again.

I wasn't worried about Julia finding them, but I'm glad Mom never did. Anyway, Julia didn't go in my room because she said it was a health hazard and she didn't want to catch the Ebola virus. Every now and then she yelled at me to bring down the dirty dishes that seemed to stack up in there. You'd think Armageddon was around the corner if the dishes weren't washed. But I'd learned to put my laundry in the hamper or I would never have anything clean to wear.

Julia didn't iron, so my clothes were wrinkled most of the time. Although she made an exception for Mom's funeral, even though she was crying all over my shirt while she did it. I don't know, maybe ironing made her cry. That's a joke.

But right now my Tony Hawk was stuck tight, and I didn't want to pull too hard in case I bent the truck or chipped the deck. So I was up to my armpits in dust bunnies, trying to work around the crap that had congealed under my bed, when the phone rang.

Only official people called on that line, like the School Board or the hospital, so it was really weird to hear it ring now. My friends called my cell, and Julia didn't have friends, only Ben. I don't know if he called her, but he'd just show up most evenings.

Mom always hated the way I answered the phone; she'd yell at me to be polite. But Mom was dead, so I just picked up the phone and said, "Yeah?"

"Hi. You the guy with a room to rent? I saw it on Craigslist."

Wow, that was quick.

"Yeah, I guess."

"Okay, cool. Can I come by later and see the room? Is it furnished or unfurnished? The listing didn't say."

I knew there was a sofa in the den, but if this guy wanted to rent the space, he'd probably want a bed, right? So I didn't know whether to tell him that the room was furnished or not.

"I don't really know. My sister placed the ad. She'll be back about six."

"Okay, thanks man. What's the address?"

Our neighborhood was okay. Quiet, boring. Ours was the smallest house on a street that realtors described as a cul-de-sac of sixties cottages. But anyone else would call it a dead-end, where our house was definitely the most rundown.

I think we were the only ones without a pool, but I didn't need one because it was only a three minute skate to the ocean, and you don't have to pay a pool guy.

So I rattled off the address and then went back upstairs to dig out my Tony Hawk. I forgot about the guy. Or maybe I didn't want to remember him, because my stomach got tight at the thought of a stranger sleeping in our den. Because Mom used to sit there to watch her soaps. Because it was her bedroom at night. Because neither me or Julia ever went in there now.

Anyway, he said he was coming over later, so I didn't need to think about it at all.

It would take me just over ten minutes to skate the two miles to the pier. All the high school kids who surfed hung out there—it was kind of our place. It was chill, pretty much like school. Maybe that's because of all the stoners. Even when the school floods, which it does a lot in hurricane season, there's no drama. A lot of grads stay home and go to the community college, so it's no surprise when they party with guys who are still in high school.

The pier picked up a good swell, and had mellow rideable waves, especially with an offshore breeze. It was kind of annoying because we all know that if it's good in Cocoa Beach, it's smokin' somewhere else. But at least I didn't have to bum a ride to get to the waves. Surfing was a huge part of my life. I was a goofy foot, but I'd taught myself to ride natural too, because I thought it was cool to do both. And it was useful for skateboarding.

Lately, only the paddleboarders were seeing any action because it had been flat for over a week now.

I thought Sean and Rob might be down at the pier, even though it was where all the tourists went. We didn't go on the pier as much as under it. In fact the last time I'd walked to the fishing hut end was over a year ago. I'd taken a date, but Erin was real picky and didn't want to walk on the sand because she was wearing some stupid, strappy sandals with high heels. To the beach. Yeah, she was pretty, but not all that smart, I guess. She didn't even wear those round-toed flat shoes that girls have when they're not wearing flip-flops. And I could tell that her feet were killing her at the lame party we went to after the beach.

I didn't ask her out again, but she still hung around by my locker forever, just staring at me. It got a bit creepy after a while. She backed off when I started dating Yansi.

That sounds bad. I mean it wasn't the reason I started dating her. She'd transferred in towards the end of our Sophomore year and all the guys thought she was hot. She had thick brown hair that hung in ripples to her waist, and eyes that were so dark and deep they seemed black.

She had a banging body too, but it was her sass that made her different. Most girls would get all dumb and giggly when you talked to them, but Yansi didn't take shit from anyone and nobody dared talk trash to her. I think some of the guys were kind of afraid of her.

I asked her out right away, but she said her dad wouldn't let her date until she was 17, so I had to wait until halfway through Junior year. But it was worth it. We'd started going out nearly four months ago and it never got old. Her dad was still pretty strict and he wasn't real happy about her dating an Anglo who wasn't even a Catholic, but he hadn't told her no either.

Today, she was babysitting her brother and little sisters, and since I wasn't allowed to be alone in the house with her, I wouldn't be able to see her until tomorrow, which sucked. So instead of spending the first day of summer vacation with my girlfriend, I'd celebrated by sleeping till lunchtime, then lounging around my house.

I skated down to the pier, feeling the faint breeze that always tasted of salt, and made sunglasses hazy. The air was growing heavy as the temperature hit the low nineties, the humidity making my t-shirt cling to my chest. I ripped it off and stuck it into the back of my boardshorts, still weaving slowly down Ocean Boulevard, avoiding potholes in the road and tourists who didn't seem to know the difference between a street and a sidewalk.

I wondered if it was worth asking 'Oh Shucks' again if they were hiring. It was a seafood place where all the tourists went, and I'd heard that tips were really good. I should have been bussing tables there this summer, but I hadn't returned their calls when Mom was sick so they'd given the job to someone else. Maybe they'd change their minds, or maybe I could hit up a couple of surf and skate shops in town to see if they were hiring.

Some of the kids in my class hated living in a small town. Everyone worried what would happen now that the Shuttle program had ended and people lost their jobs.

NASA said that it was still the Space Coast, but I knew guys where both parents worked at the visitor center, and the fear that it would close was like a shadow that followed them around. A lot of kids in school talked about going to live in Orlando or NYC one day. Not me. I liked it here. I didn't want to imagine living somewhere I couldn't see the ocean.

Some of last year's seniors were hanging out when I walked down to the shore. They were all surfers so they nodded at me, but there was no sign of Sean or Rob. I stayed for a while, listening to them bitch about the high pressure system that was sitting over us like swamp gas, sucking the life out of the ocean, reducing it to a glassy pond. Low pressure means good waves, but all the tourist shops like high pressure, because that means sunshine.

My cell buzzed with a message, and I smiled when I saw what Yansi had written.

> * Four hours of Doc McStuffins and Peppa freakin Pig.
> My brain will never be the same. Miss you.
> Want to come for supper? We're having Sancocho x *

Yansi's house was so different from mine. It always smelled of cooking, and was full of color and noise. Her brother, Mateo, was 10 and happy if you played catch with him. Her little sisters Pilau and Beatriz were kind of annoying, but cute as hell, following me around and chatting away in Spanish. I'd gotten an A in every Spanish test since I'd started dating Yansi. Her parents could speak English, although her mom not as well, but in their home it was always Spanish.

Mr. Alfaro had a weird Tom Selleck mustache, but he was quiet and reserved, and what he said was law. I didn't know people lived like that anymore. Mom had guy friends sometimes, but none of them lived with us or told us what to do. I could see that it bugged Yansi, and sometimes she said she felt like she was more American than Panamanian, even though she hadn't been born here.

I liked it there because it was different and because they always fed me, but it was hard to be around Yansi and not be able to touch her. I think I'd have ended up face down in Banana River if I'd tried and Mr. Alfaro saw me. Well, maybe not, but I was allowed inside their house for now and I didn't want to fuck that up.

She complained about not having any privacy and having to share a room with her sisters. They caught us once and told their mom. We weren't really doing anything, just kissing, but after that Yansi got hit with the rule about not having me in the house without her parents being there. There was no way we could sneak around without the kids knowing, and I didn't want Mr. Alfaro telling Yansi that she couldn't see me at all. Sometimes she managed to come over to my house by saying that she was studying at the library. Those were the only times I ever cleaned up my room. I didn't want her to think I was a pig. Somehow when she was there, I could forget everything. She had a way of making it okay.

Sean was always asking me if we'd done it yet, and the truth was that we hadn't. I was ready. I was *so* ready, but Yansi wasn't. I could wait. I hoped. But it was none of Sean's business, and he only kept on asking because I wouldn't tell him anything and because he knew it pissed me off.

Sean liked to talk shit about girls, but I think that's because he didn't have any sisters. He wasn't really into dating, just hooking up. It was one of the reasons he was always bitching about me seeing Yansi, saying that we acted like an old married couple. I think he was kind of jealous because she was so hot and really smart.

I headed home by way of 'Oh Shucks' just in case. The manager looked embarrassed and apologized, but said they didn't have any jobs. I tried 'Ron Jons' too, but they'd already taken on all the summer help they needed.

I stopped by a couple of other places on the way home, but they all said the same thing. I even looked at the ads posted on the community board at Publix. But it was just people looking for nannies and babysitters. It was easier for girls—they could always get jobs looking after kids or walking dogs. I wouldn't have minded doing that, pet sitting or whatever. I liked dogs, but adults thought girls were more responsible or something.

I was batting zero when it came to earning any money this summer. I would have liked just being a beach bum, but there was no way Julia would give me anything, not that I'd ask anyway, and I hated being broke.

I took a quick shower when I got home, but I'd left my wet towel in my bedroom a couple of days ago and it smelled rank, so I borrowed Julia's. She wouldn't mind. So long as she didn't know.

Then I heard her yelling my name.

Busted.

"Nicky!"

The whole neighborhood could have heard her. Seismometers probably measured something on the Richter scale. If they ever needed a Godzilla at Disney World, she could nail it. Probably wouldn't need a costume either.

"WHAT?" I yelled back, because I knew that would annoy her. If she wanted to treat me like a kid, that's what she was going to get.

"Get down here!"

Yeah, not happening. She only wanted to yell at me some more. I took my time getting dressed, hoping that if I was slow enough she'd change her mind about wanting to see me. That worked sometimes.

I could hear the low rumble of voices from the den, which probably meant that the dude had arrived to see the room. I could tell that Julia was being all nicey-nice, like she was a princess or something. She wasn't a princess—

she screamed when Ben was fucking her, words that I didn't know she knew.

I walked downstairs slowly and watched her while I leaned against the doorjamb. I never used to notice stuff before. Now I noticed everything, even when it made no sense.

I've been like that since Mom died. I don't know how to describe it—it was kinda like I was looking for the clue, the sign that would tell me, *this person is going to die on Tuesday*. Like Mom. Shouldn't I have known? Shouldn't there have been some sign the day before, something that told us to say everything we needed to say? To say goodbye?

But it doesn't work like that.

Right now Julia had this super sweet smile on her face that made me want to hurl, and she kept tucking her hair behind her ear and twirling it like Zoe Ward did in eighth grade when she wanted me to notice her.

Then Julia saw me.

"Why didn't you tell me that we had someone coming over to see the room?"

"You weren't here."

Her eyes narrowed and her lips got all thin. "You couldn't leave a note?" she asked, her voice rising too sharply.

That made me hide a smile because I could tell she wanted to yell some more but not in front of the guy.

"This is Nicky," Julia said to him, rolling her eyes in that chick way.

"Nick," I said, and pushed my hands in my pockets.

The guy looked at me, like really looked at me, and then held out his hand.

"Hi, I'm Marcus. We spoke on the phone. How you doin', man?"

"Yeah, okay."

I shook his hand. Julia was smiling again now and totally eye-fucking him. He was a lot like the kind of guys she used to have pictures of on her bedroom wall before she started dating Ben.

I could tell that this dude worked out a lot. I was pretty toned and had the kind of long, lean muscles that you get from surfing, but this guy was built. Funny thing was, he looked like me, but with gray eyes instead of blue, and I guessed he was maybe ten years older. I looked a whole lot more like him than I did Julia—yeah, me and Marcus could have been brothers.

"Nicky is my *little brother*, who I am going to strangle for not telling me you were coming," she said to the guy, like I hadn't spoken.

I hated it when she did that. She knew it, too.

"I can come back later?"

"No, it's fine."

Fine? So why was she making like I'd committed a crime by not telling her about him?

"How many rooms do you rent out?"

Julia's eyes flickered to mine, and I wondered if she really was planning on renting out my room.

"Just the one. Our mom died ... so we kind of need the extra money, you know?"

"Oh, sorry."

No one ever knows what to say when you tell them that your mom died. They say 'Oh sorry' but what they really mean is that they're sorry you embarrassed them by telling them someone died, as if it's catching or something. So they say 'Oh sorry' like it means something, but it's just words.

Then the dude looked at me.

"That sucks," he said.

I didn't reply because it sucks when you forgot there was a test and then you get a D, or when you miss the bus and have to walk miles, or some douche steals your last dollar because he thinks it looks cool to light a blunt like he's Snoop Dog. Those things suck.

Mom died and the world doesn't spin the same way

anymore. I wanted to say that, but I didn't. I just looked at him and nodded.

"Don't mind my little brother," said Julia.

And I was burning inside, but I didn't show it because that's not how I roll. So I just stared at her like I didn't care and that pissed her off even more. But it was her fault because she made me out to be a dick in front of this dude, and maybe I was a dick, but "us against the world," that's what she said at Mom's funeral. What a freakin' bunch of bullshit.

"It's $590 a month, all utilities included. The bathroom and the kitchen are shared—obviously."

"No problem."

I could tell Julia was uncomfortable when she told him, "It's the first month's rent plus a security deposit."

The dude just gave her a toothpaste-commercial smile, but looked her right in the eye.

"Can we say a week in advance, and I'll give you the rest when I get paid? I've just started a new job."

"Oh, I don't know…"

"Just till I get paid."

"Well, I guess…"

Ha! She'd caved already. The dude was good, because that never worked for me.

"Thanks, that's great...? Sorry, I didn't catch your name."

"Oh! I'm Julia."

And then he winked, and her face went beet red. It was kind of nauseating. I thought she was into Ben.

"Can I move my stuff in tonight, Julia?"

He was saying her name like I wasn't even in the room.

"Tonight?"

She was really flustered now and kept looking at me. But it was her deal and usually I kept my mouth shut around her, because everything I said was wrong.

"It's either that or sleep in the van," said the guy, still

smiling.

I looked out the window and saw a vintage VW camper parked outside. It had a couple of surfboards and a paddleboard secured to the roof rack. It wasn't that surprising—we got a lot of guys coming here to work the summer months and hope for waves. The surfing wasn't great during the season, but the fact that Kelly Slater was born here still pulled them in, even though the dude was really old, like 40 or something. But being an eleven time ASP world champion earned respect.

It was kind of interesting watching Julia with this guy.

"Um, well, as you can see, the room isn't furnished yet. I only posted the listing yesterday. I didn't think anyone would want it so soon.

"Well, hey, that doesn't bother me. How about you make the rent $450 and I'll get my own furniture?"

I could see my sister doing the math, or trying to, because even though she was a teacher assistant in the elementary school, she couldn't add for shit. I could have helped her out and told her she'd be losing $420 if he stayed the whole season, and that you could get used furniture for way less than that. I could have.

"Um, yeah, that sounds fair," she said.

"Great! Thanks, Julia."

"Just one thing," she said, and this time she used her school voice. I recognized it because she used it on me all the time. "I have to get up early for my job. I can't be dealing with a lot of noise at night."

That was news to me. Maybe Julia was working as an assistant teacher for the summer program. She hadn't told me. Yeah, so freakin' surprising.

"Well, I'll be working some late shifts, but I can park the van around the corner."

"Where do you work?

"The Sandbar, down by the pier. Do you know it?"

"Oh yes. I go there sometimes." She hesitated and looked at me again. "Well, I'd better get you the spare key,

Marcus."

She left us alone, and I stared at the room with the worn sofa, scuffed paintwork and sagging floorboards. It looked empty without Mom's TV and her magazines, especially now that we'd gotten rid of her broken old cot that she'd sleep on. Julia had sold the TV even though she knew I wanted it for my room.

"There didn't seem to be much swell today," the guy said to me.

I'd almost forgotten he was there.

"Nope."

"Guess I'll take my paddleboard out."

I shrugged and looked away.

"It must be pretty shitty to have a stranger come and rent a room."

I was surprised by what he said, but it was true. It sucked major ass. I hated being poor.

"I'll try and stay out of your face."

Julia walked back into the room, throwing me an evil look. Jeez, I hadn't even said anything. Maybe I was breathing too much air.

I left the room, but Julia screamed out to me.

"Nicky! I hope you didn't use all the hot water again—Marcus wants to take a shower!"

Great. The dude had only been here five freakin' minutes and he already wanted to shower. Just what I needed: Julia stressed out because of him being here. Fun times were certainly in my future. Not.

I headed for the kitchen hoping that there were some Pop Tarts left. It would be at least an hour before Yansi's mom served dinner, and I was starving.

I finally found one lousy package left all the way in the back of the kitchen cabinet. Then I heard the shower running so I guessed the new guy had made himself right at home.

While I waited for the toaster to pop, I grabbed a soda from the fridge and sat on the step outside the back door watching Julia hang out some towels on the line. I wanted a beer, but Julia would be pissed and I didn't think it would be a good idea to show up at the Alfaros smelling of alcohol. I was trying to stay on Yansi's parents' good side—although I wasn't sure Mr. Alfaro had one when it came to me.

The shower turned off at the same time the front door opened and Ben walked in. Julia had given him a key two months ago. I guess Mom had agreed to it, but I don't know because no one tells me shit. I mean, I didn't really mind, but I thought it would have been nice for someone to mention it seeing as though I lived here, too.

There were footsteps on the stairs, then I heard Ben's voice.

"Who the fuck are you?"

He sounded pissed. I guess Julia hadn't told him about renting the room out either. Funny enough, that made me feel a little better.

Marcus kept his cool though.

"Ben, right? I'm Marcus. Julia rented me the room today."

There was a pause, but Ben sounded much calmer when he spoke again.

"Oh! Sorry, buddy. I just thought…"

I could see from Julia's face that she'd heard everything as she marched past. Boy, she looked mad, and for once it wasn't aimed at me.

"*What* did you think, Ben? I'd really like you to finish that sentence!"

I followed her into the hallway, curious to see how this was going to pan out.

Marcus was still halfway down the stairs, wearing just a towel. I could see how that might have given Ben the wrong idea. Marcus looked amused, standing there with his arms crossed.

Ben looked like a dog who was about to get whipped.

"Babe, I…"

"I'm not finished!" she yelled. "Kitchen! Now!"

Then she pushed past me, and Ben followed after her, still apologizing.

Marcus looked at me. "Are they always like that?"

I thought about it for a moment. Julia yelling at full volume. Check. Ben getting his ass handed to him. Check.

"Yeah, pretty much," I said.

Marcus shook his head as he walked into his room.

"Fun," he muttered.

I heard the toaster pop and wondered whether it was worth risking life and limb by going into the kitchen, but the yelling was pretty one-sided, so I thought it would be safe.

I snuck in and snatched up the Pop Tart, juggling it between my hands, hoping it wasn't going to ooze or anything gross like that before it was cool enough for me eat.

But Julia spotted me.

"Nicky! Where are you going?"

I scooped up my Tony Hawk from the hall and slammed the front door behind me. I didn't owe her an explanation. She wasn't Mom.

Mr. Alfaro's truck was parked outside the house when I got there, and he was unloading a bunch of equipment he used for his lawn care business. I'd hoped he wouldn't be home yet because, like I said, he didn't let anyone speak English, which made it hard for me. Yansi's mom was more laidback and I think she liked me, or felt sorry for me or something, and she was always trying to feed me, which I didn't mind.

At home, Julia bought the groceries but she never

cooked anything. She didn't trust me to buy food either, in case I came back with things that weren't on the list. That was a misdemeanor, maybe a felony.

"Hola, Señor Alfaro. Can I help you with that, sir?"

He stared at me with flat, black eyes, then nodded once.

I hopped up onto the bed of the truck and passed down two weed whackers in different sizes, a chainsaw and some other shit that he used. He even had one of those old fashioned hand mowers that you pushed. I thought most people had ride-on mowers these days, so I wasn't sure when he'd use it, but I guess he did because it looked pretty banged up. Yansi said he took care of 20 yards each week, depending on what the owners wanted done, and sometimes worked on Saturdays too, but never on Sunday.

I heard their front door bang open and looked across to see Yansi standing there in these real short denim cut-offs, barefoot.

She grinned up at me, rubbing her ankle with the sole of her other foot. She did that all the time, and I told her it made her look like a flamingo. She did it now because it was sort of like a private joke for us.

She had great legs even if she wasn't that tall, with smooth, caramel-colored skin that felt like silk when I touched it. I must have let my eyes linger a little too long, because Mr. Alfaro snapped something at her, too fast for me to catch. Yansi scowled, then turned on her heel and darted back inside.

I felt guilty and annoyed—even more so when my face heated up.

Without another word, Mr. Alfaro pushed the mower toward the garage, leaving me standing in the truck.

I wasn't sure if I'd been dismissed, but after a few seconds I headed inside.

Yansi was waiting and attacked my mouth the moment the door was closed behind me.

"Ignore him," she murmured as her hands roamed under my t-shirt and across my chest.

For someone who'd never had a boyfriend before me, this girl had some moves.

I shivered as the tips of her fingers brushed over my nipples. I have no idea why they were so sensitive—I thought that was supposed to be just girls. I had to push her away quickly when I saw Beatriz watching us with solemn eyes.

"Mami, ella está besando a Nico de nuevo!"

"You little sneak!" hissed Yansi, but her sister darted away before she could grab her.

"Holy shit, Yans! You wanna get me killed?" I choked out, sounding like someone had sandpapered my throat.

We heard her mother call from the kitchen and Yansi sighed, giving me a look full of longing that was in danger of heading straight to my shorts.

"Ya vengo, Mami," she said, and walked away, smiling at me over her shoulder as she swung her hips.

That girl just about killed me. I looked down, but my t-shirt covered my semi pretty good.

I followed her into the kitchen where Mrs. Alfaro was stirring a huge pan of Sancocho. Yansi hated it, mostly because they had it three or four times a week. I could eat it every day and never get bored because her mom never made it the same way twice. Today I could smell the chicken in the stew and when I peered into the pan, large pieces of corncob were floating in it.

"Hola, Nico! Cómo estás?"

We caught up on our days while Yansi set the table, and I told her that I'd been job hunting but hadn't had any luck. Then we had a few minutes before supper was ready, so Yansi pulled me out into the backyard where we could talk without being overheard. But no touching. Mrs. Alfaro could see us from the window.

"What's up?"

I could tell by now that Yansi was pissed about something.

"Mami got a job as a nanny with some rich family over in River Falls."

"Yeah, so?"

"So," she said, sighing heavily because I'd obviously missed the point, "it means I'll be stuck babysitting *all summer.*"

"Oh." *Crap.*

"Yeah. It really sucks. And I won't even get paid. I'll never be able to see you!"

"We've still got the evenings, maybe some weekends?"

I was really pissed off about it, but trying to hide it for Yansi's sake. I guess I wasn't doing a good job because she scowled.

"You know they'll never let me out in the evenings, especially with you."

"Tell them you're meeting your girlfriends. Esther will cover for you."

"That won't work. Papi always phones her parents to make sure I'm where I'm supposed to be."

"Go for a sleepover. When her folks have gone to bed, you can sneak out."

Her eyes lit with excitement and I felt my pulse speed up.

"Yeah, that could work!"

"You could ... you could stay at my place. We'd just have to be awake early to get you back to Esther's for breakfast."

Before she could reply, Mateo came out with his football, looking at me questioningly.

"Qué pasa?"

He grinned and shook his head. "Mami says you have to go in now, Anayansi. You women have work to do."

Wow. I knew I couldn't get away with saying shit like that, and this little dude was like 10 years old!

Yansi threw him a look and muttered under her breath, "Mi hermano me tiene realmente cabreada." *My brother is really pissing me off.* If I were Mateo, I'd be watching my back.

We tossed the ball around for a few minutes before Mrs. Alfaro called us for supper.

I could tell Yansi's brain was whirling—she was really quiet and kept throwing me these searching looks. I felt uncomfortable because we hadn't been able to finish our conversation, and I knew it sounded like I was asking her to have sex with me, and maybe I was, but really I just wanted us to spend time together by ourselves—although I wouldn't say no if she offered. Obviously.

It was killing me not knowing what she was thinking.

"Nico, I heard you tell my daughter that you're looking for a job?"

I caught my name just in time, taking a second to translate in my head.

"Yes, ma'am."

Mrs. Alfaro smiled at her husband.

"It's a busy time of year for lawn care," she went on. "Raúl could use some help, if you're interested."

"Um, that's real nice of you," I said doubtfully, glancing at Mr. Alfaro's stern face. "But I'm looking for something full-time."

"It would be, but just for the summer. Isn't that right, Raúl?"

I saw the trap a good ten seconds too late. If I was working for Mr. Alfaro, then I wasn't messing with their daughter while they weren't there.

"Si. Pay is $7 an hour. Cash." He stared at me, his eyes giving nothing away. "Starting tomorrow, 7AM-4PM."

From the frown on Yansi's face, I could see that she got it, too.

I decided that I'd accept, just to stay on his good side, but keep an eye open for anything else that came up. But then my brain cranked into gear as if to say, *Dude, you aren't quitting a job your girl's father has given you!*

Besides, even though it was less than minimum wage, if he was paying me cash, I wouldn't have to pay taxes. But nine hours a day with a guy who didn't like me because I was dating his daughter?

"Wow, that's, um, great. Thank you, sir."

He nodded, his face showing no expression.

Shit.

It was going to be a long summer.

Chapter 2

The sun had sunk behind the river by the time I left their house, and the sky was flushed with color—orange and pink bleeding into the silver-blue water.

I usually felt peaceful after seeing Yansi, but now I was restless and on edge, annoyed at the way the Alfaros had railroaded me, frustrated from sitting opposite Yans all night without being able to touch her.

I walked home rather than skate; it was too dark to see potholes in the road, and I didn't want to risk trashing the Tony Hawk.

As I got closer to the house, I could see lights on in the den. There was a stranger in there. It didn't feel right. Nausea bubbled up, and I rubbed my chest as memories came flooding back; Mom sitting up waiting for me every evening, watching her get sick, watching her lose weight, watching her fade away, watching her die. I'd hated coming home some nights, but I always did because I knew she wouldn't go to bed until I was back.

Seeing those lights now was all wrong, and I nearly lost my dinner.

I stood frozen for a moment, and I could see the guy, Marcus, walking backwards and forwards, moving his stuff around the room, settling in.

Then I forced myself to move, digging out my key, and let myself into the house, wincing when the door slammed.

I hadn't replied to either of Julia's texts asking me where I was, the last one telling me to be quiet when I came home because she had to be up early for her summer job.

I was too wired to go to sleep, so I headed into the kitchen and snagged one of Ben's beers from the fridge. I knew he wouldn't mind, although Julia would be mad if she found out. Tough.

I sat on the back step, listening to the soft rumble of waves rolling up the beach. This wasn't how I thought it would be. I'd been looking forward to this summer all year. I'd imagined long days on the beach with Yansi, borrowing Mom's car to drive us somewhere quiet.

But the car was long gone, sold by Julia. She hadn't even told me she was going to do it; one day it was gone. Just like Mom.

When I asked her about it, Julia told me to grow up. I didn't even know what she meant by that. Get a job that made me miserable, like her? Worry about the price of milk or the price of gas? Worry about things that no one could control, like who got cancer, and who lived and who died? How did any of that help?

I heard footsteps and looked over my shoulder to see Marcus watching me.

"Someone's birthday?" he asked.

"What?"

He pointed to the small pile of colorful envelopes pushed into a heap by the telephone.

"Oh. Well, yeah, I guess."

I'd forgotten about those. They'd been there for so long that I'd stopped seeing them.

"Yours?"

"Yeah. I haven't opened them yet."

"Why not?"

I shrugged.

He shook his head and laughed lightly.

"Funny … I thought people usually, you know, enjoy birthdays? Isn't that traditional?"

It did seem kind of dumb now that I really thought about it. I just hadn't been able to open them before, but seeing myself through Marcus' eyes, I must have looked weird, or maybe just pathetic.

I stood up and put my beer on the kitchen table, then dragged the pile of envelopes closer. There weren't that many—only five. One from Yansi, one from Julia and Ben, Aunt Carmen who wasn't really my aunt but a friend of Mom's, one from Sean. And one more.

I opened them all, reading the jokes and dumb messages, pocketing the twenty dollar bill that fell out of Carmen's envelope, and the $50 gift card for Ron Jon's Surf and Skate shop that was from Julia. Yansi had bought us tickets to see a band in Orlando, but I hadn't been able to go. She had begged her parents for weeks to get permission just to buy the tickets, too. She went with a girlfriend instead, which her parents preferred anyway. No point wasting them.

I hesitated over the last envelope, feeling dizzy as I stared at the shaky handwriting.

Marcus sat down next to me and popped the tab on a can of beer.

"You okay, man?"

"Yeah," I said, my voice breaking embarrassingly.

I tore the envelope and read the card quickly, knowing that it was the last thing Mom had ever written. But all it said was, 'Love, Mom'. She'd been too sick to write anything else.

"Happy birthday," said Marcus, tapping his can of beer against mine. "How old?"

"Seventeen. A month ago."

He stared at me. "How come you only just opened

your birthday cards?"

I began to speak, but couldn't get the words out.

His eyes widened in understanding.

Mom died on my seventeenth birthday. Now every time I had a birthday, it would be a death-day, too.

Marcus stood suddenly.

"You up for a little stealth mission? The surf by the pier has picked up enough for some longboard action."

I didn't want to be in that house filled with memories of a sick woman who aged in front of my eyes, opening cards with shaky writing I could hardly read.

Then I remembered that I'd dinged my longboard a couple of weeks back and hadn't gotten around to resealing the top layer of fiberglass. If you ride a damaged board and seawater gets inside, it rots the foam.

"My board's trashed at the moment," I explained, "but I know a place you can go that'll work better than the pier with this onshore breeze."

"Sounds good," Marcus said, "I've got a spare you can borrow if you want to come along."

"Really? Thanks, man."

"No worries," he said with a smile.

I stood at the entrance to the den—his room now—while he rummaged in his board bag, then hauled out a nice-looking eight footer.

"It flexes a bit too much on the bigger waves, but it should work for you now."

I ran my hands along the board's stringer and scuffed up the wax with my fingernails. Yeah, this was a nice board.

Then I saw that Marcus had a guitar propped up against the wall. I pointed to it with my chin.

"You play?"

What a dumb friggin' question. What did I think he did with it? Play tennis?

But Marcus just smiled.

"Yep. Been playing since I was ten. I'm writing some

songs, working on a few things. If I can get some money together, I'm going to cut a demo to send off to record companies."

I was impressed. I didn't know anyone who did stuff like that, but I just nodded and tried not to look too interested.

"Cool."

He grinned like he could tell what I was really thinking, then he snatched up his car keys and shut the door behind us.

Two minutes later we were sitting in his van and Marcus was following my directions to Jetty Park.

"I thought the entrance was manned by security," Marcus said curiously.

"Yeah, but there's another access road that heads straight down to the shore the other side of the boardwalk. You're not supposed to drive there, but no one checks at night."

"Sounds good."

We bumped down the sandy path and he parked on the beach, leaving the headlights on so we had something to aim for, even though we could see windows lit up in the big house on the point and the Shorewood condos in the distance.

I shivered slightly, but not from cold. The sea was warm, maybe 70°F, but there was something about the way the endless blackness crawled across my skin.

I shucked my jeans and t-shirt, and Marcus handed me his longboard. So I paddled out, the ocean moving under me, the spray misting across my face and shoulders as the waves broke gently.

Two things made me peaceful: being with Yansi and feeling her warm breath on my neck while we held each other; and this, here and now … being rocked by the swell, rising and falling, listening to the waves breaking on the shore behind me. I stared into the night, breathing in the humid, salty air, before turning my board around, feeling a wave rise up, springing to my feet, curving into the clean water at the shoulder, the white foam chasing me, riding until the energy passed through and carried me away.

We surfed maybe an hour before Marcus called time-out and I caught a wave back to the beach.

He'd built up a small fire by the time I jogged over to join him. The van was between the road and us, so no one would see the flicker of low flames.

The sickly sweet smell of weed floated toward me, and I could see the bright embers glowing as he inhaled.

I plopped down next to him, thirstily eyeing the two six-packs he had lined up as he handed me a can of beer.

"Happy birthday."

"Thanks."

He passed me the blunt next, and I thought maybe having Marcus live with us wouldn't be so bad after all.

I coughed slightly; it was stronger than I was used to, and it didn't taste like he'd mixed much tobacco in with it.

"Good shit," I wheezed.

He chuckled quietly. "Yeah, got it from a friend who knows some people south of the border."

I took another hit and passed it back to him.

"So you're not into birthday cards?" he asked, his voice amused.

"No, not anymore."

He grinned and inhaled deeply.

"Yeah, they're evil. I mean, what kind of sicko sends people cards on their birthday?"

I gave a small laugh and lay back on the warm sand, staring up.

"What about other cards? You down on them, too?"

I could hear the mocking humor in his voice, but I didn't care.

It was easy being with Marcus. He didn't look at me sideways all the time, because I was 'the kid whose mom died'. You'd be amazed the shit teachers let you pull when they think you're 'acting out through grief'. The school

41

counselor said that to me shortly after it happened and I'd been caught beating up a Senior who was bothering Yansi. I wasn't 'acting out'—I was kicking the shit out of a dickhead. I didn't even get a detention.

I put my hands behind my head and stared at the sky, stars marking their way across the night, moving, moving, until they burned and died.

"Birthday cards are okay, I guess. Kinda lame. But I don't see the point of Valentine's cards. I mean, they're just embarrassing, right? That dude, St. Valentine, he got thrown to the lions or beheaded or something. What's that got to do with hearts filled with chocolate and flowers and all that shit?"

Yeah, I think the weed was getting to me; I didn't usually talk this much.

"Maybe because girlfriends take your head off if you forget to send a Valentine's Day card."

I laughed. It sounded like he'd met Yansi, although I knew he hadn't.

"I always preferred St. Jude," said Marcus, with a huge yawn.

"Who's he?"

"The patron saint of lost causes."

"Yeah? Does he have a special day?"

Marcus laughed. "What? Like Hopeless Loser day?"

"Yeah!"

"And you think people would what … send cards to real losers?"

"Or, if you were a real loser, you could send one to yourself."

He laughed slowly, drawn-out and mellow.

I must have fallen asleep after that because when I woke I was cold and the fire had gone out. The sky was the faintest gray and I could tell that dawn was only an hour away.

Marcus was sprawled out on the other side of the charred sand, our empty beer cans lined up drunkenly.

"Hey!" I said, then again, louder. "Hey!"

He grunted and sat up.

"Oh man, what time is it?"

"I don't know. Maybe 5:30AM?"

He rolled his shoulders and stretched, working the stiffness out of his neck.

"I haven't fallen asleep on the beach in a while. That must have been some good weed."

I wondered if Julia was up yet, and I wondered how much I cared that she'd be mad at me.

We climbed back into the van and drove home, some early traffic already on the road.

Marcus went straight to his room without a backward glance. Groaning, I realized that I had less than an hour before I had to be up—my first day of working for Mr. Alfaro. I stopped to get a glass of water from the kitchen, but paused when I heard voices—Ben and Julia, arguing again.

"What time is it now?"

"Ten to six."

"Damn Nicky! Where the hell is he? I should have left for work five minutes ago. He's been gone all night. All night, Ben! He could be dead!"

"Don't be too hard on him, babe."

"Why are you always taking his side?"

"I'm not," Ben replied, his voice calm like always.

"He's out all the time, doing God knows what. He doesn't listen to me. He certainly doesn't listen to you."

"Nicky's a good kid. He's had a lot to deal with."

Julia's voice was tight with irritation. "And I haven't?"

"That's not what I meant, babe."

I pushed the door open and walked inside. Julia's face was red and blotchy, her expression furious, like she'd explode any second or her head would start revolving.

Here it comes.

"Where have you been?"

I shrugged my shoulders. "Out."

"Your curfew is midnight!"

I laughed out loud at that. "Curfew! Says who?"

Her eyes bulged and the red flush on her cheeks spread to her neck. Not a good look.

"I know I'm not your legal guardian, but you should let me know where you are as a common fucking courtesy, for God's sake!" she snapped.

I stared straight at her and she was the one who looked away first.

"Well, there's no one else to worry about you, is there? You should do what I say!"

"Not gonna happen."

Her expression rushed from shock to anger to something else that I didn't recognize. I left the room before she lost it completely.

I heard Ben's voice as I trudged up the stairs. "Maybe you're right about having kids—if they grow up like him."

I think he was trying to make a joke of it, but he should have known better.

"I just can't talk to Nicky anymore!" Julia ranted. "Whatever I say he bites my head off, or just looks right through me."

"He's 17. Everyone's like that at his age."

"I'm 23, Ben! I didn't sign up for this. I'm not 'mom' material."

I stopped to listen to the rest.

"You're doing a great job," Ben said, and I wished I could have laughed out loud. "He'll come around."

"He missed so much school last semester. I never knew where he was. His grades are slipping. If he doesn't make *some* effort, he won't even get through high school let alone college."

Ben's voice was even.

"College isn't for everyone. There's always work for a plumber. I could ask my boss to take him on as an apprentice when he's 18—although Nick would have to complete his GED. But it's good money."

"I don't know what to do with him." Her voice dropped, and I strained to hear her. "Maybe he'd be better off in a foster home. It would only be for a year—just while he finished High School."

Sweat broke out all over me and my heart lurched. I'd always wondered, but now I knew.

I yanked open my bedroom door, letting it bang into the wall, then slammed it behind me. I fell face first onto the comforter, burying my head, muffling her voice that said everything.

Ugly, angry thoughts bubbled rapidly, and I pounded the pillows, fury burning through me.

We'd never gotten along. I'd always been in the way, the annoying younger brother, the mistake that should never have been born. She wanted to go off and live her boring life with boring Ben, play it safe. Fuck her. I didn't need her.

When the alarm went off on my phone half an hour later, I hadn't slept for even a minute. A glance in the mirror showed red eyes with dark shadows underneath. I looked like hell. Felt it, too.

I threw myself in the shower then dressed quickly in an old pair of boardshorts and ratty tee. I didn't have time to make any breakfast, so I just grabbed a loaf of bread and shoved it in my backpack, along with a wrinkled apple and a bottle of water. I remembered my baseball cap at the last minute. The high pressure was still sitting over us, and it was going to be in the mid nineties today.

I could already feel a trickle of sweat in my armpits and down my back as I skated to the Alfaros' house. I hoped I'd get to see Yansi—something that would make this shitty day a little better.

But Mr. Alfaro was waiting for me, his arms crossed, his face a hard, blank line.

He didn't say anything, just jerked his chin toward the truck. I went to open the passenger door, but he laid his hand on my arm and motioned at me to sit in back with the equipment.

Great. I was so insignificant I didn't even rate sitting in the truck's cab.

I tossed my backpack and skateboard in, then jumped on and slumped against the side of the truck. As he pulled away, I glanced up at the house's windows and saw Yansi. She smiled and blew me a kiss.

Suddenly, the day was a little brighter.

By lunchtime, I had learned one essential truth: Mr. Alfaro was a fucking slave driver and wanted to kill me. Maybe that's two truths, but I was too tired and pissed to think straight.

I started by spreading about 20 wheelbarrows of lava rocks. After that, I lost count. Next, I crawled on my belly in dust and spider webs and shit under some lady's deck, trying to find a leak in a pipe that fed her sprinkler system and fishpond, hoping like hell that there weren't any snakes. Then Mr. Alfaro made me scoop green slime out of the same freakin' pond, until I was filthy and stinking.

I got all the crappiest jobs that he must have been saving up, and he never said more than ten words the whole time, just pointing and grunting.

Finally, he signaled me to come take a break. My lips were cracked and dry, and my shoulders and back felt burned. I'd taken off my t-shirt hours ago when it was soaked with sweat. It had dried stiff and covered in white salt marks. I pulled it on and tried to wash my hands using the garden hose. I'd drunk two bottles of water, but I'd sweated so much I didn't even want to piss. Not that the lady of the house would have let me inside. She came out to study the beds where I'd spread the lava rocks and looked at me like I was shit on her shoe. But then she gave Mr. Alfaro the same look, heading back inside without a word.

I wondered how many lava beds there were in front—anymore than two and I was out of there.

I sat in the shade of the truck and drank some more water then stared at the loaf of bread I'd brought to eat. It was totally unappealing, and I decided I needed to get my shit together and pack a better lunch tomorrow. If I was still alive.

I knew Mr. Alfaro was watching me, even though it looked like he was half asleep, his eyes black slits. But every now and then he took another bite of his tortilla, chewing it slowly. It smelt amazing and had my stomach groaning. I forced down another dry slice of bread, nearly choking on it, but hungry, too.

The owner of the house came out again, passing us as she headed toward the new Benz parked beside the three-car garage. Then she pinned her irritated gaze on me.

"You!"

I glanced nervously at Mr. Alfaro, but his face showed no emotion.

I stood up, feeling uncertain, brushing the crumbs from my t-shirt.

"You're new," she said accusingly.

"Yes, ma'am. Just helping out Señor Alfaro for the summer."

Her lip curled. "Really. Is that the best you can do, working for some Hispanic?"

My jaw dropped open as she shook her head impatiently and marched away.

I was totally embarrassed, knowing that Mr. Alfaro had heard every word. I stood there, having no clue what to say, and I couldn't meet his eyes.

I sat down again, my appetite gone. What a bitch! I wondered if Mr. Alfaro had to put up with crap like that every day. It sort of made some sense now, why he always insisted on speaking Spanish at home. I would too if I were him, and some white bitch spoke to me like I was scum. Or even worse, couldn't bring herself to say a single word to me.

I wondered why we hadn't driven somewhere else to

eat our lunch, even if we did have to come back later.

My eyes flickered over to him and I realized he was watching me again. My cheeks reddened, but I hoped that he wouldn't be able to tell the difference because of all the sunburn.

Weirdly, I felt like I should apologize or something, but that would probably have made it worse.

Eventually, Mr. Alfaro stood up and jerked his chin at the mountain of lava rocks next to the wheelbarrow. I supposed that meant I should start on the front yard.

The afternoon passed pretty much the same as the morning. By 4PM, I was nearly keeling over. I was hungry, thirsty, sunburned and every muscle was crying out. I thought I was pretty fit, but everything hurt. Mr. Alfaro just kept going, moving through the day like a swimmer with slow, even strokes.

He dropped me at my house, and drove away without speaking. I was pretty annoyed about that. Would a 'thank you' or 'gracias' have killed him? I wasn't even being paid daily—I'd have to wait until the end of the week for my money.

I limped into the kitchen for more water and just my luck, Julia was there. Jeez, didn't she have a life?

"Where the hell have you been? You look terrible and God!—what is that smell?!"

"I've been working," I grumbled.

"Working?" she said suspiciously. "Doing what?"

I could have ignored her, but fighting took more energy than I had left.

"Yard work for Yansi's dad."

"Yard work?"

Was there a fucking echo?

"Yes."

"Oh…" she hesitated, testing whether or not to be pissed about that. "Well, okay then," she said at last. "How much is he paying you?"

"How much is the summer program paying *you?*" I

asked sharply.

Her lips tightened, but I think she must have realized she wasn't going to win that one.

"Whatever, but if you're earning money you should start helping out. A contribution to the grocery bill would something with the amount you eat."

That's when I lost it.

I pulled the half eaten loaf of bread out of my backpack and threw it at her.

"Fine! Have the fucking bread! I ate half. You want a dollar for that?"

I shoved a hand in my pocket and tossed a handful of quarters onto the kitchen table where they bounced and skittered to the floor.

"Don't yell at me! You're acting like a child."

I wanted to throw more than fucking bread and a handful of change, so I stormed out of the room and headed for the shower, ignoring her shouted words.

I locked myself in the bathroom and stood under the water until it ran cold. My skin stung and my muscles ached. Even though my stomach growled, I lay down on my bed and fell asleep.

I woke up shortly after midnight, wondering why I was conscious. My eyelids felt sore and were tender when I touched them. Shit on a stick—even my eyelids were sunburned.

I sat up drowsily, and immediately my stomach rumbled. I was so hungry my backbone was sticking to my ribs.

I pulled on a pair of jeans and stumbled into the kitchen then stopped dead. I realized what had woken me: a woman giggling.

A blonde girl with huge tits spilling out of a tank top was sitting on Marcus' lap, her mouth glued to his face.

Was *everything* going to make me lose my appetite on this fucked up day?

"Oh, hey man," said Marcus, looking up and pushing

her away. "Didn't mean to wake you. This is Gina."

"Dina!" giggled the woman, slapping his shoulder playfully but fluttering her false eyelashes at me. "He's cute! You wanna party with us?" and she held out a bottle of tequila.

"Um, no, I'm good, thanks. I was just, um, just gonna get something to eat."

"Me, too," laughed the woman as she licked her lips.

Oh hell, I did not want to know that.

Marcus smiled. "Come on, peaches. Let's take the party back to my room. See ya, kid."

Shaking my head at the weirdness of the day and world in general, I made myself a baloney sandwich and then, as an afterthought, another two for lunch the next day.

And then finally, finally, the day really was over, and I headed back to bed and fan-fucking-tastic beautiful oblivion.

By the end of my first week the alarm on my phone had become an instrument of torture. I was so tempted to just ignore it and go back to sleep.

But two things made me haul my ass out of bed. One was that last night Julia had laughed when I dragged myself home, and said that I'd never make it at this job. The second was that Yansi had texted me and said that she wasn't working on Saturday, and did I want to do something.

Hell, yeah! And I was counting on Mr. Alfaro paying me, so I could take her somewhere nice.

I was pretty much used to the work and had learned to pace myself. Mr. Alfaro did a ten day rotation, so I'd already met a lot of his customers, although quite a few were out when we were there. Maybe they went to work in air-conditioned offices, sat on padded chairs behind desks and never broke a sweat. The women had maids and nannies and cleaners and kids at summer camp, so I wondered what they did all day. Although a lot of them seemed to make shopping into a hobby. I'd never understood that. I mean, you can only wear one pair of sneakers at a time, right?

Most of his customers were polite but vague, their smiles sliding away as if it was too much effort to keep one fixed to their face, or to meet your eyes. But a couple were nice. One lady gave us fresh lemonade so sweet I nearly went into diabetic shock, and another had homemade cookies. On those occasions Mr. Alfaro would lean on his spade or his weed whacker and talk in formal English, his face grave and serious. I don't think I'd ever seen the man smile. If it wasn't for the fact I saw him chewing his food, I'd have doubted he had teeth.

At 4PM on Friday, I wanted to yell 'quittin' time!'. I stood by his truck, half tempted to stand at attention, but I didn't think Mr. Alfaro would find that funny.

When he saw me, he nodded slowly, then reached into his wallet and counted out a bunch of notes. I watched every dollar bill land in the palm of my hand, eyes narrowed, counting hungrily. It was more than I'd expected and I realized he'd paid me for the half hour of my lunch break. I was surprised and I wondered if he'd made a mistake. But Mr. Alfaro didn't make mistakes, and I wasn't about to argue with him.

I muttered, "Gracias, señor," and shoved the money in my pocket as I went to climb in next to the mower. Then I felt his hand on my arm, and he pointed with his chin at the cab of the truck.

I must have looked dumbstruck, because he pointed again at the passenger door, then paced around to the driver's side.

A weird feeling settled in my chest, something like I'd won an award, something like pride. The only thing I'd ever been good at, I mean better than other people, was surfing. In every other single part in my life, I was average, ordinary, just one of the guys. But now, being allowed to ride up front after sweating my guts out all week … it felt damn fine.

He dropped me back home and I walked inside wearing his silent approval like armor. Julia's shit wouldn't touch me today.

She was sitting on the back porch drinking coffee when I walked into the kitchen.

"You survived the week then," she said.

I peeled $100 from my small pile and laid the bills on the table. That was my reply.

I heard her calling after me as I walked upstairs, but she was easy to ignore.

I showered slowly, letting the hot water wash away the week. One more night before I could see Yansi, and then we'd have the whole day together.

Mr. Alfaro had made damn sure we didn't get the chance to see each other during the week, although he couldn't stop us talking on our cells or texting. Thinking about her, wanting her and not seeing her was torture. I woke up every morning hard enough to pound nails. Every morning and right now. I wanted to feel bad that I jerked off thinking about her. I knew I should, but I couldn't.

I didn't feel like hanging with the guys, but it was Friday and even though I was exhausted from a week of back breaking yard work, I'd arranged to meet up with Sean and Rob. Sean had gotten a car from his parents for his sixteenth birthday and they even paid for his gas, so tonight we were going to drive to Melbourne, eat junk, talk trash and see a movie.

I'd learned by now that I'd only survive going out after work if I took a quick nap like some old guy. I stretched out on top of the sheets wearing just a pair of boxers, because it was too danged hot and Julia said we couldn't afford to run the A/C. I dozed, vaguely aware of voices in the house, before it occurred to me that I could hear Julia, and she was laughing.

And I felt a pang of grief, cold and solid in my stomach, like I'd swallowed a rock. I hadn't heard her laugh in a long time. No one had.

I lay there listening, certain it wasn't Ben who made her laugh. When she talked to him, she sounded pinched and irritated, like how she talked to me, but now her laugh was open and loose.

And then I heard Marcus' laughter, floating up weightless.

I remember this, I thought. *We used to laugh in this house.*

Chapter 3

I'd known Sean almost my whole life. I wondered sometimes whether we'd be friends if we'd met in high school instead of third grade, because he could be kind of a dick. But when Mom got sick, he stuck around. A lot of people didn't because it's a major downer when someone's dying. Nobody wants to be around you, like the silence will break apart if someone laughs or cracks a joke.

But Sean stayed. He drove me to the hospital after school every day, and sometimes he'd sit with Mom and tell her all the dumb shit that we did, and I'd see this look on her face like life was normal again, even though she had these tubes all over her. I couldn't make her look like that because life wasn't normal and never would be again and I tried, I really tried, but the words choked me and filled my mouth with cotton. So I'd smile like I was the one who was sick.

Sean never expected anything from me during those days, and he even laid off Yansi. I couldn't figure out why those two didn't get along. They tolerated each other, that was all. But with Mom dying, they must have agreed to a truce. I don't know, they never told me. I asked Yansi why she didn't like Sean and she said, "he's a dick," which I knew. And I asked Sean why he enjoyed making her mad and he said, "she's a chick."

But even though he acted like a douche sometimes, I knew Sean was solid.

It pissed me off that he resented the time I spent with Yansi, and it was true I didn't hang with the guys as much, especially at school. But even though he was all about 'bros before ho's', he was the first person to ditch a party if he hooked up with someone. He had a casual thing going with Lacey Russo who was a year ahead of us in school. I think he knew her through his brothers. They hung out at parties, or disappeared into locked rooms at parties. Whatever, good for him. I was glad one of us was getting some action.

I could have cheated on Yansi. It would have been easy, because she was almost never allowed out in the evenings, and not to parties, not with me. And it wasn't like I hadn't had offers, because I had. I wasn't squeaky-clean either because sometimes I wanted to, just to know what it was like. But I knew Yansi would dump my ass real fast if I so much as kissed another girl. Not that anyone else really did it for me anyway.

Mom gave me 'the talk' when I was 12. It's in the top two of most embarrassing moments ever. The other is changing into my boardshorts on the beach when I was 13, and managing to leave my dick waving in the wind. Sean nearly choked to death he was laughing so hard.

But 'the talk' was a whole other level of excruciating. Mom brought out a pack of condoms and rolled one over a banana to show me how it was done. I couldn't even think about having a piece of fruit for months, and I haven't been able to eat bananas ever since. There are some things that scar a guy for life.

After that, she talked about feelings and how shitty it was (without using that word) when somebody you cared about treated you badly. I always wondered if she was talking about my dad, but I didn't have the balls to ask. She looked so sad, I felt all sort of hot and queasy inside, like I wanted to punch the fucker who put that look on her face.

So I can't cheat. And that's Mom's fault.

Before Yansi, I'd made out with a lot of girls, even getting to third base once, when Wendy de Luca sucked my cock at a party. I lasted about ten seconds, which felt like a world record at the time.

But I didn't cheat.

It was kinda fun hanging with Sean and Rob on Friday night, even though the movie was lame. Sean started hitting on a group of girls who were sitting behind us. He was the annoying guy that everyone kept frowning at and shushing, and the funny thing was, even though he spent the whole movie trying to persuade the girls to come to the beach with us after, as soon as the movie was over and the lights came on, he decided they were dogs and we had to head out fast. See what I mean? Asshole.

Instead, we drove back to Cocoa Beach and when Rob said he'd gotten hold of some weed, Sean cheered up and we headed down to the pier.

I was surprised to see Marcus pulling up at the same time as us. I thought he'd be working. I hadn't seen him since the night I met Gina or Dina or whatever her name was, but tonight he had a dark haired girl with him that I'd never seen before.

He looked up and nodded when he saw me.

"Hey, Nick. How you doing?"

"Hey! This is Sean and Rob. Marcus is our roomie."

We joined the small group of people hanging out. I knew most of them vaguely because they'd gone to our school and graduated a couple of years back, and some because they were surfers.

Jonno, a guy who'd been our high school quarterback last year was drinking from a quart of whiskey.

"You new in town?" he asked Marcus.

"Yeah, moved in a couple of weeks ago."

"You surf?"

"Every chance I get."

Jonno saluted him by raising his bottle.

"A day without waves is a day wasted."

Marcus laughed.

"I'll drink to that."

Rob started rolling a blunt and I made myself comfortable on the sand, listening to the waves, half an ear on the conversation. I never got tired of talking about surfing; where was the best break, the most awesome wave you'd ever ridden, the worst wipeout. It was our own language and it separated us from civilians—people who didn't surf.

"You got a favorite break?"

When Marcus answered, I could tell by his voice that he was smiling.

"A few. Bali is the place, man. Great waves, cheap food."

"Cheap women," said an older guy named Frank, and everyone laughed, even the girl Marcus was with. "Padang. Now *that* was special."

Marcus nodded in agreement. "Nusa Dua had a gnarly left and right just before the rip."

I could tell Sean was drinking it in, his eyes intense and glassy at the same time. We'd talked about taking a year off when we graduated, leaving town, surfing our way around the world. I didn't know if I'd be able to afford it now. I hadn't told him that. I suppose part of me was still hoping I'd find a way, but part of me couldn't imagine leaving Yansi for that long. I hadn't told him that either. But with Mom dying, I couldn't imagine staying. That was the bit I hadn't told anyone.

"Oh man! I'm totally going there!" Sean said, the weed making his words slow like he was sucking on licorice. "There hasn't been any decent surf here for two, three weeks now. It's driving me crazy."

"Yeah," said Rob. "And even before that it was typical summer mush … just shitty surf."

There was a general mumble of agreement.

"I don't know why you bother coming back here," griped Sean.

Marcus just smiled.

"Working the summer season is the quickest way to get some cash: tourist tips are usually pretty good."

"Yeah, but you could be in Maui or Bali."

I could tell that Sean was turning into some sort of Marcus fanboy now. This could get embarrassing quick.

"What's the biggest wave you've ever ridden?"

Everyone pitched in their answer. I'd ridden a 12 footer once, and it had scared the crap out of me—not that I was admitting that to *anyone*. But, man, the adrenalin rush was with me for days.

"Mavericks, northern California," said Frank. "The waves were topping 20 feet and the swell just kept getting bigger. By the time the waves were 35 feet there was only one surfer left: Jeff Clark. Everyone else had called time-out."

"Freakin' A!" muttered Sean, in an awed voice. "What about you, Marcus?"

I sucked on the blunt that Rob passed to me and imagined traveling the world, ripping across monster waves. My dreams drifted out with the sweet smoke. Anywhere but here … maybe.

"Nazaré in Portugal was pretty wild," said Marcus, leaning back on his elbows. "It was topping 30, 35 feet when I was there."

Everyone went quiet. When someone told you that they'd ridden a thirty foot wave, you paid some fucking respect.

"What was it like?" breathed Sean. "Surfing a wave that big?"

Marcus paused.

"It was ... intense. I was sitting in the line-up with two other guys and I could see all these people on the beach. I wondered what they were looking at and then I realized it was me—like they were waiting for a train wreck or something. And then the horizon went black and I knew this was my wave. You start paddling for the peak and it's getting higher and higher and you're paddling up hill and this wall of water is rearing up behind you; then just as the nose starts to drop, you're standing up and ... imagine a two-story house chasing you down the wave; the wind's roaring and you think you're shouting but you can't hear your own voice; and you know that if you wipeout they'll be picking your carcass out of the seabed; and your thighs are starting to cramp because the water's so cold and your balance is the only thing keeping you alive; and the spray is whipping past you like an express train; and all the time the wave is threatening to snap its jaws shut; so you're pushing and pushing and part of your mind is ice cool and part of it's burning; and then the wave starts curling over and wrapping around you and the light is green all around; and you don't know if you're gasping or holding your breath; and then you're spat out the other side like you've just been born; there's no past, no future—just the moment."

He shrugged.

"It's like nothing else on earth."

We were silent, and I think all of us were imagining it, riding that monster wave, surviving to tell the tale. And nobody ever challenged him about it, because we all he knew he'd told us something real.

"But Pe'ahi off Maui was my favorite," he said.

"Why's that?" asked Jonno, breaking the tension.

Marcus chuckled quietly. "Because the water's warm!"

All surfers dreamed about Hawaii. It was like the Holy Grail of surfing. Yansi liked to bust my balls about that—she didn't really get the whole surfing thing. She preferred to lie in the sun, watching me. Yeah, did something for a guy's ego, that's for freakin' sure.

Someone else rolled another blunt and that got passed around too, along with Jonno's whiskey and some beer that Sean had snuck out of his brother's room.

Marcus' date had gotten bored and walked away to talk to some other people. Frank watched her leave then turned to Marcus.

"Hey," he said, "what about you and that piece you were with last night?"

"Who's this?" asked Jonno.

Frank laughed. "Some stuck up tourist. She wasn't so stuck up after, was she? Are you seeing her again while she's here?"

Marcus shrugged. "No, she wasn't my type."

Frank raised his eyebrows. "She had a pussy, didn't she? So, what *is* your type?"

"Single mothers."

Jonno laughed like he couldn't believe what he was hearing.

"What? You're kidding! Why?"

Marcus shook his head, smiling. "They know the score—they've got lower expectations." He paused. "And I like kids."

I wasn't sure if he was being serious, and I didn't know how to feel about that. Mom had been a single mother. Did that make *her* fair game? I felt a little sick thinking about it, or maybe that was the weed. I sat up quickly, kind of dizzy.

Marcus was watching me. He shook his head slightly, smiled before he nudged my shoulder and passed me a can of beer.

I popped the tab and drank it down, suddenly thirsty.

We sat around drinking for hours that night, and I washed away the week in beer and cheap talk, and it felt like being happy.

I couldn't remember too much about getting home,

except that at some point I was in Marcus' van, and then I tripped going up the stairs, landing heavily. I made it to my room, crawling into bed fully dressed. I wasn't sure if I imagined the voices swirling over my head.

"Thanks for bringing him home."

"No worries."

"Well, I appreciate it."

And then I passed out.

Hangovers suck. What happened to 'make the punishment fit the crime'?

My mouth was dry and I suspected that my breath reeked worse than the bottom of a parrot's cage. For the second Saturday in a row, I'd woken up face down on the bed with drool gluing my cheek to the pillow, and my head feeling like someone had shoved bricks inside then rattled them around.

And, *oh fuck!* I was supposed to be meeting Yansi in less than half an hour.

I'd been looking forward to seeing her for a whole week, and now all I wanted to do was hide under the sheets and sleep for a month.

I dragged myself into the shower, but someone had used up all the hot water. I shivered and shook under the cold spray, and that woke me up like nothing else could have.

At least I didn't need to shave more than once a week, because if I had to shave right now I'd probably cut off an ear, maybe my whole head. Sean's mom made him shave every other day, saying that he looked like a homeless person when he wore a little scruff. They fought about that because he said girls liked it. I wasn't so sure. I remember Yansi and her friend Esther talking about stubble burn and how Esther had been caught by her parents because her face, neck and the top of her tits were scratched red after one party.

Rob didn't have to shave at all, although he swore he did.

I remember last year when I first sprouted two hairs on my chest—I was so proud I thought I'd better tie them together in case they decided to disappear back in. Mom asked me why I started walking around the house without my shirt all the time. I guess I was waiting for someone to notice that I was a man. No one ever did, so I put my shirt back on. They hadn't noticed my chest hair at all; I blamed it on being blond.

I swallowed two Tylenol and headed for the kitchen.

Yansi and me didn't have big plans. I'd wanted to take her out, but she wouldn't let me spend any money on her. I was working on it. Instead, we were going to hang at the beach with Esther and another friend of theirs, Megan. Yansi had to promise her parents that she'd be in public with me the whole time during our dates. She didn't want to break any promises, but we found every which way to bend them.

I just wished I was in better shape to make the most of seeing her. I don't know what I was thinking to get so hammered. I didn't think. What a fuckin' tool.

Julia was drinking coffee in the kitchen with Ben when I walked in.

"Morning," said Ben, a huge ass smile on his face.

I grunted something unintelligible and shoved two slices of bread in the toaster then hunted through the fridge for something to put on them.

"What have you got to say for yourself?" snapped Julia.

I was tired, hung-over and she was already on my last nerve. "What?"

"Coming home drunk, stinking of whiskey and marijuana! It was a good thing Marcus was there otherwise

I'd have been getting a call from the police."

I didn't even bother answering, but that was wrong, too.

"Well? Say something!"

"Like what?"

"An apology would be nice!"

"For what?"

"For God's sake, Nicky!" she yelled.

Ben winced and stared at his coffee.

I folded my arms and leaned against the fridge, watching Julia's face change color from white to red to an ugly purple.

"Can you even get my fucking name right?" I said quietly. "It's Nick. N.I.C.K."

Julia's nostrils flared.

"How are you going to amount to anything if you spend your life drinking and smoking away each pay check? You need to start saving now if you're ever going to be able to afford to go to college, even community college. Because God knows there's nothing left after paying Mom's hospital bills."

That was news to me.

"Maybe I don't want to go to college."

"Don't be ridiculous," she hissed, her lips peeled back from her teeth like the rabid bitch she was. "What sort of job would you get without a degree?"

"Like you?" I spit back. "Two years of community college so you can be a teacher's assistant for ten bucks an hour. Maybe I'll work in a bar, like Marcus."

"Don't be stupid. You can't. Not till you're 18, unless you want to wash dishes. Hardly a great career move. And anyway, you know I want to continue to get my bachelor's so I can become a teacher. But you are just so…"

I was sick of her telling me what to do, and that every choice I made was the wrong one. I wasn't even thinking clearly; I just wanted to be left alone.

"It's my life. I'll leave school if I want to."

"The hell you will!" she shouted

"You can't stop me!" I yelled back.

She paused, and for a moment I thought that might be the end of it, but she was just reloading her weapons.

The toaster popped, making me jump a little, but Julia just took the opportunity to launch her next attack.

"And your great life plan is what? Go surfing? You can't spend your whole life as a surf bum."

"Why not?"

I didn't mean it. Or maybe I did. Julia got me so mad, it was hard to think straight.

She took a deep breath, as if willing herself not to yell. It wouldn't work; there were about 10 seconds left until she went nuclear.

She spoke slowly, like she was talking to one of the grade school kids she worked with.

"Do you want to be like Frank? A perpetual teenager?"

"Frank's okay."

Frank had been part of the surf scene as long as I could remember. He'd always been around, working some, catching waves, hanging out. What was the problem?

"How are you going to support yourself? Just one dead-end job after another? Oh, *there's* ambition!"

She aimed hit after hit, until it was me who lost it first.

"At least I won't be miserable like you!" I shouted.

She looked stunned.

"What? I'm not miserable!"

"Yeah, you are. You're always moaning about your job: the kids, the teachers, the other assistants. I'm not going to live like *that*."

"Everyone complains a bit about their job. I love what I do."

I shook my head and stared right at her.

"You're so full of crap. I don't know how Ben puts up with your shit."

She was on her feet trying to take a swing at me before I even realized what was happening. I stumbled back as Ben grabbed her around the waist.

"Don't talk to me like that!" she screeched, spit flying from her lips.

"I'll say what the fuck I want!" I bit back. "This is *my* house too, whether you like it or not. I know you're trying to get rid of me. I know you'd rather see me in a foster home. Well, fuck you! You're not Mom."

"Thank God for that!" she screamed. "Who'd want a shitty kid like you? Not even your own dad wanted you!"

Then all the color drained from her face, and she raised her hand as if she was reaching for me.

I shrugged her off and charged out of the house, breathing hard. Shaking and feeling like I was going to throw up, I scrubbed at my eyes furiously. My knees gave way and I slumped onto the small patch of grass next to our short driveway.

I heard the door open behind me and didn't think I could take round two. I pushed myself up and stumbled away.

But it was Marcus, not Julia, who caught my arm.

"You okay, kid?"

I took a deep breath, knowing he must have heard every word.

"Yeah, I guess."

"She's just being a big sister."

I shook my head, and my voice cracked. "I just get so sick of her telling me what to do all the time."

There was a beat before he responded.

"I think it's in her job description."

"She's always talking about grades and college. I don't even know if that's what I want. What do you think I should do?"

I looked up, but he just shook his head and gave a small smile.

"It's your life, Nick. I can't tell you how to live it."

I closed my eyes, my body sagging as the tension pooled in my head.

"Wish I could say the same for Julia," I sighed.

Marcus laughed and thumped my shoulder. "Come on. You need a ride somewhere?"

I was still bitching about Julia by the time we got to Yansi's house, but I was feeling in a marginally better mood.

Marcus just let me talk, nodding and laughing occasionally.

The girls were all waiting by Megan's car as we drove up. I was surprised when Marcus turned off his engine.

"This is where your girl lives?"

"Yeah."

"How long you been dating?"

"Uh, nearly four months."

His eyebrows rose in surprise.

"So long?" Then he laughed. "Didn't figure you for the one steady girl type."

I wanted to ask what he meant, but he was already out of the van and grinning at the girls.

"And who are these beautiful ladies?"

They started giggling and even Yansi was smiling at Marcus, which kinda pissed me off.

"This is Megan and Esther, and this is my girlfriend Yansi."

"Anayansi, actually," she said, and threw me a hard look.

What the fuck?

She stared at me, unblinking, and I shoved my hands in my pockets because I didn't know what else to do with them. Marcus introduced himself to each of them and then kissed Yansi's hand.

I scowled, but he just winked at me.

"I'm warming her up for you," he whispered. "You look like you need all the help you can get."

From the expression on Yansi's face, he could be

right, but I had no freakin' clue what I'd done to deserve the ice-age look.

Marcus left soon after that, but by then my mood had taken another dive.

"Oh my God, he is so freakin' hot!" Esther shrieked at a volume that had me backing away. "Does he have a girlfriend?"

"Yeah," I muttered. "Several."

They ignored me, so I climbed into the back of Megan's car, shoulders slumped and head leaning against the seatback. Yansi slid in next to me, but when I tried to take her hand, she snatched it away.

"How's the hangover?" she hissed.

I might not have been feeling too sharp, but I could see that she was pissed about something.

"Are you mad at me?"

"Good guess!" she snapped, then stared straight ahead.

Megan plugged in her iPhone and I didn't know if she really wanted to listen to Taylor Swift, or if it was supposed to cover up the sounds of our argument.

For a whole week, all I'd wanted was to kiss the hell out of my girl, and now she was acting like a total bitch. I felt the headache that had been threatening to re-emerge all morning, blossom behind my eyes.

I massaged my temples with my fingers, then gazed tiredly at Yansi.

"Are you going to tell me what the fuck I'm supposed to have done, or do you want to yell at me, too?"

She pressed her lips together and I could see Megan smirking at me in the rearview mirror.

"Fine," snapped Yansi. "Two words. Erin. Lenz."

I stared at her, surprised and confused by the fury I saw there.

"Is that supposed to mean something to me?"

"I thought you were different," she scoffed.

I rubbed my eyes, unable to dredge up the reserves of

energy to fight with her.

"Yans, I have no idea what you're talking about," I said, watching her wearily through a haze of exhaustion. "I went to see a movie with Sean and Rob and then we hung out at the pier. I had a few drinks and ... okay, I was totally trashed ... Marcus drove me home. End of story."

"Huh. So you're saying you didn't see Erin last night?"

Erin? I didn't remember seeing her...

"I'm saying that I haven't got a fuckin' clue who was at the beach last night. I was wasted, okay?"

"You look like shit and I can smell the alcohol on you."

Her words were still harsh, but her tone had eased considerably.

I pulled her hand into mine, soft and small, and a wave of something like peace rippled through me.

"Yans, I swear ... I would never cheat on you. You know what I think about that. Maybe Erin was there, I don't know. But even if she was, I don't give a shit."

She looked into my eyes, measuring the truth, then sighed and leaned her head against me.

"I'm sorry. It really sucks not being able to go out or go to parties or anything." Her lips twitched upward. "It would be easier if my boyfriend wasn't so hot."

I blinked a couple of times and began to smile.

"Yeah? I thought you said I looked like shit?"

She laughed. "Comparatively speaking."

And I knew she'd forgiven me, even though I hadn't done anything that needed forgiving, because she kissed me.

For the first time in a week, I felt her lips on mine, soft and so fucking sweet; gentle pecks at first. Then she slid her arms around my neck and pulled me towards her. I held her waist and kissed her back with an edge of need and desperation that shocked us both.

She gasped in surprise and my tongue slid into her

mouth, stroking and licking against hers. She moaned quietly, and the sound went straight to my dick.

I couldn't stop my hand trailing down to her bare thigh, and I felt her shiver. I was ready to lay her down right here, but Megan's whiny voice reminded me where I was.

"God, you guys! I don't need a live porn show in the back seat while I'm driving!"

Esther turned around in her seat to stare at us, muttering, "Speak for yourself," which I thought was seriously creepy.

Yansi just laughed and tossed her long hair over her shoulders, but her eyes were wide and sparkling, and I knew she was as turned on as I was.

I closed my eyes and leaned my head back again.

"You're gonna kill me," I muttered.

She grabbed my hand and squeezed it. "Aw, poor baby! Want me to kiss it better?"

I groaned again, but my lips turned upward in a smile, too. I opened one eye and she looked smug, her eyes flicking down to my boner.

I was surprised that she was being so, I don't know, flirty? Was that the right word? Whatever the reason, I loved it—and hated it, because it just made me want her more, and I was already struggling with the boundaries she'd drawn.

I took a long breath, and closed my eyes, enjoying the warmth of her hand in mine, her thigh pressing against me … and prayed the hard-on would disappear by the time we arrived.

We were driving down to Satellite Beach to meet up with some girl that Megan was friends with. Yansi knew her a little and said she lived in a condo next to the park. A whole bunch were supposed to be coming. I'd have been happy if it was just me and Yansi, but she didn't get to see her friends any more than she got to see me. It was fair.

The motion of the car and the soothing press of

Yansi's fingers had me drifting back to sleep. When the car jerked to a halt, I nearly got whiplash, only the seatbelt holding me back.

"Holy crap!" Esther yelled, as Megan looked at her sheepishly.

But at least it had woken me up.

Yansi had her hand clutched to her chest and took a deep breath. I couldn't resist planting one on her plump, rosy lips—goddamn, they looked so juicy.

She laughed quietly and then pushed lightly on my shoulder.

"Save that thought," she whispered.

Yeah, as if I'd be thinking of anything else now.

I climbed out of the car, squinting in the sunshine before pulling my sunglasses over my eyes. They were fake Aviators, and Yansi said they made me look like Zac Efron. I was kind of pissed when she told me that, because I don't look anything like that dude. But then she said she had a thing for him, so I guess I didn't mind that much.

I felt Yansi's hand slide up my back and I turned to grin at her.

"No you don't!" snapped Megan. "Not until we've got everything out of the car and down to the beach."

She grabbed a fistful of my t-shirt, dragged me around to the trunk, pointing at two enormous coolers.

"Carry those!" she ordered.

"Yes, ma'am," I muttered under my breath, while Yansi laughed at me openly.

Then she grabbed a bunch of beach towels and followed me down the trail.

"You have a great ass," she whispered.

"Yeah?"

"Oh, yeah!"

"It's all yours," I challenged her. "You only gotta ask."

"Maybe I won't ask; maybe I'll just grab a hold," she laughed.

"Fine by me."

As the trees thinned out, I could see people already laying out beach towels, and a couple of guys throwing a football. Some of them I knew, but there were several I didn't. I thought maybe they went to Viera or Rockledge schools.

Yansi laid out two towels for us while Megan took charge of the food and Esther was eye-fucking one of the guys playing football. Maybe more than one.

I tugged off my t-shirt and plopped down next to Yansi. She was wearing some real short cut-off jeans that showed her butt cheeks, and a tank top that was cropped above her belly button. She looked incredible.

"How come you were allowed to leave the house like that?" I teased.

She smirked at me and pointed to her sweater.

"I tied this around my waist. Papi couldn't tell the difference."

"And your mom?"

Yansi laughed. "She just shook her head and said to tell you hi."

I really liked Yansi's mom.

Just then a girl walked past wearing the smallest bikini I'd ever seen. It was only a couple of triangles that covered her nipples, and a thong that covered ... well, not that much. I couldn't help looking. No straight guy could.

"Stop staring at that slut," Yansi whisper-yelled, her eyes narrowing dangerously.

"I can't help it," I said, unpeeling my eyes. "She's got a bitchin' rack ... but yours is better."

Yansi slapped her hand down on my stomach then shook out her fingers.

"Ouch! Your stomach is so hard! You hurt my hand."

"Is that my fault, too?"

"Yes!" Then she lifted up onto one elbow to study me. "You've gotten more ripped since you started working for Papi."

In just one week? I didn't think so, but if Yansi liked the way I looked, I wasn't gonna argue.

"Yeah?"

"Oh my God, yes! Megan and Esther were just saying. They always thought you were hot, but when you took your shirt off, they were practically drooling."

I squinted up at her, trying to hold back a smile.

"You know, I'm kinda shocked. You let them talk about your boyfriend like that?"

"Not just you," she smirked. "We rate all the hot guys."

I closed my eyes and winced. "I don't think I want to know."

"It's okay, you're sittin' pretty in the number one spot."

A huge grin stretched across my face, and my ego swelled like my dick.

Then her smile slipped away. "I'm sorry I was being a bitch before. I mean, about Erin. I do trust you, it's just that…"

I looked up at her.

"Just what?"

Yansi rolled her eyes. "It's Erin. She's such a skank—guys only like her because she'll sleep with them. It creeps me out that you ever dated her."

"Jeez, Yans, one freakin' date over a year ago!"

"I know, I know. But you did go out with her so you must have liked her then—or maybe you just wanted to get laid."

"For fuck's sake!"

"Well, why did you ask her out? Was it just because I wasn't allowed to date?"

I took a deep breath, trying not to get irritated.

"Yeah, kinda. A bunch of us were going to a party and Se— the guys had been going on at me because I was the only one going stag. I just thought, you know, it would be fun … and I knew Erin would say yes."

Yansi side-eyed me.

"But it wasn't fun. She was a pain in the ass." I paused. "Why are we still talking about her?"

Yansi shrugged. "I was jealous."

I rolled onto my side. "You don't need to be. I'd never…"

"I mean a year ago. I really, really wanted to go out with you. I was so furious with Papi that he wouldn't let me—not just you, any guy who asked me out." She sighed. "But I liked you right away. You were different—you didn't flirt with all the girls; you just talked to us like we were humans. The other guys were so immature. And I knew you weren't gay…"

"What?"

Yansi grinned at me. "Well, it's one of the possibilities when a guy seems too good to be true. But Wendy de Luca said definitely not."

She raised her eyebrows challengingly and I had to look away.

"Yeah, I heard about that," she said, nudging my side. "I also heard you were a really good kisser."

"Want me to remind you?" I offered.

"Nah, I have a good memory."

She laughed as I grumbled quietly.

"I was really surprised when you asked me out because the girls told me that you didn't date. Half of them had crushes on you. Some guys would have been total players, but I don't think you even noticed half the time. And all the guys respected you. So when you were nice to me, they were, too. It just really helped, you know, being the newbie."

I laughed. "Yans, that had nothing to do with me. Believe me, every guy in school wanted you, but you were kind of scary. I mean, when Kevin Clayton said that shit about you in the lunchroom, everyone expected you to go off crying. Most girls would have, but Sean told me you handed him his ass without breaking a sweat. Jeez, I would have loved to see that."

Yansi laughed. "Yeah, well he shouldn't have called me a bitch just because I wouldn't go on a date with him. Anyway, the only guy I wanted to say yes to was you. I was just so mad that I couldn't. I didn't believe it when you said you'd ask again when I was 17. I mean, I didn't expect you to wait," she looked across at me, "but I hoped you would. So when Erin went around bragging that you'd asked her out a month later, it really hurt." Her voice dropped to a whisper. "I know she still wants you."

"Who cares? I don't want her, I want you. So nothing else matters."

Yansi smiled. "And that's what makes you different."

I leaned across and wrapped my arms around her, pulling her down for a kiss, showing her that I meant what I said—that I didn't want anyone else.

After a few minutes, she pulled away and laughed softly. "I think Papi is going to tell Pilau and Beatriz that they can't date until they're 30. Mami says every time I have a date with you he gets another gray hair."

I grinned up at her then scooted down to kiss the bare skin of her stomach, feeling her muscles shiver. "You want to really give him something to worry about?" I asked, only half joking.

"Maybe I do," she replied, her voice husky.

"God, you're so beautiful."

"You're pretty hot yourself," she whispered, reaching up to kiss me again.

"It's good to know you only want me for my body, Yans. What are you going to do when I'm bald, take my teeth out at night and have a gut bigger than Kim Kardashian's ass?"

"Dump you," she said.

I burst out laughing. "Wow, that's harsh!"

"Live with it!"

"Guess I'll have to."

"Ha! Like you guys don't do the same thing. Sean's always going on about tits and ass. I don't think he ever looks at a girl's face."

"He looks—it's just not the first thing he looks at. By the way, he thinks you have great ass-ets."

Yansi scrunched up her nose and pushed my shoulder hard.

"Oh gross! You let your friend gawk at me!"

"Well, you know Sean. And 'no' isn't really a word he understands."

"He's even more annoying than usual lately."

I didn't reply because that was true; I just didn't know why.

He'd been drinking a lot more than he normally did too, and smoking his damn head off. He said he was coming today, so I hoped we could hang later.

"By the way," Yansi said quietly, dropping her voice. "Papi's really impressed with you."

I turned on my side to look at her. "He is?"

She laughed lightly. "Yeah, he thought you'd quit after the first day."

I lay back and closed my eyes.

"He wasn't the only one," I said bitterly. "Julia didn't think I'd make it either."

Yansi was silent for a moment then squeezed my hand.

"I told Papi that he was wrong, but you know what he's like. He just said, 'Una acción habla mas que mil palabras'."

Actions speak louder than words.

"Maybe I'll just fuck up and then everyone will be happy."

She didn't say anything, but she didn't need to. Besides, I was boring myself with the pity party.

Yansi leaned her head against my shoulder and I slid my arm around her. Then she picked up my free hand and started playing with my fingers.

"I made you some Yiyimbre."

Damn, I loved those spicy gingerbreads.

"You did?"

"Yes."

I kissed her hair.

"Thank you."

"You're welcome."

Warmth flooded my chest, and I closed my eyes as she snuggled into me.

When she rested her hand on my stomach, a soft groan escaped me, and I could feel the blood instantly heading south.

"Let's go find somewhere," I whispered to her.

Her dark eyes burned and her cheeks flushed.

"I don't know, Nick…"

"Please, Yans. Please."

I could hear the desperate pleading in my voice.

"You know I want to…" she said quietly.

"Then let's go."

I was standing and tugging her hand, but she was resisting me.

"I want to … but I'm afraid I'll let things go too far," she said, staring up at me.

I closed my eyes and took a deep breath before flopping down next to her again. I'd promised myself I wouldn't be one of those guys who pressured their girl to have sex. But waiting was getting harder. No pun intended.

"Okay," I said quietly.

Yansi bit her lip. "Don't be mad."

I opened my eyes and lifted my hand to her cheek. "I'm not mad, Yans. I can't help wanting you—especially the way you look in those little shorts, but I can wait."

God, I hoped I wouldn't explode first.

She sighed. "I know you could have pretty much anyone you wanted. I know half the girls in our class are sleeping with their boyfriends and…"

I stopped her words with a kiss. "I can wait. I

promise. Just because I'm horny as hell, it doesn't mean I'm going to screw anything that looks at me."

"Are you sure?"

Her reply made me kind of pissed, and it wasn't like Yansi to be insecure.

"I said so, didn't I? Jeez, Yans, have I ever given you a reason to doubt me?"

"No, but…"

"But what?"

"I know it's harder for guys."

I stared at her in disbelief.

"For fuck's sake!"

She shook her head. "Sorry, I know you're not like that. I'm being dumb. Just kiss me."

She pressed her warm lips against me and all the irritation rushed away. She kept kissing me, her tongue fighting with mine, her breasts crushed against my chest, until I'd forgotten my own name.

Eventually, she pulled back, flushed and breathless, and I could hear catcalls and cheering behind us.

"Oops!" Yansi giggled. "I did say it was too easy to get carried away with you, cariño."

I lay back breathing hard.

"Yeah," I croaked, then grabbed my t-shirt and draped it across my hips.

Yansi looked at me questioningly as I raised my eyebrows.

"Oh!" she laughed, her beautiful eyes glinting with mischief.

Yep, I was a goner. Could guys my age have heart attacks?

Then someone plopped down next to me.

"Get a room, you stallion," slurred Sean, with a laugh.

Yansi threw him an irritated look then stalked off to talk to her girlfriends.

"How you doin', bro?"

"Awesome! Your man Marcus is one cool fucker. He

fixed me up with some grade-A shit. You want some?"

"Nah, I'm good," I said, sitting up reluctantly. "If I smoke anything today, I'll fall asleep." I'd already felt my eyelids closing in the warm sunshine.

Sean laughed loudly. "Yeah, right! Nothing to do with the fact that your tight-assed *girlfriend* is here," he spat the word venomously.

"Hey!" I said, elbowing him in the ribs. "Don't talk about Yans like that."

"Whatever," he slurred, then lurched to his feet. "Let me know when she gives you your balls back."

I watched him stagger away, crashing into the bunch of guys playing football.

"Asshole," I muttered.

Yansi was right—something was up with Sean, but the mood he was in, I didn't think he'd be letting me in on what was bugging him. Maybe we could hang later in the week—if I wasn't working or sleeping.

I yawned and stretched. If I didn't get up and do something, I'd be spending the day with my eyes closed. I watched Yansi talking to Esther and Megan. Esther saw me and shook her head.

"Girl time!" she yelled.

Yansi laughed at the expression on my face, then blew me a kiss. All the guys whooped and yelled, and I felt my cheeks heat up. *Fuck 'em; just because they didn't have a girlfriend as hot as Yans.*

I decided to go for a swim. The tide was way out, and the beach was wide and flat. The light gray-brown sand was soft as sugar and burning hot. I broke into a jog, relieved when the ripples splashed up my legs. I dove into the water, the light turning hazy as I opened my eyes, a slight sting from the salt, but one I was well used to.

The beach seemed distant when I surfaced, and I was amazed how far I'd swum. Yansi was right—even in just a week of yard work, my muscles had gotten stronger. It felt good. It felt really good. I swam further, enjoying the silky feel of the sun-warmed water on my skin. When I turned to look at the beach again, I could just make out a figure standing on the shore watching me.

She raised a hand and waved.

My girl. Looking out for me. And then the sudden realization hit me, *I love her.*

I was so surprised I nearly sank, and then panic started to set in. I must be wrong. I liked Yansi; I liked her a lot. But it wasn't love, no way. I couldn't love her. Love was too big, too risky, and people you loved died.

But the idea wouldn't go away. With every beat of my heart, the truth pulsed through me, *You love her, you love her, you love her.*

It was the scariest fucking thing ever.

She was waiting for me, paddling at the edge of the water, stunning in a pale yellow bikini that showcased her curvy body; her long hair loose, begging for me to tangle my fingers in it.

I love her.

"Hey, you," she smiled. "The food's ready. But I wasn't going to put out the Yiyimbre till you got back in."

I offered her a weak smile, afraid to meet her eyes, knowing that she was too good at reading me.

She frowned. "Are you okay?"

"Just ... tired," I stuttered.

Her raised eyebrows told me that she didn't believe me, but she didn't call me on it either.

"Okaaay," she said slowly, and held out her hand.

Her skin was hot against mine and darker. I stared at our joined hands, feeling a jolt of painful pleasure, as if someone had jumpstarted my heart. Maybe she had.

She didn't try to talk to me as we walked back to join the others. Unlike most girls who seemed to think they had to talk 24/7 to keep a guy interested, Yansi didn't make me talk when I didn't want to. And right now I couldn't. Words kept sticking in my throat, and I felt dumb in more than one way.

When we joined the others, at least I had the distraction of loading up a plate with some food. I knew Yansi wasn't buying the whole 'tired' excuse, but I knew she wouldn't force the issue in front of other people either.

"Oh my God, my parents are so stupid!" laughed a girl. "They totally believed me when I told them I'd never smoked weed and I never would. Are they serious?"

"Yeah, well your mom thinks Santa Claus is real and that you're still a virgin!"

"Bitch! Like you can talk?"

"At least your parents let you have your own car. Mine are so pathetic—they say I have to share with my sister. I really hate them."

Yansi threw me a sympathetic look and moved our towels further away. She knew I couldn't stand it when other kids whined about their parents, calling them losers and assholes. I'd have given anything to be able to complain about curfews or parent-teacher conferences. Julia did some of that stuff instead now, but it wasn't the same; it never would be again.

I didn't feel hungry anymore, so I set the plate down on the sand and pulled my sunglasses over my eyes.

"You never talk about your mom," Yansi said quietly.

I didn't reply.

"I wish I'd known her."

Mom was already sick when Yansi and I started dating. We didn't know at first. Or if Mom knew, she didn't say anything. I guess I just hadn't noticed, or noticed but not realized what it meant. I remember small things that she did or didn't do—not finishing the take-out food, even though it was her favorite chicken enchiladas; losing weight even though she'd been on every diet known to woman, and it had never made any difference; and just being tired all the time.

I remember her asking me why I was late back from school one day. She knew I hadn't been with Sean, because he'd stopped by on his way home, looking for me, pissed when I wasn't there. And I admitted that I was seeing someone—someone I liked a lot.

I thought I'd get another lecture about respecting women and being safe—but I didn't. She just gave a small smile and said she was glad that I'd found someone.

"When can I meet her?" she asked.

I told her, *Soon, maybe*, but I hadn't meant it, and then it was too late.

Mom knew it as well, because in small ways, she started preparing us, me and Julia. Suddenly, it was important for her to tell me that that main valve for the house's water supply was at the back of the garage, and that the electricity bill was monthly. I listened halfheartedly, itching to be outside, surfing or skating or shooting the breeze with Sean; Julia pursed her lips and kept looking at her watch. And I don't know why Mom didn't scream at us: *Pay attention! I'm not going to be here to hold your hand.*

And I didn't bother to listen when she told us to wash dark loads and white loads separately in the machine; and Julia was impatient, saying she already knew that; Mom, tired and defeated, trying to pass on a lifetime of advice in just a few short weeks.

Because that's the thing about cancer … even when the doctors give you a deadline, it still sneaks up on you. They don't like to be too certain—I suppose they can't. But they never say, *You're not going to need to order a turkey for Thanksgiving this year*, or, *I don't think you'll get much use out of your Christmas sweater.*

So despite everything, I think dying took Mom by surprise. And she forgot to pay the phone bill. We only found out when the landline stopped working and it took weeks to reconnect. So we didn't have any internet either. And that's at the same time as having to pick out a coffin, even though Mom had left instructions that she wanted a cremation. She said not to pick a real expensive one because it's only going to get all burned up anyway.

Julia said Mom wanted a cremation because she was afraid of the dark. I thought it was because she was creeped out by the thought of being in the ground with all the worms and bugs and then they'd ... you know. But she'd always hated yard work too, even though she liked it to look nice. So it might have been because of that and because she didn't want to put us in the position of tending her grave. But I'm just guessing because I was too chicken shit to ask her anything real when she was dying.

So Mom never met Yansi. I think she would have liked her though.

Mom always had a soft spot for Sean, even when he was the reason I got detention every afternoon for three weeks for putting saran wrap over the toilets in the staff restrooms when we were in ninth grade. I think she felt sorry for Sean. And he made her laugh.

The second to last thing Mom said to me was, *Don't forget to put out the recycling.*

The last thing I said to her was after the nurse had given her a morphine shot because the pain-relief cannula didn't seem to work anymore. I said, *Don't rub where she's injected, Mom, or it'll bruise.*

So the very last thing she said was, *It hurts.*

Why didn't she tell me about my dad? Why didn't I ask? Because that would mean admitting something real. But I didn't ask and now I'll never know. But shouldn't she have told me?

It really sucks being pissed at someone who's dead.

In the days leading up to the funeral, I wondered what sort of things I'd tell people if I knew I was dying. Well, I wouldn't tell Julia anything, because she already knew everything there was to know, or that's what it seemed like. I didn't even like the willow coffin she picked out because I thought it looked like a hamper. She said that was stupid and that Mom would have chosen it for herself. I don't know—Mom hated doing laundry as much as I do, so I didn't think she'd like being stuck in one, but

Julia started crying again, so I didn't say anything after that.

I guess I'd tell Sean that he always stops paddling for a wave about two seconds too soon, which means he's never at the best place to pop up, which means he loses a lot of waves that he should have caught. I'd tell Mrs. McInnery, my math teacher, that all the students laugh at her because she has a mustache, and not because they don't like her. I'd tell Erin Lenz that sleeping with half the guys in Junior class is never going to make her popular. I'd tell Yansi that asking her out is the smartest thing I've ever done, and that waiting for her to turn 17 before I could ask her out again is the second smartest thing I've ever done.

And I'd tell myself to ask my dying mom about my sperm donor father, because I'd never get the chance otherwise. But then again, maybe I'd tell myself not to bother, because I had one really great parent, and that's more than some people get.

"She'd have liked you," I said to Yansi.

"Really?"

"Yeah," I said. "She'd have loved you."

Yansi smiled.

Maybe she knew that was the closest I could get to telling her myself.

Chapter 4

I lay in bed with the curtains drawn back and the window wide open.

Not that it made a damn bit of difference. The air was heavy with a damp heat, and I could hear the sound of mole crickets, crackling like radio static. I was so used to them, it was almost white noise. But tonight, I couldn't get the sounds out of my head.

I shoved the wrinkled sheet completely off my body, trying to find a cool spot on the bed, and wished again that Julia wasn't such a bitch about having the air-conditioning on.

A couple of weeks ago, I casually mentioned that Mom used to let us have A/C in the summer, and my sister nearly took my throat out. Yeah, over-reaction much.

She acted like just saying Mom's name was a blasphemy or something.

Sean said that I shouldn't take Julia's shit, and that half the house was mine, too. I hadn't really thought of it like that until he mentioned it. But I guess he was right: I owned a house. Well, half a house. I imagined drawing a line down the middle. We could have half the bath tub each, but the toilet would be on my side, and I'd make her pay a toll every time she used it. But then that would mean she'd get the half of the house with the coffee maker and the fridge. Maybe I could get a used fridge for my half of the house, then I could have cold soda and leave the door open all night to cool my room, too. Or maybe just buy an air-conditioning unit and hope she didn't notice the increase in the electric bill.

We'd have to share the computer because I needed it for school, and Julia used it for work. Mom had bought it two years ago, so it was kind of ancient now. Maybe I'd let Julia buy me out and I'd get a new one with that and the money left over from work. Then I could watch porn whenever I wanted.

Sean had a really good stash of DVDs that he'd borrowed from his brothers—the kind of borrowing where nobody knows that you borrowed it and you don't give it back either. I had the stack of magazines that he'd finished with, too. Although I got a bit queasy at the thought of used porn mags. A guy's gotta have standards, even if they're low ones—and some of the pages were stuck together, which was kind of gross.

Not that I needed photos like that to get a boner. Seeing Yansi in that little yellow bikini today—that had given me spank-bank material for months.

She'd let her hair loose and it hung down to her waist, all thick and glossy. I imagined wrapping it around my hands and losing myself in her sweet, spicy scent.

Just thinking all that had me good and hard, and seeing as it didn't look like I'd be getting to sleep anytime soon, I decided to go with the flow.

I kept a small bottle of lotion that I'd swiped from Julia's side of the bathroom cabinet for times like now. I mean, you can use spit, but it's not so good, and ... you know ... chafing.

So I reached under the bed and squirted some of that

fruity shit onto my hands. It smelled kind of sweet, but I'd shower it off in the morning.

It felt good to touch myself. Hell, I'd been doing it since I hit puberty. When I was a kid, I imagined some actress off of the TV or a model in Julia's magazines. Sean liked Pamela Anderson, and made me watch a ton of 'Baywatch' reruns. I'd always preferred brunettes, like Megan Fox. But these days, I couldn't help but think of Yansi's hands on me, imagining what it would feel like to have her mouth, her body around me.

Holy shit, that image always worked quickly. My legs stiffened, my heart rate went up and I was breathing hard like I'd just paddled out through a set of eight-foot waves. My dick was throbbing like a mofo and that amazing tingling sensation started shooting around my body. I broke out into goose bumps on my chest, and the head of my dick became super sensitive so it was almost too much to touch it on the up-strokes. My butt muscles clamped up and my toes curled. I could feel the cum welling up, like filling a glass with water until…

I jerked all over my stomach, thick trails of cum, and imagined doing that on Yansi's chest. I felt a bit guilty for using her like that, but not really all that much.

I lay there catching my breath. It amazed me that a couple of minutes of beating the meat was more exhausting than half a day of yard work for Mr. Alfaro. Weird. Maybe God didn't want you to enjoy sex too much, so it was rationed by how fit you were. They should tell you that in gym class—you'd have guys lining up for extra workouts.

Yeah, I had some strange thoughts when I was spiraling down from having shot my bolt.

Sean said he had hallucinations, like someone was whispering in his ear when he was coming down. He said it freaked him out so much this one time that he thought someone had come into his room. He'd ended up slapping his school book across his stomach to hide the mess.

Two pages of 'To Kill A Mockingbird' got glued together so he never did find out what happened when Boo Radley went into Scout's bedroom. I don't think he cared either, but he had to tell Mr. Donovan that he dropped carbonara sauce on it. I don't think Mr. Donovan believed him. Maybe he thought Sean was jerking off to ninth grade literature. Maybe English teachers would like to think that books turn students on that much.

It happens a lot in school. Not in the bathrooms so much, because they're pretty disgusting. I'm just saying that if you're a substitute teacher, look out for the kid sitting at the back, or the one whose desk is kind of away from the others. Oh, and sweaters lying over people's laps when it's pushing a hundred degrees in the shade. Not just dudes either. Macie Peters would do it and let you watch if you paid her $10. I didn't have the money, so Sean cut her a deal: $15 so we could both watch. That was pretty nice of him, I thought. That's when we were in eighth grade.

I didn't tell Yansi that sort of shit: I wasn't dumb. I mean, she probably knew, but it was in the bro code.

I was just falling asleep when Julia started moaning, her headboard thudding against the wall. I threw my pillow over my face. I *so* didn't want to hear my sister getting nailed.

I made a mental note to sneak into her room tomorrow and move her freakin' bed away from the wall. Sheesh. A guy shouldn't have to listen to that in his own house.

Sean's brothers had been back from college for a few weeks, and I'd been invited to go eat dinner with the family.

I'd known Sean since third grade, so I'd met his

parents a bunch of times, although not really that many for the length of time we'd been friends. I never felt all that comfortable in their house, and Sean preferred hanging out at my place anyway. I'd always thought it was because his older brothers were ragging on him, but even when Patrick moved out last Fall, Sean still preferred my place.

I'd heard him complain about his parents enough times to know that they put a lot of pressure on all their kids. Plus, his older brothers had been lettermen and Sean wasn't into that ego bullshit. He partied, he surfed. I guess that was one of the reasons we were friends.

The few times I'd had dinner at his house, it had always been kind of formal—like his mom insisted on setting the table with silverware and napkins. At my house, it was takeout, TV dinners or sitting on the rickety back porch while Mom charred something on the grill.

When Mom died, Mrs. Wallis made a point of coming over with a pot roast and meals to put in the freezer. Julia thanked her and made small talk; I watched Sean's mom as she tried not to notice the peeling wallpaper or sagging sofa. I hated seeing my home through her eyes.

Sean had stood awkwardly, hands in his pockets, cringing when his mom offered "sincere condolences". She'd met Mom maybe five times in eight years and they hadn't really got along. Whatever.

I wasn't sure why I was being asked for dinner now. Maybe because Sean's brothers were home, or maybe Mrs. Wallis thought it was the right thing to do since Mom died.

But Sean was like my brother, so I wasn't going to say no.

He had three real brothers, all older than him.

Dylan was 23, and had graduated in the same year as Julia. He was in med school at Florida State now and didn't come home all that often. He was okay. He told great stories about anatomy class and what it was like dissecting some poor bastard who'd donated his body to medical science. He brought a finger home once when he was pre-med. Dylan didn't do cool shit like that anymore. But you don't want to know what happened to the finger; I'm just saying the next door neighbor's dog was sick for three days—probably the formaldehyde.

And it didn't seem so funny after Mom died.

Aidan was 22 and had graduated from U of SC in Business and Marketing. He'd just scored some fancy internship with an advertising agency in Chicago. I only knew that much because Sean had griped about his parents making a big deal of it. I don't know, maybe it was a big deal, but I couldn't imagine working in an office all day. I liked Aidan. He was the one who'd taught me to surf when I was eight, and we'd spent a lot of hours together catching waves. That's why it seemed so weird that he was going to live in a city so far from the ocean.

Patrick had just finished his first year at MIT and was planning to major in Aerospace Engineering. He was also a dick, and I was glad when he moved away. I wasn't looking forward to seeing him now. He used to beat the crap out of Sean until he grew big enough to hit him back.

But, like I said: family of over-achievers. Sometimes I didn't envy Sean his car and allowance.

He was quiet on the ride over. I knew why and didn't blame him. Hell, I'd be quiet with all that weight of expectation pressing down on me.

I don't know if Mom wanted me to be anything. She always said she was happy if I was happy. But she was proud of Julia going to college. It was only community college to get her AS degree in Elementary Education so she could get a job as a teacher assistant, but it meant she was the first person in our family to study after high school. The money was shit: $10.23 an hour. Hell, if I went to college, I'd want to earn more than that—something that would make sitting in a classroom for years worthwhile.

I don't think Sean had a choice about going to

school. His parents started a college fund for him before he was born. The only choices he had were Florida State, where Mr. Wallis had gotten his bachelor's degree; Ole Miss, where Mrs. Wallis went before she got married; or U of SC because Aidan had gone there. They already knew he wasn't going Ivy League.

Sean had the air turned up real high, so I was shivering even though I was wearing jeans and it was 90 degrees outside and damn near 90% humidity, too. It was one of those evenings where it felt like you could wring out the air and make it rain.

But it was the tension in Sean that made me the most uncomfortable.

"You okay, man?"

He shot me a sideways glance.

"Sure. Why wouldn't I be?"

I shrugged. If he didn't want to talk, that was just fine by me.

"No reason."

He looked like he was going to say something else, but then changed his mind.

He fiddled with his iPhone and tried not to wince as the car lurched toward the curb. The beat of 'Damned If I Do Ya' came through the speakers. It wasn't music to slit your wrists by, but it was close. I would never admit it to Sean, but I preferred Jack Johnson.

"You seeing Yansi tomorrow?"

"Nope. She's got church then family time."

He pulled a face. "Fuckin' family time. It's overrated, bro. You're better off without it."

"Nice to have the choice," I muttered.

There was a moment's silence.

"Sorry, man. That was a shitty thing to say."

I stared out of the window. "'Sokay."

"Fuck, I mean it. You're my brother. You're more family to me than any of *them*. Hell, your Mom practically raised me. She was the one who taught me to hold the toilet seat up in case it fell when I was taking a wiz and cut off my johnson."

I laughed out loud. "Mom said that?"

"Yeah! Freaked me out, too! I've never forgotten it. I was nine. I pissed in the tub for a month after she told me that."

I had to hold my stomach, I was laughing so hard.

"Seriously! Your mom was a legend."

The smile slid off my face, and I sighed. "Yeah. She was."

We were both silent for a moment.

"You miss her," he said at last.

I couldn't take talking about her in the past tense anymore.

"You grow a vagina this week?" I snarked. "Because you're talking like a pussy."

Sean laughed. He knew exactly what I was doing, but he didn't call me on it. It was times like this that I remembered why I put up with the sorry fucker.

When we got to his house, the driveway was full of cars. I felt a stab of jealousy that everyone in Sean's family had their own rides, and then I wondered how come his other brothers all drove Beamers when he had a Toyota, even if it was a new one.

Sean must have guessed that part of what I was thinking.

"You sure you want to hang with the bougies?"

I grinned. "You bet!"

Sean looked relieved. He probably thought I was going to bail on him, but if he lived at my place and knew that the only option for food was Cheerios or baloney, he'd be hittin' up the Wallis house, too.

As soon as we were parked, Patrick and Aidan came around from the side of the garage, arguing and shoving each other jokingly. Patrick was carrying a basketball and threw it straight at Sean so it would have slammed into his chest if he hadn't caught it in time.

"The kids are here," laughed Patrick.

"Asshole," Sean muttered out of the corner of his mouth.

Aidan came over to shake hands.

"Hey, Nick. How you doin', man? Sorry about your ma."

"Yeah, thanks," I said awkwardly, shoving my hands in my pockets.

I hated it when people said stuff like that to me, but I hated it more if they pretended it hadn't happened. I guess there isn't really a good way to bring it up. Although Jesse in my homeroom probably won the prize for the most crass comment.

"Hey, heard your mom died. Rough break. Did you know corpses piss and shit themselves because the muscles don't work anymore?"

Sean would have punched him in the face if I hadn't gotten there first. I didn't get detention for that either. I got sent to the guidance office, and was allowed to do what I wanted for pretty much the rest of the day.

I almost hoped Jesse would say something else dumb the next day too, because then I could have another day of slacking off. But he didn't. Guess someone 'had a word with him'. He avoided me after that, although it was two days before he could see out of his left eye and another week before the bruise faded. Guy was a harmless dick really.

Sean tossed the basketball into a bush and smiled as Patrick cussed him out.

"Welcome to the Brady Bunch," muttered Sean.

We all walked into the house together, but it was only when I was side by side with Patrick, that I realized I was a couple of inches taller than him. I'm not generally the kind of guy who holds a grudge, but I got a kick out of the fact that I could look down on him. He seemed kind of pissed about it, too.

Mrs. Wallis came out to corral the troops and send us

to wash up. Yeah, really. Like we were first graders or something.

Patrick rolled his eyes but Aidan just laughed and gave his mom a hug. I saw Sean watching, something like envy on his face. The expression quickly faded.

When Mrs. Wallis saw me, she came over, acting really formal.

"Good evening, Nicolas. How are you coping, dear? And how's that lovely sister of yours?"

Nobody called me 'Nicolas' except her. I asked Mom once and she said that wasn't my name. Maybe Mrs. Wallis thought it would make me sound like a kid whose parents were members at the country club. It didn't. I thought it was kind of amusing, but I knew it irritated the hell out of Sean. He thought his mom was pretentious. I had to agree.

"Yeah, okay thanks. She's good."

She nodded quickly and gave me a practiced smile. Damn, her teeth were white and really, really big, like Tom Cruise big. I wondered if she'd had more work done on them.

"Do take a seat, dear," she said, pointing at the straight-backed dining room chairs.

I always felt like an imposter when I had to sit down to dinner like this. I couldn't imagine why people enjoyed it; it gave me gut-ache, sitting there all tense, waiting to drop something or spill something. At the Alfaros' house, nobody cared about that. I had to concentrate because it was all in Spanish, but even with Mr. Alfaro there, it was always noisy and fun. Not that I talked that much, but I liked being there. Here, I felt like I was taking a test.

Sean hated it, too.

Dylan wandered in, looking at something on his phone, but he turned it off when Mr. Wallis came in and sat at the head of the table. He always sat there; I guess he wanted to let everyone know that he was in charge.

Aidan and Sean brought the food in while their dad started grilling me.

"So, young man, what have you been up to this summer? Being a beach bum, like my youngest, I presume."

I shot a look at Sean and he pulled a face before darting back into the kitchen to carry more dishes.

"No, sir. I've been working."

Mr. Wallis looked surprised.

"Really? Doing what?"

"Yard work—lawn care."

He looked amused.

"Well, at least it won't be too challenging for you."

Bastard. I felt my cheeks heat up with a mixture of anger and embarrassment. When Sean walked back in I knew he'd heard because he looked pissed, but he didn't say anything either. Maybe my father was a prick for not caring enough to want to see me even once, but at least I didn't have to live with a prick for a father every day of my life.

Aidan looked at me sympathetically while Patrick just smirked at his father, sharing in the holy fucking joke of me doing yard work to make some money.

Mrs. Wallis said grace and then told us to pass the food around.

Patrick went into a long monologue about MIT and how he'd decided to choose his major. He made it sound like NASA would have a big hard-on for him once he'd finished his degree.

"And what are your plans for college, Nicolas?"

I was poised with a piece of roast pork halfway to my mouth. I laid my fork on my plate and looked up.

"I don't really have any plans at the moment."

Mr. Wallis looked like I'd just dropped my pants and pissed on the table leg.

"Surely you have some idea?"

"No, sir. I guess I just want to graduate high school."

He snorted in disbelief. "A high school diploma won't get you far these days. You need a college degree unless you want to spend the rest of your life mowing other people's lawns."

As he hadn't asked an actual question, I didn't reply. But he hadn't finished yet.

"Even Sean, who isn't at all academically gifted, will be going to a good school. You have to plan ahead. Your mother must have wanted something better for you than yard work."

He spat out the last sentence and the table fell silent. Aidan looked pained, and even Dylan and Patrick seemed uncomfortable. Sean was pissed and about to say something, so I answered before he could rile up his old man.

I looked across at Mr. Wallis and met his eyes. "She said she wanted me to be happy."

"So your mother had no ambition at all for you? You have none for yourself?"

"Nick wants to be a shaper," Sean said, unable to stay quiet for a moment longer.

I hadn't told many people that, because it seemed like a pipe dream. But I'd shaped three surfboards for myself in the last two years, starting from a block of solid foam, adding the stringer down the center for strength, covering it with fiberglass cloth, and glossing on the top layer that made you high if you breathed it in too much. Sean had been around quite a bit while I was doing that. The first board had been shit and impossible to balance on because I hadn't got the rocker right, but the next ones had been pretty good.

Mr. Wallis laughed. "Really? Is surfing all you boys think about?"

"You have to be pro surfer to be a shaper and sell surfboards," Patrick stated like I was too dumb to have thought of that. "You have to win competitions."

"Nick was runner-up at Ron Jon's," Sean said hotly, talking about the surf festival that was held at the pier every Easter. About fifty thousand people showed up to watch this year.

Patrick looked surprised, but I could tell he was impressed and trying to hide it.

"Runner-up isn't winning," Patrick went on, his voice smug. "And the Junior section doesn't count."

I didn't bother to tell him that I was runner-up in the men's pro-am shortboard. Sean had loaned me the money for the $150 entry fee, and Julia had forged Mom's signature for parental permission because I was under 18 and Mom been too weak to hold the pen.

The winner was a pro surfer named Michael Dunphy. He'd been cool, chatting with me, giving me some tips, and when he heard that Yansi was from Panama, he told us about a trip he was taking down there and the awesome surf spots he'd be hitting up around Isla Grande and Bocas del Toro.

"Nick will win next year," Sean said. "Won't you, bro."

I shifted uncomfortably in my chair. I hated everyone talking about me like that. And I wished I had Sean's confidence in me winning. I'd have to put in a lot of hours, and what with school and work, I didn't see how I'd have the time.

Anyway, I'd only done the comp for a bet, although the prize money came in handy. But I wasn't great as a competition surfer; I preferred being at an empty break with a consistent 8-10 foot swell, with one or two buddies or by myself.

Older guys called it being a 'soul surfer'. I don't know about that—I just liked doing my own thing.

"Nice job, Nick," said Aidan. "That's pretty cool! Maybe we could all head out to Shark Pit some time. You can show us how the pros do it."

"Hell, yeah!" said Sean, and immediately got called on his cussing.

Shark Pit was a great beach break not far from us, that worked at its best when a large northern swell came in. It was a place where mostly locals went, and virtually a secret spot.

"We should show Marcus," Sean continued.

"Who?" asked Patrick.

"Nick's roomie."

Mrs. Wallis looked taken aback. "You have a roommate? A school friend?"

"No, we rent out a room at home."

Mrs. Wallis looked like she was having difficulty understanding the concept.

"We put an ad on Craigslist," I clarified.

It didn't seem to help much.

"You rent a room?"

"Yes," I said, trying not to roll my eyes.

"Your house must be bigger than I remember," she sniffed.

"We rent out Mom's old room," I said quietly.

Wow, no wonder Sean wanted to get wasted all the time if that was what it was like for him at home.

I was allowed to eat the rest of my dinner in peace after that.

When we'd cleared the table, we headed out to Sean's room to play on his Xbox.

"Sorry about the inquisition," he mumbled. "Dad's always like that when the four of us are together. He probably thinks it'll make me want to be more like *them*. And Mom's just ... what the fuck ever. I can't wait to tell them I'm taking a year out for our surfari."

I rubbed a spot on the back of my neck.

"I don't think I'm going to be able to afford it now."

He looked at me in horror.

"You gotta, man! You gotta! I'm counting on you, bro. I've got to take some time out from school or my head will fucking explode. Come on! You *promised.*"

I sighed and stared at my sneakers. They were just about trashed. A new pair would cost most of what I already had saved.

"I don't have the money and..."

He shook his head furiously. "You'd be a shoo-in for financial aid in college."

"Maybe, but…"

"And you've got a year to save up! You can…"

"I can what?" I snapped. "Take another fuckin' backbreaking job so I can pay for it? And what about college? Just because your parents think I'm dumb as dirt, it doesn't mean I don't want to go."

"Don't lump me in with *them*," he yelled. Then he gave a hollow laugh. "They think I'm dumb too, so don't worry about it. At least you're acing Spanish."

I gave him a wry grin. "See! Girls are good for something other than screwing."

"Speaking of which … what about you and Yansi? Have you plugged that hole yet?"

"You did not just say that!"

I threw a pillow in his face to make my point.

"That means you haven't!" he laughed.

"Don't go there, man," I said, a slight warning in my voice.

He held up his hands in surrender, then looked more serious.

"Nick, we've been talking about this trip for two freakin' years. Don't bail on me now, man. I *need* this."

I sighed and leaned back against his bed. "Maybe I can do three months. If I work the rest of the year, maybe I'll have enough."

"Eight months?" he wheedled.

"Okay, four! Final offer."

"Ah, fuck," he said, shaking his head. "I'll talk you into it."

"Whatever, man!" I laughed.

Chapter 5

Sometimes one bad decision leads to another, and another, and another, and without even realizing it you're some poor bastard with the house of cards crashing down on top of you. It seemed solid at the time.

It started when Trey's parents went away for the weekend. I didn't know Trey that well—he was one of the graduating seniors, just one of the guys who surfed on weekends.

It's like an unwritten rule that when someone's parents go away, the party's at their place, especially if they've got a pool. Then you hope that no idiot tweets it or you're overrun with strangers and tourists.

I heard about the party from Sean, and he heard about it from Rob, and Rob had been invited by Trey's sister who he knew from pol-sci, and he'd bumped into her when he was buying more grip-tape for his skateboard. That's small towns for you.

I didn't mention it to Yansi because I knew that she'd be pissed at not being allowed to go. Yeah, not the smartest thing ever. Because, like I said, small town, and word gets around.

Trey's family were well off. Maybe not rolling in money, but his mom and dad both worked, and Trey and his sister were planning on going to expensive Boston colleges. Plus, each had their own brand new Ford SUVs, so they seemed well off to me. I wondered if Trey knew the price of a gallon of milk.

The evening began just the same as all the others had that summer.

It had been a long day—hot, hard work, and the end of my second week working for Yansi's old man. Today it had been a new client for Mr. Alfaro, and a garden gone wild, if the scratches up my arms were anything to go by. I'd spent the afternoon wrestling a tree stump out of the sun-dried dirt; a small tree—but a fucking enormous bastard of a stump. I won in the end, and felt like a gladiator, sawdust and blood fresh on the ground. And a strange satisfaction looking down into that hole, the defeated stump on the back of Mr. Alfaro's truck. *Now who's the man, motherfucking stump!*

Exhausted, I'd fallen asleep for a couple of hours when I got home, my alarm waking me after what seemed just a minute. Then I stumbled to the shower like one of the zombies from *Day of the Dead*, but with better hair.

The hot water felt like heaven and the only thing that would have made it better was if Yansi was there with me. Just thinking about her hands sliding over my body had me too hard to think straight.

But even after taking care of that, I was still out of the bathroom in less than 10 minutes.

Julia used to spend two hours getting ready for a party when I was a kid. It drove me crazy because she'd hog the bathroom, and one time I even had to take a piss in the backyard because she'd been in there for so long and wouldn't come out until she'd glued on her false eyelashes.

I like girls with makeup just fine, but false eyelashes

seem like cheating. It's like when you cop a handful, and you're aching for soft, warm flesh, but instead you get one of those padded bras or even a pair of socks. That happened to Aidan once. Fact.

But Julia didn't go to parties anymore or hardly ever, although she still had a set of false eyelashes that she kept in the bathroom. They creeped me out, looking like spiders in a jam jar. Freaky.

These days, she just stayed in with Ben, watched a movie and ordered take-out. Yawn.

I couldn't afford to buy take-out for myself, and I hated her choice of movies. Just sayin'. I usually mooched some food then headed out. I don't know how Ben put up with all that chick flick shit. But he didn't seem to mind. He didn't seem to mind about much at all. Or maybe she kept his balls in a box in the closet. That seemed possible, too. Or maybe she was really good at giving head—the thought made me gag.

Ben was in the kitchen when I went to hunt for food. I could have hugged him—in a bro way. Yeah, really, because he was phoning for pizza and automatically ordered me a spicy meat feast with extra cheese when he saw me. He might have been boring, but he was okay—treated Julia good, which I thought was cool of him, even when she was a total bitch. Maybe he had a few screws loose, but like I said, nothing fazed him.

I wondered if he was like that at work, fixing people's plumbing; slow, steady, treading calmly through the day. Trustworthy, yeah; but boring, oh yeah.

Julia was slumped in front of the TV, watching some reality show. She said she hated them, but she always watched them. Cue laughter.

"Pizza in ten minutes," said Ben, sitting next to her on the sofa and slinging his arm around her shoulders.

"Ugh, it's too hot," she moaned, so Ben shifted his arm away again.

He didn't even roll his eyes. I would have. In fact I

did. I couldn't figure out why the hell anyone would date my sister. I suppose she was kind of okay looking, but dear sweet baby Jesus, she could complain about having sand on the beach.

I turned away and stared out at the weed-filled back yard.

"God, I'm so bored!" whined Julia. "How come we have to stay in every night? Why can't we go out and do something for a change?"

Even though she was talking quietly, I could hear her complaints all the way across the living room and into the kitchen. Not that our house was large or anything, but I could hear every word. Ben answered easily, like he always did.

"You said we're saving money."

Julia made a sound like she wanted to disagree but couldn't deny it, and I really wanted to laugh.

There was no soda in the fridge, so I poured myself a glass of water. I knew she'd bust a blood vessel if I swiped one of Ben's beers in front of her.

But when I walked into the living room, it was my turn to get chewed out anyway. Guess she really was bored.

"Where are you going tonight, all dressed up?"

Dressed up? That was funny. I was wearing ripped jeans and a band tee. But I'd had my weekly shave; maybe that was what she meant.

"Out," I said shortly, more from habit than because I wanted to make her mad.

"Out where?" she snapped.

I considered whether or not to answer, but I couldn't think of a good enough reason not to tell her, unless I just wanted to piss her off some more. And I was feeling mellow because, hey, stump-killer here.

"Party," I said.

Her eyes narrowed.

"Where?"

"A friend's."

"Could you be more specific?"

"No one you know."

She ground her teeth.

Ben coughed and threw me a pleading look. Okay, so maybe she did get to him. Maybe the guy was one click away from postal after all.

I headed back to the kitchen to swipe that beer. Suddenly, I was feeling like I needed it. Ben followed me.

"She just worries about you, bud."

I considered that while I took a long drink of beer. Did she worry? Because last I'd heard she was planning to put me in foster care. Like I'd fucking let her.

Yeah, I'd found my reason not to answer her. Sorry, Ben.

Then I heard the front door open and Marcus walked into the living room. Nice timing. He could be Julia's distraction.

"Hey, Julia," said Marcus. "'Sup?"

"Hi! I thought you were working."

"No, night off."

"Are you going to that party with Nicky?"

Wow, straight for the jugular.

He laughed lightly. "Well, I'm going to *a* party. Couldn't say if it's the same party Nick's going to."

He strolled into the kitchen and a knowing smile crossed his face when he saw me sitting on the back porch with Ben, both of us drinking beer.

"Hey, guys."

"Hey."

"If it is the same party, I don't want Nicky getting drunk," Julia yelled after him.

Ben shook his head, and padded back into the living room.

"It's Friday night," I heard him say mildly. "Give the kid a break. We used to party at his age."

"Don't tell me how to handle Nicky!" Julia snapped.

Great. So now I needed handling. There was an awkward silence.

Marcus winked at me and helped himself to a beer as well, then leant against the doorjamb looking into the living room.

I stayed on the porch, pressing the cold can against my head, trying to calm the fuck down from a sudden burn of anger that hadn't been there two minutes ago.

"What are you guys watching?" Marcus asked.

I bet myself a dollar that Ben was feeling pretty good about Marcus' interruption now.

"Some weirdo film about a kid who wants to screw a granny."

"Ben!" snorted Julia. " 'Harold and Maude' is a classic! It's about love and life and possibilities."

"You're kidding!" Ben laughed. "Some old wrinkly screwing a freaky mama's boy who's got a horse fetish."

"Hearse, not horse!" Julia argued back sharply.

"Whatever," yawned Ben. "Can't we watch something else?"

"No. Anyway, Marcus likes this film, too."

Ben coughed discreetly, but was smart enough not to challenge her directly.

"You'd rather watch 'Die Hard 4', wouldn't you, buddy?" he asked, sounding like he was begging.

"I'm easy," Marcus replied.

Ben chuckled.

"Yeah! That's what I heard. Last night, huh? Lucky bastard!"

Julia's reaction was shocked, and it made me want to laugh out loud.

"Ben! I'm sitting right here!"

Ben coughed again.

"Sorry."

"And I don't think it's something to joke about!" Then Julia opened fire on Marcus. "You shouldn't treat women that way."

He looked surprised at being the subject under attack.

"What way?"

"Like objects!" she clipped out.

Ben groaned. "Leave it alone, babe."

Julia ignored him. He was probably used to that.

"You shouldn't just sleep around."

Marcus laughed.

"I'm not forcing anyone … I like women. And women like me."

But Julia was starting to snort smoke and fart fire. If she'd grown wings and a forked tail, I wouldn't have been surprised. Sometimes I couldn't believe we were related. Well, half related.

"And one night stands?" she snapped. "How do you justify that?"

Marcus continued to stand there casually drinking his beer. "I didn't think I had to."

"You know what I mean! It's just using people. Using women."

There was a long pause, then Marcus said, "Maybe they're using me."

I think he had a point.

Funny enough, Julia didn't.

"Oh, come on!"

Marcus didn't reply, so she changed tactics. She should have been a lawyer. My sister loved to argue. Me, not so much.

"Don't you want to meet someone special? You know, settle down? You can't keep drifting all your life, can you?"

Why the hell not?

Marcus' reply was casual.

"I'll let you know."

"I mean, what do you want to do with your life?"

I could hear Ben clearing his throat, and I imagined him wishing he was anywhere but here. He hated arguments, too. God knows why he was with Julia.

"Jeez, babe! Give the guy a break."

Ben was probably thinking the same thing as me—that we shouldn't piss off the guy who paid us rent money.

"I'm sure Marcus can answer without your help!" Julia hissed.

Ben surrendered and retreated back to the kitchen for another beer. He looked at me and muttered, "Hurricane Julia is about to make landfall."

I wanted to ask him why he put up with her. No way I'd let some chick talk to me like that. Yansi was ballsy, but she wasn't a bitch.

"Isn't there anything you want to do?" Julia said to Marcus. "I mean, anything *more?*"

Marcus' voice was calm, but I thought he sounded like he was getting pissed. There was an edge to his voice that wasn't there before.

"I go where I want, when I want. I earn my money stateside in the summer, and go somewhere warm with waves in the winter. I'm happy. How many people can say the same?"

I didn't think she'd have a comeback to that, because hell yeah! It sounded good to me. Really good.

But Julia wasn't finished.

"That's fine when you're 27. But what about when you're 37? Or 47? Or 57? What then?"

Marcus laughed. He freakin' laughed at her. Guy should get a medal.

"What do you think I should do? Get married, then have 2.5 children, get a 'real' job like you, get a mortgage? Then what? Wonder where my life went? How is that way better? I mean, husbands are kind of irrelevant, aren't they?"

What?

"What?"

Julia spat the words like someone had put mustard on her PB&J sandwich instead of peanut butter.

"Well, what's the point?" asked Marcus coolly. "Women don't need them. You do fine without us. Nicky is all right without a dad, isn't he?"

Ben threw me a worried look, and my brain crackled with sudden tension.

"You think?" Julia's brittle laugh carried clearly into the kitchen, sending nervous tremors throughout my body. "You don't think Nicky is fucking up his life? He's drunk or high every weekend. You've had to carry his sorry ass back here once already. He has no clue what he wants to do with his life. You think Nicky is doing okay?"

I felt sick, hearing what she really thought of me.

There was a pause and Ben said quietly, "She doesn't mean it like that, buddy."

I couldn't look at him, and I just gripped the can of beer in my hands a little tighter. I worked, I gave her money for groceries, I went to school, I wasn't flunking out. What more did she want? Why was it never enough? I chugged the beer and tossed the can into the backyard where it landed in a patch of overgrown grass.

"But the way you live," huffed Julia, "it's so rootless? Don't you miss your family?"

Marcus snorted. "No, not particularly."

Right now I was feeling pretty much the same. I wouldn't miss Julia if she moved to Mars. In fact, I'd throw a fuckin' party.

Julia's voice was tight, as if Marcus was casting some judgment on her. Maybe he was. Maybe we looked like a bunch of pathetic losers to him.

"What's wrong with getting married and having kids?"

Marcus laughed, his voice colder now.

"Nothing. Marriage is a great institution. If you like institutions."

"Then what *do* you want?" Julia persisted.

"I want something more than that."

"It sounds like less."

"It's just not for me."

"Not ever?"

There was a long pause, real long, and I was straining to hear what was happening. But then Marcus spoke again.

"Julia, I don't sleep with my friends."

Ben stood up and walked out into the backyard, kicking my empty can and staring at the weeds. He didn't look happy. I guess everyone has a breaking point. I didn't know why, although I could take a damn good guess, but Ben had just reached his.

Julia's voice was unnatural, and a high-pitched laugh escaped her.

"I should hope not!"

There was another pause.

"I didn't mean to embarrass you," said Marcus.

I wondered if maybe that's exactly what he wanted to do after the way she'd tried to tear him apart, his life, the way he lived. She tried to do it to me often enough.

"No, of course not. I'm not..." she stuttered.

Marcus must have walked out of the room, because his voice was fainter now.

"Think I'll go take a shower. Later."

I looked outside where Ben was staring at a crack in the concrete slabs that paved the grill area.

I stood up and walked into the living room.

"What the fuck was that?"

Julia looked guilty, then bristled immediately.

"I don't know what you're talking about. And don't curse."

"That with Marcus. Seriously, sis, were you *hitting* on him?"

"Don't be ridiculous!" she snapped, but my eyes narrowed when I saw her lips tremble. "Of course I wasn't! Ben's in the kitchen and ... and I don't even find Marcus attractive!"

Smelled like bullshit to me.

"Whatever helps you sleep at night," I laughed coldly.

"But good to know you think I'm a fuck up."

A dull red flooded her cheeks.

"I didn't mean…"

"Save it!" I snapped. "I don't give a shit."

I didn't even stay for the pizza. I'd throw up if I tried to eat it now. I was hot with fury, and cold and raw at the same time.

I stormed out of the house, taking pleasure in the flakes of paint that shivered down from the cracked doorframe as I slammed the door behind me.

Which was why, four hours later, I was totally shitfaced, having drank God knows how many beers and shots of tequila.

My head was pounding in time to the music leaking through the walls.

"Oh, man, you're wasted!" sniggered Sean, his words soft and slurred, like unset Jell-o.

I stared up at him and grinned. "Yeah!"

He collapsed down next to me on the sofa, sucking on a blunt.

"This will sober you up," he said, passing it over.

I wasn't sure I wanted to be sober; my head was too crowded when I could think straight. I was happy floating away on a sea of alcohol, but I sucked in the smoke anyway because I was too hammered to say no.

The sweet smell got stuck in my nose and made my eyes water.

I was still in a confused haze when Erin Lenz flopped down into my lap and wrapped her arms around my neck.

"Shotgun," she whispered and mashed her mouth against mine.

I coughed in surprise, and she inhaled my smoke.

"Thanks," she said, making herself comfortable.

Sean was pissing himself laughing. I tried to push her off, but she clung to me tightly.

"Why don't you like me?" she murmured loosely against my neck. "I've always liked you."

I pushed again, but she tightened her grip then started kissing up my neck.

I tried to unhook her hands, but every time I freed one, she'd grip onto my t-shirt with the other. It was like wrestling an octopus.

In the end I gave up, leaving her plastered across my chest. I closed my eyes, too tired to fight her off. I figured if I fell asleep on her, she'd give up.

Sean nudged my shoulder. "Lacey's here. Gonna see if I can hook up."

"Yeah, man," I muttered, without opening my eyes.

As an afterthought he said, "She might have some speed. You sure could use it—although you look like you've got your hands full right now."

I wanted to say something, but I couldn't wrap my mouth around the words.

Erin must have gotten bored, because when I opened my eyes again, she was gone.

I started feeling like I might throw up, so I shouldered my way through the crowds of drinkers, dancers, slackers and stoners, until I found an empty bathroom upstairs. I heaved a couple of times, spitting out damn near pure alcohol. My head spun, or maybe my head was still while the room spun around—it was hard to tell. My stomach lurched again, and I clung onto the sink. When the wave of nausea subsided, I drank some water from the faucet, then stumbled into the bedroom and passed out on the bed.

I was dreaming about Yansi. We were in my bedroom and it was dark, which was strange because my room never got fully dark; the curtains were too thin, the streetlights too bright, but now it was filled with shadows. She was kissing my neck and it felt so good, and I said her name, but her lips murmured against mine, silencing me.

Her hands slid across my chest under my t-shirt, and her fingers traced the ridges and planes of my abs, stroking lower. Then her hands were on my belt, and I liked this dream because normally she called time-out on going this far.

Even though I was so totally wasted, I was still getting hard, with her warm hands rubbing firmly across the denim. Then she tugged down on my zipper and I struggled to open my eyes, wanting to see this, urging her on by rocking my hips into her hand.

She dragged my cock out of my jeans, and I hissed softly. Her warm, wet mouth closed over the tip and I groaned as she sucked hard. Part of me wanted to say, *not here, not like this*, but I didn't want her to stop either. Up and down, hot and wet and tight, and I couldn't breathe.

Her head disappeared, and my cock wept silently, but then I could feel her right over me, lowering herself down and I lost a little more of my mind.

Oh fuck, that felt good—soft and heated silk as the head of my dick sank into her, stroking me from all around like nothing I'd ever known before. Shit, I was gonna lose it fast. Too fucking good.

Her tongue was against my throat, and my body was thrusting, thrusting, sweat and heat; her humid breath across my face.

It was awkward and rough and I couldn't find a rhythm. Then her musky scent hit me and my eyes snapped open.

Some girl, not Yansi, and I was sick and horrified and hard as I fucked her or she fucked me.

"Come on, babe," she moaned, scratching at my chest and shoulders.

I did and I didn't want to stop. Couldn't stop. And I came in her and on her and on me. And she slumped down onto my chest, hot and heavy, breathing vodka fumes into my face. I pushed her limp body away and stumbled to the bathroom, splashing cold water on my face and traitorous cock.

There was a light above the sink and when the yellow bulb flicked on, I had to squint against the brightness.

When my eyes adjusted, I took a deep breath and

turned back to the bedroom.

Erin's face surrounded by a mop of dirty blonde hair smirked up at me.

"Hey, Nick. Some ride, huh? Where's your precious Yansi now? She doesn't put out. She doesn't know how to party."

She crawled off the bed and pressed her tits against my back. My head was still spinning, and my stomach rolled with disgust and regret. I struggled to stand up as she wrapped herself around me again, and I pushed her away so she crashed back onto the bed.

"You fuckin' bitch! I can't believe you did that!"

Her eyes widened in surprise, then she laughed harshly.

"It wasn't just me. You were hard, babe. You can't deny it. I've still got your cum inside me."

She saw the appalled look on my face, and her smug expression slipped a little.

"Don't worry. I'm on the Pill."

That was only one of my worries, but my brain still wasn't fully functioning.

"Jesus Christ, Erin! I was drunk. I was passed out asleep, for fuck's sake!"

She leaned up on her elbows, staring at me critically.

"You don't look that drunk."

She was almost right, disgust sobering me quickly. Although I wouldn't have tried to drive a car, the last five minutes had cleared my head considerably.

"Are you so desperate for a fuck that you wait until a guy's passed out?"

Her face darkened and she scowled.

"I'm not a slut. You asked me out on a date once. If it hadn't been for that Mexican bitch, we'd still be dating."

I swore loudly and she backed up the bed a little, wary now.

"Are you really that deluded? We had one lousy date. One goddamn awful date where I couldn't wait for it to end so I could get rid of you. That had nothing, nothing to do with Yansi. You're a whore and you're sitting there with your panties God knows where, and you're calling *her* names. I don't want you. I'll never want you. Is that clear enough? Have you got that through your dumb skull?"

Her mouth trembled, but then she sat up straight and tossed her hair over her shoulder.

"Clear. Very clear, *Nicky*. You don't want me. Fine. But your precious Yansi won't want you either now."

A shock of electricity passed through me, then my shoulders slumped and I sat on the bed tiredly, resting my elbows on my knees.

"So, that's it. You wanted to fuck things up for us."

There was silence for a moment, then she rubbed my back and I cringed away from her touch.

"Am I that bad?" she asked, a crack in her voice.

I glanced over my shoulder and saw the glint of tears in her eyes.

I hated it when girls cried—that was my Kryptonite. I felt like shit, even when I wasn't to blame. And I didn't know if I blamed her or blamed me or blamed this whole fucked up situation.

"This should never have happened," I said quietly. "But I shouldn't have called you a ... those things I said."

Her lips trembled and tears started to trickle down her cheeks, carving salty tracks through her heavy makeup.

"I can't believe you were so horrible. You've always been nice to me. I thought ... I thought..."

"You thought wrong," I said firmly.

I looked down, studying the new calluses on my hands, and she sighed softly. Then I felt the mattress move and the rustle of material as she straightened her clothes. I hoped she found her panties.

"I won't tell anyone," she said. "Your dirty little secret is safe."

The door closed behind her and I was alone.

Guess I wasn't a virgin anymore.

It wasn't as great as I thought, and definitely not how I'd imagined it happening. I thought it would be something I wanted to remember forever; now I couldn't forget it fast enough.

And what the hell was I going to say to Yansi?

I don't know why, but I thought Erin would keep her word. But it didn't mean that other people hadn't seen us—or heard us.

I wanted to get the fuck away. I looked for Sean but found Rob, asleep on a pile of coats. I shook his shoulder, but he swore softly then rolled over and started snoring.

I had no choice but to walk, feeling the weight of every step, more and more appalled by what I'd done.

I was *that* guy—the one who cheated on his girlfriend. Maybe the apple didn't fall too far from the tree after all. Not that I knew anything about my dad, except that he hadn't stayed.

I wished again that I'd asked Mom about him before she died. Right now I wanted to know that I wasn't really like him, or that I could change, or something. Because I sure as shit couldn't wish this night away.

What was the right thing to do? If I told Yansi, she'd be hurt and probably dump my ass, and I wouldn't blame her. But maybe that was the selfish thing to do—just lay everything on her so I could feel better. Maybe the best thing would be to say nothing. But what if she found out later? She'd never trust me again. Hell, *I* wouldn't trust me again.

Not that I'd been completely at fault, but there was a moment when I could have stopped Erin, when I *should* have stopped her.

And the fact that it was a girl that I'd taken on a date once, and who'd made no secret of wanting me—that made it worse.

Although I don't think there was anything that could make it better.

By the time I got home, I was almost sober. It had

taken me nearly two hours. I was tired, hung-over, and pissed. At Erin, at myself, at the whole fucked up situation.

I dragged myself into the shower, shivering when I realized that the water wasn't hot, but at least it washed the scent of Erin off of me. If I had to smell that perfume ever again, I'd throw up.

I lay in bed, my body exhausted, but I couldn't sleep. I kept going over it all in my head: should I tell Yansi or not? I mean, what was the point? It might make me feel better—or possibly not—but it definitely wouldn't make Yansi feel any better. I'd always thought that confessing was a selfish thing to do. Yansi said that when she confessed to her priest it always made her feel worse because now he had to carry her burden. That's how she put it. That must suck: having everyone dump their shit on you, week in, week out.

I thought I could trust Erin, so it depended on whether or not anyone else had seen us. We'd been in an empty bedroom; I didn't remember anyone looking in, but hell, the state I was in, I might not have noticed.

By dawn, I still hadn't made a decision. I forced myself to close my eyes, but was awake an hour later.

The surf was crappy again, so I took my Tony Hawk and skated into town along the road as there were hardly any cars around. The pier was empty except for a couple of old guys fishing. I sat on the sand and stared at the ocean, wondering how the hell life had gotten so freakin' complicated.

Yansi was having a family day, and I didn't know whether I was happy or not about that. Usually, not. But right now, I didn't know how I could face her.

I stayed until the beach started getting busy, then I dragged myself home.

I spent the rest of the day doing laundry, which freaked Julia out. She kept making lame jokes about me not feeling well, until I snapped at her, and then she chewed me out and said I could do my own damn laundry forever. Then she ran up to her room wiping tears from her face.

When she was still crying ten minutes later, I knocked on her door to apologize. In between her telling me to 'grow up' and then to 'fuck off', I worked out that Ben had dumped her. I guess he hadn't been too happy with whatever had gone on with her and Marcus. When she told me to fuck off for the second time and then threw a book at my head, I took the hint and left her alone.

You could say it was a pretty crappy Saturday in the Andrews house.

Like a total pussy, I was still ignoring Yansi's texts, deciding that I'd tell her tomorrow that I hadn't charged my phone.

Well, it seemed like a good idea at the time. But when Sunday rolled around, I spent the whole day surfing and hanging out at the pier, knowing that she'd have church and then be with her family again.

The next day at work was sheer hell. I felt guilty every time Mr. Alfaro looked in my direction, and my attention was shot. He had to tell me three times how to stake the saplings in a mini orchard that a client wanted. I was supposed to be trimming back the surrounding eucalyptus trees to decrease the shade, but I don't think he thought I was safe with a chainsaw. I was so out of it, I'd probably have cut off my own leg. In the end, he sent me to give the saplings a good watering—something I couldn't screw up too badly.

I still hadn't replied to Yansi's texts, and I'd deliberately left my phone at home today.

When the day finally finished, I staggered into the house and climbed the stairs to my bedroom almost on my hands and knees. I felt sick to see that she'd blown up my phone with eight texts and 12 missed calls. I had a bad feeling about this, but I was too chicken shit to call her up.

I decided I'd shower, eat something, *then* call her.

So, I was slumped in front of the TV eating a grilled

cheese sandwich with baked beans—yeah, I know—when I heard a car pull up outside.

I assumed it was Julia, so I didn't bother to look out of the window.

But when she walked into the living room, Julia wasn't alone: Yansi and Megan were with her.

Yansi looked like she was about to cry, and Megan just looked ... I didn't give a shit how Megan looked—my eyes were on Yansi.

"Is it true?"

I froze, and she must have seen the guilt on my face.

"Oh my God! It *is* true! I didn't believe it, even though everyone told me it was. How could you, Nick? After everything you said about ... about waiting, and it didn't matter. How could you do it? With *her?*"

I tried to answer, tried to find the words, but all I could do was stare with an appalled expression on my face.

"Yans..." I choked out.

She strode forward and slapped my face, rocking my head to the side with the force of the blow.

"Yans, please..."

"I *hate* you," she screamed, then gasped something in Spanish that I couldn't catch.

She ran out of the door and I started to follow her, but Megan blocked my way.

"She doesn't want to talk to you. Asshole."

Then she turned on her heel, and the next thing I heard was the car screeching away from the curb.

I sank back onto the sofa, nausea swirling in my stomach, my cheek burning from where she'd hit me.

"I can't believe it. My own brother."

Julia was standing at the door, her arms folded, a disgusted look on her face.

"You fucked some skank at a party? Well, Anayansi has done the right thing dumping your ass. After everything Mom said to you about respect, and you turn around and do this."

"I didn't!" I yelled. Then more quietly, "I mean, I did, but it wasn't like that!" Frustration heated my voice.

But Julia laughed coldly.

"Really? You were just walking along and oops, you fell dick first into some girl."

"Pretty much, yeah," I muttered, half to myself.

"God, you men are so pathetic," she grit out, her tone disbelieving. "Some slut drops her panties and you've all got your tongues hanging out. You forget you've got wives and girlfriends and…"

"You don't know what happened, so just shut the fuck up!" I shouted, leaping off the sofa. "You weren't there! You don't know what it was like!"

"Did you fuck some girl?"

I took a deep breath.

"Yes, but…"

"There is no 'but'!" she yelled, pointing her finger in my face. "Guys like you are disgusting and pathetic. I can't believe my own brother…"

"You wanna tell me the reason Ben broke it off with you?" I spit at her. "Nothing to do with the fact you were like a bitch in heat every time Marcus walked into the room." I laughed flatly at her shocked expression. "Yeah, I know about that. The difference is that I gave you the benefit of the doubt and didn't go screaming at you, because I've *seen* Marcus in action and I know what he's like. Not that he'd be interested in a crazy bitch like *you*. And you know what else? How the fuck Ben put up with your whining and complaining all these years is a freakin' mystery. Guy deserves a gold medal. No wonder he dumped *your* ass."

Her face creased and I thought she was going to hit me, too. I tensed, ready to grab her arm if she did. But instead she sank onto the sofa and started crying; ugly, heavy tears that made her mascara run and her nose fill with snot.

She looked so defeated and hopeless that I felt like a

complete douche.

I sat down next to her and tried to put my arm around her, but she shoved me away.

"I'm sorry..." I began.

She cried harder, making weird choking sounds and wiping her nose on her sleeve. I didn't know what to do, so I sat there listening to her cry, until finally it sounded like she was stopping. I darted into the kitchen and grabbed some tissues so she had something else to wipe her face with.

She snatched the tissues from my hands and muttered a quiet, "Thanks."

"I'm sorry," I said again, lamely.

"I'm not," she snapped, sounding more like herself again. "You're still a jerk."

So much for an apology.

"Yeah, well, if you want to blame anyone, blame yourself," I said tiredly.

"What?"

"You're always acting like you can't be bothered with Ben; always telling him he's an idiot or boring. I mean, yeah, he is boring, but no guy needs to hear that."

She stared at me, her face streaked with tears and mascara.

"I don't do that."

"Um, yeah, you kind of do."

"I love Ben," she hiccuped.

"Really?" I shook my head, "Well, maybe you should tell him that sometimes."

"I do!" she protested.

"When was the last time?" I challenged her.

She didn't answer.

"You treat the guy like furniture, Ju."

"At least I didn't cheat on him while I was drunk at a party!" she snapped back.

"Yeah, that's kind of your fault, too," I sighed, trying to rub away the headache that seemed to be building again behind my eyes.

"What?"

"If you hadn't told Marcus what a fuck-up I was, I'd have stayed to eat pizza with you that night," I chuckled without humor. "I got so wasted because I hadn't eaten all day; then I passed out. When I woke up, Erin was sitting on my dick. True story. So think what the fuck you like."

The truth was that I still did the deed so I had to take responsibility for my actions—and I should have manned the fuck up and answered my damn phone when Yansi called me.

I stood up tiredly and headed for the stairs, each one feeling like I was climbing a mountain.

I lay face down on the bed, reliving the moment when Yansi had asked me, 'Is it true?' I'd had two days to think what I should say to her, but when it came to it, I couldn't even speak. That was it; we were finished. And it was my own damn fault.

My cheek throbbed. I held onto the pain, because it was all I had left.

I was still dazed by what had just happened. I couldn't believe that Yansi had gone off at me like that. Well, I could—and I didn't blame her—but she wouldn't even listen to me.

I dug my hands into the covers and pulled the pillow over my head as my throat closed up, and I felt the burn of tears starting. I forced them back along with the pain in my chest.

Yansi was gone and I'd never even had the chance to tell her that I ... how I felt about her.

I couldn't even bring myself to think the 'L' word, let alone say it. Not that there was any point now.

Losing Yansi was worse than losing my mom. I know that sounds fucked up, but watching Mom get sicker and sicker, weaker and thinner every day, seeing her in so much pain, I wanted her to die. I wanted her to give up. I sat by her fucking hospital bed day after day *praying* that tonight was the night when she'd die. If I'd had the guts, I'd have done it myself. I could see the look on her face when she woke up, asking, *Why am I still here?* And I'd say, "It's okay, Mom. You can let go now. Please just let go, Mom. We're going to be okay. I promise we'll be okay. We'll look after each other."

So yeah, I wished my mom would die. And then she did, and I missed her so much. Not the sick woman, the woman who smelled of piss and shit because she couldn't control her body anymore: that wasn't my mom.

I remembered the woman who made me pancakes and cinnamon rolls for breakfast, and loved to laugh and dresse up to go out on the town with Aunt Carmen. Her hair was so pretty—before it all fell out.

My mom was beautiful, and the cancer made her ugly.

I didn't even register when Julia knocked the first time. The second time, I ignored her, but she came in anyway.

I felt the mattress move as she sat down, and when she started tugging at the pillow, I didn't fight it.

Knowing that whatever lecture she felt the need to give was on its way, I sat up and slumped against the headboard. But she surprised me.

"I'm sorry, Nicky," she said. "Sorry about Yansi. I know that you … that she meant a lot to you."

"Yeah," I muttered.

"Tell me what happened?"

So I told her the whole sordid story again, but this time she listened without yelling.

"That's really fucked up," she said softly, once I'd finished.

"I know." My voice was bitter.

"Did you tell Yansi everything?"

I shook my head.

"Why not?"

"I didn't get the chance, did I?"

"But this happened on Friday. You've had since then to tell her. Didn't you think…?"

"Of course I fucking thought!" I snapped. "I've thought about nothing else. I nearly cut my damn foot off at work, because I was thinking about how to tell her!"

"So why didn't you?"

"Because! Because it seemed … selfish. I get to tell her—big confession, right? And she has to hear that … I've been with another girl. I thought … I just thought that it would be better that she didn't know, but now…"

Julia shook her head sadly. "I don't think Yansi sees it that way. But I get it, I do. In your own messed up way you were trying to protect her. But it must look to her like you just got caught."

"I know," I said wearily. "I've blown it with her."

Julia sighed. "Maybe. Maybe not. Give her a day or so to cool off, then try texting her. Don't give up if she's what you really want, Nicky."

"Are you ever going to call me 'Nick'?"

"Probably not," she said, shrugging her shoulders, a small smile on her face.

We sat in silence for a moment, lost in our thoughts.

"So, what about you and Ben?" I asked.

I'd gotten used to having him around, and even though Julia hadn't seemed that happy with him, she was a helluva lot more miserable without him. I knew what that felt like.

"Are you guys trying to work it out?"

Her face twisted and she looked down at her hands. "I guess I'm better at giving advice than taking it."

"Ben's a good guy," I said. "He'll see that you didn't do anything."

"You don't even like Ben," she murmured. "You think he's boring."

"No, I don't." She skewered me with a look. "Okay, I do think he's boring," I admitted. "But he's still a good guy. Puts up with all your crap."

She sighed. "I guess he reached his limit."

"Then ... you were ... hitting on Marcus?"

Julia stared out of the window. "I don't know. Not really. Maybe I was. He's just so ... I don't know, different. He's been all over the world. I've never even left Florida, except to stay with Aunt Carmen in Detroit after she moved away. And I've dated Ben since I was 18. Maybe I was bored, but..."

"But?" I prompted her, a little bit amazed that she was really talking to me.

"But I don't know. I don't know if I would have ... gone through with it. I mean, yeah, Marcus is hot..." she smiled at the look of revulsion on my face. "Well, he is. Obviously. But ... he's not Ben. But I don't know ... and that's why I haven't called Ben."

I nudged her shoulder. "Give him a few days then try texting him. I hear that works sometimes."

She gave a quiet laugh. "Thanks for the advice."

"Anytime."

She sighed, then looked up to meet my eyes.

"Look, about Yansi ... she's just hurt right now; her pride's been dented. No girl likes to think that her boyfriend is sleeping around..."

"I'm not!" I protested hotly.

"I know, but ... that's how it looks ... like you've gone from her bed to that skank's and..."

"I haven't," I interrupted. "I mean, me and Yansi ... we haven't ... done that..."

The words trailed away as Julia stared at me.

"Oh for fuck's sake! I'm not sleeping with Yansi! Okay?"

"But ... I thought..."

"Well, you were wrong," I said sourly.

She looked at me carefully.

"So ... this thing with Erin ... are you sure you weren't just aiming to get laid or...?"

"No! I didn't want it to be with her!"

Her eyes grew wider, and she chewed on her lip before speaking.

"Nicky, are you saying … are you saying that this … with Erin … was that your first time?"

I couldn't meet her eyes, so I studied the hole in the hem of my t-shirt.

"Yeah."

"Oh."

There was silence, and after a few seconds I couldn't stand not knowing what she was thinking. When I looked up again, her face was pitying.

"I'm so sorry, Nicky. No one's first time should be like that."

I sighed.

"Yeah, well. Too late to do anything about it now."

"I just thought … I just assumed that you'd been sleeping with girls for years."

I looked at her curiously.

"Why did you think that?"

"Well, Sean…"

"What about him?"

"He's been hooking up with Lacey Russo for about a year now—I know her sister, and she told me. She was furious because she caught them at home once while their parents were away. And Sean's always talking about some girl or other that he's banging…"

That was true, although I wasn't sure I always believed him.

"And he was forever going on about girls you'd met at parties," she continued, "so I just assumed that you were both…"

"You assumed I was sleeping around. Fuck. You assumed I was cheating on Yansi all this time!"

Julia's expression was guilty.

"Well, that's how it looked."

A lot of things made sense now: why Yansi and Sean hated each other so much. She thought he was encouraging me to dip my dick in every girl who looked at me; and he thought she was uptight and possessive, keeping me on a leash when I wasn't getting any.

I was so dumb not to have seen all that before.

"It made me angry to think that you were behaving like that after everything Mom went through."

I chewed over my question before I asked it.

"Do you know what happened with her ... and my dad?"

She frowned. "No, she never said. I was only five—I don't remember any guy in particular." She looked at me sympathetically. "You never asked her?"

"I meant to..."

She nodded. "Yeah, I get that."

Julia's dad still sent her birthday cards. He lived in Alberta now and had a new family. But at least she knew who he was, and he knew who she was. I didn't even know if my dad knew that I existed.

"Mom kept a box of documents in the loft space above the garage," she said tentatively. "There might be something in there..."

I swallowed the lump in my throat. "Maybe I'll take a look sometime..."

She nodded, then stood up and smoothed down the covers where she'd been sitting

"You're not bad for a little brother, Nicky. When you're not being a giant pain in my ass."

"Ditto."

She smiled and closed the door behind her.

Wow. I guess that's what you call having a conversation.

Chapter 6

Julia was doing better. She'd gone around to see Ben, and she said they talked and decided to take a break for a while. She wasn't happy about it, but I didn't think it was such a bad idea. Not that I said that to her. Hell, no! But if she really was bored with Ben, having some more time apart might make her see if she really wanted him or not.

It only took a week before Ben was back with Julia. I guess he'd forgiven her or something. I'd heard her talking on the phone late at night—crying sometimes.

I don't know what she said to him, but it must have worked. Or maybe he missed her. I guess it was possible.

One morning I woke up, and he was sitting in the kitchen drinking coffee, just like always.

I was actually pretty happy to see the guy. He was calm, and somehow seemed to handle the craziness that was Julia.

I was grateful, too: any more 'bonding' time with my sister, and I'd have been joining the crazy train myself. As it was, for the past 10 days, I'd had to listen to her overanalyzing everything Ben had said or not said, done or not done, for hours. I had no idea girls spent so much time talking about guys like that. I really wished she had a girlfriend she could talk to.

And it made me wonder what Yansi was saying to Megan or Esther about me. Nothing good, I guess.

Megan had never liked me all that much, and Esther had liked me *too* much. So it was anyone's guess what they were saying. All I knew was that Yansi wasn't talking to *me*. She was refusing to take my calls or return my messages. I was still working for her old man, but I didn't know how long that would last if she told him what I'd done. Probably less than a second.

I was bored and miserable.

Sean had gone to North Carolina for a week to see his grandparents, and Rob was spending a week in the Bahamas with his family.

So I decided to go for the offer Marcus had made of bussing tables at the Sandbar a couple of evenings a week and on Saturdays if they needed me.

This summer was turning out to be less fun than dental surgery. I wasn't even sure it was my fault. What happened with Erin, hell, no one could blame me for that. Well, Yansi could. And did.

I showed up the first evening wearing the uniform tee and a clean pair of jeans. They were still slightly damp because I'd forgotten to wash them the day before and they hadn't had time to dry fully. I'd have been more comfortable in shorts but Steve, the manager, said all the guys had to wear long pants, even though I wouldn't be serving customers.

My training took all of five minutes: clear tables, stack the dishwasher, press the button, empty the dishwasher, and any of the shit jobs that no one else wanted to do, like cleaning the ashtrays from the patio. I didn't care much, and even if I did, I could use the money. I got a share of the tips at the end of the night, too.

It was my second evening shift, and I'd been allowed a 15 minute break while it wasn't busy. I was sitting outside when I told Marcus what had happened with Erin. I was hoping that he'd tell me what to do, or at least have some ideas ... because he was older and had a lot of girlfriends, I guess.

But after laughing his ass off, he didn't seem to think it was important.

"It happened. Either your girl will get over it or she won't. If she doesn't believe you, then move on. And it's a great story—I might have to use that some time."

"But it's true!" I complained. "I was wasted. I didn't know what the fuck I was doing."

Marcus laughed again.

"Keep telling yourself that, kid, but from anyone else's point of view, you fucked some girl who was all over you at a party when your girlfriend wasn't around. No guy would blame you. But I gotta tell you, I don't think ... what's her name? Yansi? I don't think she's the forgiving type. She'll be bringing it up in every argument you ever have."

"Yansi isn't like that."

He glanced over, his expression amused.

"They're *all* like that. They say they're not, but they are."

"Not her."

He grinned as he shook his head, then closed his eyes, sitting back in his chair, face to the setting sun.

"Sure she is. She's a ball buster. Why do you want to get her back when you could have any chick? Je-zus! You dated her for four months; you work for her old man ... before you know it, she'll have a ring on her finger, a kid on the way, and you'll be standing in front of her priest saying 'I do'."

He shook his head.

"Don't let them tie you down, kid. That's a shortcut to being miserable for a very long time."

He looked at me slyly.

"Emma asked me if you were single."

"Who?"

"Chick with the rose tattoo on her shoulder."

I knew who he meant. She was one of the servers and had started at the Sandbar a couple of days before me.

"What did you tell her?"

Marcus smiled. "I said she should ask you herself."

I frowned. "I'm trying to work things out with Yansi."

"Then tell her that," he said, sounding bored. "It's your life."

That was Marcus' answer to pretty much everything.

I wanted to ask him some more, but break time was over.

I went back to bussing tables, clearing glasses from the happy hour rush.

Then Frank walked in with an older guy that I'd seen around but didn't know. Marcus set them up with a couple of beers without being asked. I got the impression that they stopped by at this time every evening.

They were talking about the crappy surf conditions when a noisy group of girls came in: out-of-towners. From the way they were swaying, I guessed they'd already been partying somewhere else. One of them was wearing a bride's veil and a tiara. It was pretty clear they were on their way to a bachelorette party. Or maybe this was the party.

Instead of taking a table, they perched on bar stools and fluttered their fake eyelashes at Marcus.

"Four Mojitos, gorgeous, and a Sea Breeze," said one of them, throwing her American Express card onto the bar.

"Coming up," said Marcus, smiling easily.

"Anything else coming up?" she giggled.

The girl wearing the veil laughed, sounding a little embarrassed.

"Holly! Leave the poor guy alone. Sorry about her," she said to Marcus. "She's just had a bit too much to drink."

"No problem," Marcus replied, easily. "I hope you guys have fun tonight."

But then someone else caught their attention, and they all started laughing their asses off.

"Oh my God! Did you *see* what that woman was wearing?" shrieked one of the others in the party as they all laughed loudly.

"I know! There must be a trailer park around here."

"Whose idea was it to come here anyway?"

"Think of it as a sort of sociological experiment, Tanya!" laughed the bride

"Who knew you could get BOGOF tattoos?"

"Oh God! Totally!"

Wow, these women were trashed. And loud.

One of them grabbed my ass as I passed with a tray of glasses.

"The scenery isn't bad though."

I nearly dropped the tray, and the glasses clinked together dangerously.

"Hey!" I complained.

"Aw, he's cute!"

She drew out the word in a sickly way.

Marcus raised his eyebrows.

"Sounds like she's a sure thing, kid."

I tried to tear myself away from her claws and glanced over my shoulder. The woman winked at me and did this gross thing with her tongue that I guess was supposed to be hot, then she pinched my ass. She looked older than my sister. I shook my head—no freakin' way.

"Yeah, cute ... if you prefer brawn to brains," snickered the one named Tanya, and I felt my cheeks heat up.

"Who doesn't?" laughed another.

"Oh my God! You're such a slut, Libby!"

"I like to be able to at least have a conversation with a guy."

I couldn't believe they were talking about me as if I wasn't standing right there.

"Who needs conversation if the guy looks like him! Come on, you've got to admit these surfer-types are hot?"

Marcus came from behind the bar to help me, taking the tray so I could pry their hands off me.

"No molesting the staff, ladies," he smiled.

"Like minimum wage is such a turn on," snapped the short one. "Oh, please!"

What a bunch of bitches. I wondered what collective noun my English teacher Mrs. Lord would give them: a pack of bitches? A coven of bitches?

"Is it always like that?" I asked Marcus.

He grinned at me.

"If you can't handle the heat..."

I was kind of afraid to go near their end of the bar for the rest of the evening.

"Look at those legs," said Frank, scanning up and down the one who'd grabbed me. "I wonder how far up they go. I wonder how far up them I could go."

Frank's buddy shook his head. "No chance, bro. They're a bunch of stuck up princesses. I fuckin' hate this time of year."

Frank shook his head in amazement.

"Are you kidding? It's when all the talent arrives! Long legs and short skirts. Gotta love summer."

The older guy snorted. "Vacationers from the city or flying in from NYC, looking down their noses at us, like we're a bunch of hicks. Prices go up, everywhere is busy, and I can't park outside my building."

Then Steve, the Sandbar's owner joined in.

"Yeah, well summer is the only time most of us make any money. Without visitors this place would be screwed."

I hadn't thought about it like that before. But especially since the Shuttle program had wound down, a lot of people had lost their jobs. Transient workers always came to this part of Florida, but more kids than usual had left during Junior year because their parents went to look for work in other towns.

The funny thing about living in a place where people come for their vacation is that you always somehow sort of feel like you're missing out.

Vacationers come with their spending money, all excited because they're seeing the ocean or the beach, or renting a boogie board for the first time, and it's stuff that you've known your whole life. And they always tell you that you're lucky to live here.

And I guess it's true, because even though I was brought up in Cocoa Beach, I love to look at the ocean. I love to watch and work out what sort of mood it's in today.

Is it going to be an easy paddle-out day, or is it going to be a gnarly bitch that chews you up and spits you out? Or is it going to be mirror flat, only the faintest pulse telling you that the waves aren't dead, they're just resting.

On the crappy days—what they'd call crappy because there's no sun, even if there are awesome waves— vacationers head to the city or Disney World or Universal Studios; but on the good days, they all come back to the beach, so all the best days of the year, there's a bunch of strangers everywhere, and the locals get the leftovers.

It makes some people mean, and if they get the chance to piss off a tourist, they will. But all the businesses want tourists because it's money.

Then there's all the part-time, seasonal work; not much full-time or even that well paid.

Me, I'd be happy working in a surf shop forever, renting out boards or teaching people to catch their first wave. I think that would be a pretty cool.

But if you want the kind of job that needs a college degree, you have to quit the beach and head for the city.

Mostly.

Or you can be a teacher.

But how many people like school so much they want to spend the rest of their lives in a place that smells of disinfectant and guys who haven't learned that deodorant is their friend?

Maybe a few jocks and some of the princesses love high school, but it's hard work being popular.

I get along with most people. I hang with the jocks, smoke with the stoners, and get invited to all the cool parties as well as the slacker parties.

I'm kinda second rung popular—maybe because I don't care about any of it.

Sean's brothers were all popular, playing on the football team or going out for baseball. I think that's why his parents give him such a hard time because he only ever wanted to surf or party. But to be first rung popular, you gotta always be 'on', like happy, so people want to be around you.

You've gotta go to all the parties, and make them cool just because you're there. If you're a dude, you've gotta get Bs or you'll get kicked off the teams, and you've got to sleep with the cheerleaders, even if you think a girl is dumber than dirt. And if you're a girl, you've got to have the looks and the right clothes and sleep with the right guys.

Or you gotta be real smart and hot—like Yansi.

God, I missed her.

I'd sent her 23 text messages, seven emails, and had tried to call her twice—one time going straight to voicemail, and the other she cut me off before I could do more than breathe.

The difference between me and my sister: I already knew what I'd lost—I'd never needed or wanted any time to think about it.

But it was kind of cool talking to Julia. More like she thought of me as an adult for a change.

I mean, not always: she still nagged me about leaving

dirty dishes in my room, but she didn't seem pissed at me all the time like she used to.

Yeah, I liked it.

I was just getting to the end of my shift when Steve, the manager, walked into the kitchen, a harassed look on his face.

"Hey kid! Nick! Can you stay a couple more hours? The dishwasher's broken again and I need to get all this shit cleaned up before we open in the morning. You're good, right?"

Ah hell. I really didn't need this. It was already nearly eleven, which meant if I did two more hours I'd have less than five hours sleep before Mr. Alfaro tried to slave-drive me to death.

He frowned. "You want the work or not, kid?"

"Yeah, sure. No problem."

He nodded curtly. I sighed as he walked away, throwing an evil stare at the stack of dirty dishes and glasses.

Marcus dropped into the kitchen on his way home and looked at me sympathetically.

"Rough break, kid. Guess I'll see you tomorrow."

"Yeah, sure. Night, Marcus."

He winked and left me with my arms covered in suds up to my elbows. Sometimes my life really sucked.

Two hours later, with my hands red raw, I headed home. By the time I dragged myself up to the house, I was too exhausted to think straight. I felt in my pocket for my keys, and then remembered that I hadn't picked them up after my shower because I was supposed to be riding with Marcus.

Fucking great.

The lamps were still on in his room, a crack of light visible between the curtains. I peered in to check he was still awake, then froze.

Marcus was sitting back on his bed, resting on his elbows, while the woman who'd worn the bride's veil in the bar was on her knees, obviously giving him a blowjob. I recognized her because she was still wearing the tiara.

I knew I should look away, but I couldn't; I was mesmerized as her head bobbed up and down between his legs.

Suddenly, Marcus opened his eyes and stared straight at me. I stumbled back, tripping over the uneven paving stones, and landing on my ass.

Shit! Did he just see me watching him getting blown like I was some freakin' perv?

Hot embarrassment flooded through me. I slunk away in the dark, heading for the back door, hoping Julia still kept a spare key hidden in an old beer bottle.

I snuck into the house feeling like a creepy stalker.

They were making other noises by the time I climbed the stairs, and I knew that Marcus was fucking her. Was that a normal thing for a bride at her bachelorette party? I didn't think so. At least I hoped not.

With that thought, I collapsed face down on the bed, still wearing my beer-smelling clothes, my hands stinking of cigarettes from the ashtrays that I'd cleaned.

I was asleep in seconds.

Even so, the next day was rough. I worked through it in a haze, twice slicing my arms on pampas grass, and once tripping over the hose that I was using to water the borders, and faceplanting in the dirt.

Mr. Alfaro didn't say much but I could tell he was pissed, because at the end of the day he made me sit in the back of the truck again. I didn't know if it was because of Yansi or because I'd worn on his last nerve at work by fucking up again. I didn't really care, so long as he didn't lecture me.

I was looking forward to a lot of sleeping when he dropped me off, but Sean was sitting on the doorstep drinking one of my Dr. Peppers.

"Come on, Nick! I've been waiting for you, man!"

He made it sound like it had really put him out.

"Fuck you, I've been working."

I'm not even sure he heard me because he just carried on talking.

"The swell's three foot and clean—best surf we've had in weeks. Julia let me in, so I've got your thruster."

I peered up to see that he'd secured my longboard to his roof-rack already. Good thing I'd fixed the ding a couple of days ago.

Then he pushed open the passenger door and yelled at me to sit my ass down. I waved tiredly at Rob who was grinning at me from the back seat.

I closed my eyes while Sean drove, listening to him and Rob describe some party that they'd been at the night before and all the verbal vomit telling me that I should have been there, and that he and Sean had been so wasted, he'd slept till mid afternoon.

Lucky bastard.

A few miles north of the pier, Sean slowed down.

"Hey, isn't that Jonno's truck?"

I looked up and saw a blue Silverado parked at the side of the road. Behind it, I could see a good swell running up the shore.

It seemed like a whole bunch of people had the same idea, because several other cars and vans were parked on the shoulder.

Rob jumped out and unstrapped our boards, while I tried not to fall asleep standing up.

"Wake up, loser!" Sean laughed, slamming my board into my chest.

I grunted and then tucked it under my arm while we headed down to the beach.

Jonno was propped against a large rock when we

arrived, sucking on a blunt like his life depended on it.

"'Sup?"

"Not much. Offshore. Clean rides. Three to six knots."

Sean nodded. "Cool. You seen Marcus?"

Jonno laughed. "Nah, man. Last known whereabouts leaving the Sandbar with some chick."

I remembered what I'd seen the night before and turned away, feeling uncomfortable. Then I heard the engine of a vee-dub, and saw Marcus' van pull up next to Sean's car.

"Speak of the devil," said Jonno, passing the blunt to Sean.

When he tried to pass it to me, I shook my head. I'd be out cold if I tried to smoke anything right now.

Marcus jogged toward us, his surfboard under his arm.

"Hey, guys! 'Sup?"

"Nothing. As usual," Sean answered, yawning widely.

"Yeah, just another lousy day in paradise," laughed Rob.

"Fuck, you're cheerful," Jonno chuckled, shaking his head.

Rob grinned. "We're trying to cheer up this miserable fuck," and he pointed at me.

"Yeah, why?"

"His girlfriend dumped his ass when she found out he'd been screwing around."

I was majorly pissed. It wasn't even true, and he knew it. And he said it in front of the guys we were hanging with. They all laughed their asses off when Rob started to tell them what had happened with Erin, and I must have looked like I wanted to smash his face in, because he backed off. But by then, the word was out and it was too late.

Then Jonno said I was learning from the master, meaning Marcus, and they all acted like I'd done something cool. And the dumb thing was, if it had happened to anyone else, I'd have been laughing too, and think it was the funniest damn thing I'd ever heard.

But it wasn't a joke and it had cost me.

"You're in the best place for breaking in fresh pussy!" laughed Jonno. "Paradise has got nothing on *that*."

And he pointed to three girls in bikinis who'd arrived in a jeep. Chicks always hung out where guys surfed. I don't know why, because any guy who's serious about surfing will always pick a good surf over a girl, no matter how hot she is.

Well, maybe not, if it was Yansi. Not that she'd give me the time of day now.

Marcus glanced at the girls then looked away. "So is anyone else going in?"

"Yeah, I'm in," said Rob.

"Me, too," nodded Sean. "Jonno?"

Jonno grinned. "I think I'll just watch the scenery a bit longer. What about you, Nick?"

Marcus looked at me and raised his eyebrows. "Little brother likes to watch, too. Don't you, Nick?"

I was so fucking embarrassed, I didn't know where to look. I could feel my cheeks flushing, so before he could say anything else, I tugged off my t-shirt and picked up my board, ignoring the girls and Marcus.

No one seemed to think anything of what he said, but *I* knew what he meant.

I paddled out through the small breakers to the line-up, sitting there on my board, enjoying a rare moment of peace.

It wasn't long before a set started rising up.

"That wave's got my name on it!" yelled Sean, and four of us started racing to catch it.

Only two of us made it, and I leapt to my feet as I shot down the face of the wave, carving twice and whipping the tail around, before the energy ran out and I bailed.

I surfed for nearly an hour before my body began to protest. I was beyond tired, and all I could think about was sleeping.

Marcus had already finished by the time I walked out. I noticed he was talking to one of the girls from the jeep.

She was cute, different from the usual blonde beach bunnies. For a start, she had real short hair—shorter than mine—and it was a rich dark brown, and very shiny. She wore huge sunglasses and was slim with small breasts. Classy. Not the kind of girl who usually looked interested in Marcus. Or maybe I just didn't know shit.

The two other women were sitting in the jeep looking bored.

"So, Mr. Surfer," she said, "you surf and you bartend. What else can you do?"

Her accent was sexy and I guessed that she was Italian or maybe French.

Marcus looked surprised by her question, but answered quickly.

"I can cook. Have dinner with me?"

"But you are American. Americans can't cook."

He laughed. "I didn't say I cooked well."

The woman shook her head, clearly puzzled. "Then why would I have dinner with you?"

I couldn't help smiling. This chick wasn't going to make it easy. For once Marcus would have to work for it.

He paused, thoughtful. "Don't you like a challenge?"

She shrugged. "I don't like badly cooked food."

"I can make coffee."

Jeez, the guy was practically begging, but the woman sneered at him.

"My little sister can make coffee."

Marcus looked totally frustrated, running his hands through his hair.

Then she said, "You can teach me to surf."

He looked surprised at that. "Oh, okay, sure. When…?"

"Tomorrow afternoon."

"Sounds good."

She smiled for the first time, and I could see why Marcus was interested: her smile was stunning. I found myself smiling back at her, even though I don't think she'd noticed me.

"Ciao!" she said, then turned around and jumped into the jeep.

"I'm Marcus!" he yelled after.

"Camille!" came her answering cry as the jeep roared away.

After that, she started showing up at the Sandbar in the evenings. A couple of times with a girlfriend, but mostly by herself. She'd sit at the end of the bar and talk to Marcus when he wasn't busy. It didn't stop him flirting with the other customers, because he said that was how he made such great tips, but I never saw him do anything more than flirt. Even when he'd been given a girl's phone number, he tossed it when she wasn't looking.

Julia asked me why Marcus wasn't home so much anymore, so I told her about Camille. I thought she'd be pleased, but she just shook her head and said that she felt sorry for the girl. I don't think anyone else felt sorry for her; other girls looked annoyed and jealous. Julia also said that guys like him didn't change.

I wasn't sure she was right about that because life changes you whether you want it to or not. I didn't feel like the same person I was at the beginning of the summer.

Julia had changed, too. She seemed … older. I was beginning to understand why she was such a miserable bitch most of the time; having no money was like a constant toothache that you couldn't do anything about. When you tried to ignore it, it just throbbed like a bastard.

None of my friends had to worry about shit like if there'd be enough money to pay the next bill that came in. Julia did most of the worrying, and I knew that giving her a hundred bucks a week toward groceries helped, but the rest of my money wasn't going to last long if I spent it on take-out pizza and getting wasted, like my friends.

I hated that I had to think about this stuff. It wasn't fair. And I hated that it made me feel like a whiny pussy. So I didn't say anything. Sean knew and he tried to help by throwing in a few extra bucks when we were with the guys. But I didn't want him paying for me either, so I didn't hang out as much as I used to.

I was miserable. And I missed Yansi the way I'd miss an arm or a leg.

I spent my downtime with Sean and Rob, and Marcus when he wasn't on a date with Camille. We surfed, hung out, smoked some shit, drank beers, and talked trash. Normal stuff.

The next day, instead of heading straight for the shower and a nap after work before I hauled ass to the Sandbar for job number two, I snagged one of Ben's beers and sat out on Mom's old lounge chair in the back yard. I was hidden from the kitchen window, which was deliberate. I didn't need a lecture from Julia about drinking again.

I heard her car pull up outside and the front door slam. Ben was with her, and they were talking about me. Again. Oh joy.

"I don't like him spending so much time with Marcus."

"As long as *you're* not spending time with that fucker," Ben growled.

There was a long silence before Julia spoke again.

"He makes everything look too easy. It's not good for Nicky. He needs to know that life isn't always going to be a breeze just because he's good-looking."

"Babe, your mom died and Nicky is working his ass off during his summer vacation. He already knows that life isn't easy. I'm just glad he's got Yansi. She's a real nice girl. She'll keep him grounded."

I winced. I guess Julia hadn't gotten around to telling

him that newsflash. I was grateful, even if the reasons she'd kept it from him weren't exactly unselfish. My guess was that she didn't want to tell him that I'd fucked another girl at a party, in case it reminded him that she'd had a thing for Marcus, or made him think that cheating ran in the family. For all I knew, it did.

"Yeah," Julia said quietly. "Actually, they broke up."

Oh.

"You're kidding?" I could hear the disbelief in Ben's voice. "I thought they were solid. It's obvious he's crazy about her."

"I know. He's been so miserable since she dumped him."

I really hated that freakin' word.

"Wow. Poor Nicky. What happened?"

God, I was so hoping he wouldn't ask that.

"I'm not really sure." *Thanks, sis.* "But you know girls are always throwing themselves at Nicky. Thank God he's totally oblivious half the time."

Huh?

"Sounds like Nicky."

What girls? Other than Erin?

There was another pause. "So … what are you going to do about your renter."

"I don't know."

"You could always ask him to leave."

Julia sighed. "We need the money."

"You'll find someone else to rent the room…"

"I don't know. I don't think so. I mean, the season's already started and what if I couldn't find someone? Besides, I don't think Marcus plans on leaving town, so he'd still be around."

I knew that Julia had already had 'the talk' with Marcus and decided to let him stay, although it didn't sound like she was admitting that to Ben.

Basically, she'd told Marcus that he was a bad influence on me, encouraging me to drink, smoke, and treat women like shit.

I only knew because he told me. He got a big ole laugh out of it, too.

I'd gotten a version of the same talk direct from Julia—the whole, "Marcus isn't someone you can rely on," speech.

Just because he turned her down.

No matter what she said, I still thought that was what happened. But I was in no position to get all judgey on her ass. Or his.

I wasn't in any shape to criticize how other people lived their lives.

The next time I saw Camille, she was screaming at my sister.

Wait, let me back up.

It was a night when I wasn't working at the Sandbar. I was meeting up with Sean and we were going to make the most of a small swell at Jetty Park before hitting up some party that he'd heard about. Lacey was going to be there and he wanted to get laid.

I'd already decided not to get shit-faced; no way I was going to let another situation like the one with Erin happen again.

I was still texting Yansi every day, even though she never replied. But Ben was back with my sister, so maybe I'd get a second chance, too.

Julia was in a good mood. She and Ben were going out on a date, which shocked the hell out of me because they never went out. Anyway, she'd gotten all dressed up and was hyper and excited. It was slightly unnerving seeing her like that, especially because she was wearing a short, clingy dress and a ton of makeup, but it was nice to see her happy for a change, too. She was even being pleasant to Marcus.

He was in the kitchen cooking. Not heating shit up like Julia did, but actual cooking. I didn't know he knew how. I could make eggs, so long as they were scrambled, and I could make pancakes from a packet mix. But he was chopping vegetables and even doing something with a bag of a mixed greens. I was impressed.

He said it was because Camille was French so cooking mattered to her. I thought she was Italian because she said 'Ciao' but Marcus said everyone in Europe said that, even the Germans. I wasn't sure I believed him, but that's what he said.

Julia was impressed, too. She couldn't cook for shit.

I was sitting in the backyard drinking a soda, waiting for Sean, while Julia was waiting for Ben to text her that he was outside.

I pulled out my phone and sent my daily text to Yansi.

* Miss you *

I knew she wouldn't answer, but it made me feel connected to her in some small way.

Julia was ragging on Marcus, not in a mean way, but like they were friends. It was nice. Relaxing. It felt good having no tension in the house for once.

"So who's the lucky woman tonight?"

"Camille."

I could hear Julia's laugh float out through the open door.

"Wow! The same one for over a week! Is that a record?"

"Yep. Same girl. Have you got a bigger saucepan?"

"In the other cabinet. So, Camille, huh? What does she do?"

"She's a nurse."

I could hear the surprise in Julia's voice. "Oh! I didn't know. Well, that's … great."

There was a knock at the front door and Marcus went to answer it.

I could hear Camille's sexy accent down the hall.

"I have brought wine—a Bordeaux. I thought we should certainly have good wine if you are cooking and the food is bad."

"Who says the food will be bad?"

"You did. You said you can't cook. And you're American."

They walked into the kitchen where Julia was still waiting for Ben.

"Who is this?" snapped Camille.

Her eyes flashed dangerously.

"You live with a *woman?*" she shouted, clearly outraged. "Who is this tramp?" And then she screamed several things in French.

Marcus was surprisingly calm. If it had been me, I'd have been looking for a Kevlar vest.

"No, I mean yes I live with her, but … this is Julia. She's my landlady. I told you about her."

"Landladies are old women!" scoffed Camille. "She is not so old!"

I badly wanted to laugh, but I wondered if Julia would let rip. I was amazed when she didn't.

"Honestly, Camille," sniffed Julia as she checked her phone, "he's all yours. Good luck with that—you'll need it. Right, I'm out of here. I'm meeting Ben. My boyfriend. Have a nice evening."

The front door slammed, but the kitchen was silent.

"Babe…"

"She really is your landlady? You are not sleeping with her? I don't share, Marcus. You know this. It is, how you say, a deal breaker for me."

I didn't want to listen to their private conversation, so I coughed loudly before walking back into the kitchen.

"Hi, Camille," I muttered.

Camille looked surprised then she gave me a small smile. "Ah, the little brother. Hello, Nick."

"Yeah, I'm out now, too."

"Party?" asked Marcus, grinning at me.

"Yep, Sean's giving me a ride."

"Have fun. Don't do anything I wouldn't do. Say hi to Erin."

He seemed to think that was funny as fuck, so I just nodded and left them standing in the kitchen.

I didn't have to wait long before Sean showed up. He was in a good mood and tossed his car keys to me.

"You drive. I'm going to get the party started."

He cracked open a bottle of beer and scooted down into the passenger seat so he couldn't be spotted by any passing cop cars.

The guy having the party lived over in Palm Bay which was a 20 minute drive away. It was more the kind of place where people played golf than surfed. But Craig was one of the guys who hung out at the pier sometimes.

The house was a large bungalow surrounded by vacant lots. It made it a good place to get rowdy, with no neighbors nearby. Cars were lined up and down the street, and I parked Sean's so it wouldn't get blocked in. I had to be at work for 12.00 the next day and I didn't want some douche to have me stuck there all night. I already knew that Sean wouldn't be driving home later, so either I had to stay sober or we were sleeping on the floor.

The party was just getting warmed up when we walked in. I said hi to a few people and was getting a nice buzz from my second bottle of beer even though I hadn't planned on drinking. But then I saw the one person I had no interest in talking to.

"Hi, Nick."

She stood too close and pulled the beer from my hand, taking a long drink before passing it back. I shook my head and folded my arms across my chest.

"Can't even share a drink with me, Nicky?"

I sighed and leaned against the wall.

"What do you want, Erin?"

She shrugged. "Nothing. Just wondering how you are. I haven't seen you around much. You don't hang with us like you used to."

"I've been working."

"All work and no play makes Nick a dull boy."

And she wet her finger in her mouth, then tried to run it down my neck.

"Jesus! What is it with you?" I snapped, pushing her hand away. "I thought we'd already had this conversation? I told you: I'm not interested!"

She pouted and stood with her hands on her hips.

"Just seeing if you changed your mind."

"Fuck's sake, no! But thanks to you, neither has Yansi."

I tried to walk away but she caught my arm.

"I didn't tell her."

I shook her loose. "I know. But someone did. So whether you wanted to or not, you fucked things up for me."

"What's so special about her anyway?"

For once her tone wasn't hostile, but resigned, almost weary."

I was going to brush her off, but she looked so sad. Like I said, I'm a sucker for girls' tears.

I wanted to give her an answer that would show her that I meant what I said—something that would make her back off once and for all.

"Seeing her … talking to her … even getting a text message from her … it makes my day better."

Erin's face fell as I pushed away through the crowd, snagging another bottle of beer as I went.

I sat outside and chugged it back, trying to wipe the last few minutes from my mind. I probably needed bleach. Talking about Yansi hurt too much. I closed my eyes and leaned back.

A bunch of people were jumping in the pool, guys canon-balling to splash water over the girls. I recognized one of them: Emma from the Sandbar. Her rose tattoo stood out. Only a few of the older guys had tats, but none of the girls. I wanted to get one but Mom would never let me. I guess I could do whatever I liked now, but it just didn't seem important anymore.

She must have recognized me because she came and sat next to me.

"Hey, Nick. How's it going?"

"Yeah, good."

We sat in awkward silence for a moment.

I was hyper-aware of a pretty girl sitting by my side in a wet bikini.

I shifted uncomfortably and tried not to notice that her nipples were staring at me like a couple of car headlights.

"Is Marcus here?" she asked at last.

Oh fuck, yes! Distract me with words.

"No."

More words, please!

"Oh? You guys seem to be joined at the hip these days. Is he seeing his girlfriend?"

I glanced across at her. She didn't seem upset. Thank fuck for that. I couldn't deal with two moody girls in one night.

"I don't know," I said, lying through my teeth. "Maybe."

She smiled. "Oh, you think I care!" Then she laughed. "No, I can spot a player a mile away, although he seems to be really into that French girl. You're more my type."

She grinned at my expression.

"Don't worry. I nearly peed myself when Marcus told me you were only 17—I'm definitely no cougar!"

I didn't know what to say to that. I didn't even know

how old she was: 21 or 22, maybe.

She nudged my shoulder. "Don't freak out."

"I'm not," I mumbled, shaking my head and taking another long drink of my beer.

She laughed loudly, causing several heads to turn in our direction.

"You really are too cute for words. Enjoy the party, Nick."

As she sauntered away, I had to squeeze my eyes shut. That ass in that bikini.

I was kind of mad at myself—it was Yansi that I wanted, not Emma. But my body wasn't listening. Stupid fucker was the one who'd gotten me into this mess in the first place.

I was so tempted to get trashed, but I didn't. Sean tried to make me join in a game of beer pong but I waved him off and said I'd catch up later. I finished my beer, tossed the empty, and went to hunt down a game of pool.

When I got there, Emma was bent over the pool table, her tight ass waving at me. Then she looked over her shoulder and winked.

I spent the next two hours getting thrashed and losing horribly—sometimes I really thought God hated me. It was mutual.

Chapter 7

The box was a plastic crate, the kind that they sell at Walmart to put kids toys in. At least it had kept out the worst of the Florida humidity from where it was stored in Mom's garage.

I brushed off a decade of spider webs then carried it into the house, tipping the bundle of papers onto the kitchen table and started sorting through them.

Julia had gone out with Ben—I don't know where.

Things seemed better between them … better even than before. Maybe they were both trying harder. It made me wonder what would happen if they decided to be roomies or get married.

I guess it would be okay if Ben moved in; he practically lived here already. But if they got married, they wouldn't want Julia's little brother living with them. I didn't know what that would mean for me, and the thought freaked me out.

I sifted through the contents of the box, not certain what I was looking for.

There were photographs from Julia's high school graduation, old school reports, pictures of me with gap teeth grinning at the camera, old birthday cards, newspaper cuttings about Cocoa Beach and the year I won the Under-11s surf contest, and photos of Mom as a kid standing with people I guessed were her parents. They'd died before Julia was born, but that was all I knew. I wished now I'd asked Mom more about them. I didn't even know their names.

Most of the time I liked my English teacher, Mrs. Lord, but that crap she'd spouted about time being a great teacher—what a load of horseshit. Time was a crappy teacher, because it just reminded you of all the things you should have done, but couldn't do fuck all about now.

I almost missed the thin sheet of paper that had been folded into the size of a postcard.

Certificate of Live Birth
Florida

Name: **Nick Dalano Andrews**
Date of Birth: **May 5, 1997**
Time of Birth: **2300**

Certifier's Name: **C. Meade Gregg**
Mother's Maiden Name: **Eleanor Andrews**
Mother's Current Surname: **Andrews**
Father's Name: **Robert Alan Croften**
Date Registered: **September 20th, 1997**

So that was his name, Robert Croften. Or maybe he was known as Bob Croften or Rob Croften. Did this mean that he knew about me after all? I wasn't sure.

It was the strangest feeling, seeing his name in black and white. I was part of some guy that I knew nothing about. Half of my DNA was his. Did I look like him? Did I act like him? Did we have any mannerisms that were the same? Maybe he surfed? Maybe I got my love of the ocean from him? Maybe I was left-handed because he was?

And maybe it didn't matter because he didn't give a fuck about me.

If Julia moved out, I'd be completely alone. What if she wanted me to move out? Where would I go?

Suddenly, all her irritating habits didn't seem so bad.

I shoved the papers into a pile with the birth certificate on top.

I rested my head in my hands, trying not to think about Bob Croften who had a son that he'd never seen.

"Hi."

My head shot up, wondering if I'd imagined her voice.

My jaw dropped open when I saw Yansi standing there, and my throat began to burn.

"What … what are you doing here?"

"I was walking over here to see you and … I bumped into Julia and Ben. She said you were in, so…" She hesitated. "But I can go…"

"No! Fuck, no! Please don't go. Just … stay, please."

She nodded jerkily and fiddled with the strap of her purse, before pulling out one of the battered kitchen chairs and sitting down.

She stared at the table and I knew I should say something, but I couldn't think of a single damn word.

"So," she said at last. "You look … good."

I blinked rapidly before managing to choke out a reply.

"Thanks. You, too."

And she did, she really did. I hadn't seen her for two-and-a-half weeks, so she could have worn a sack and she'd look hot to me. But she was wearing a pale pink tank-top and short jean skirt, and her hair was loose, falling in thick, silky strands that I wanted to wrap around my hands while I kissed her. But I couldn't: I didn't have that right. Not anymore.

But now I looked more closely, her eyes were tired, dark rings only partially hidden with makeup.

She bit her lip and glanced toward the door, as if she was thinking of leaving.

"Um," I said, beginning to panic. "Can I get you a soda or a water or something?"

"Can I have a water, please?"

"Sure! Sure!"

I leapt to my feet, relieved to have something to do.

We couldn't afford bottled water, so it had to be from the tap, and it wasn't very cold. I handed her the glass and shoved my hands in my pockets.

She took a sip and put the glass down. I don't think she really wanted a drink; she was probably just being polite.

One of the things I'd always loved about me and Yans was that we could talk about anything. But not now. It was awkward and embarrassing and I had no fucking clue what to do to make it any better.

She glanced up at me and smiled weakly.

"Are you going to sit down?" she asked, squinting at the chair I'd been sitting in.

I slid into it, cringing as the legs scraped across the floor tiles too loudly.

"So, this is … strange," she whispered.

"Um, yeah," I agreed, running my hands through my hair nervously.

"How've you been?"

Shit without you. "Okay, I guess. You?"

She sighed. "I've been better."

Me, too.

"I'm sorry," I said helplessly. "I'm so fuckin' sorry."

She nodded as her lips twisted to the side. "I know." Then she looked up. "Erin came to see me."

I was so surprised, my eyebrows shot up and my mouth dropped open, but no words came out.

Yansi smiled faintly.

"Yeah, that was about my reaction."

"What ... what did she want?"

My voice sounded high pitched and strangled, as if someone had squeezed my balls hard.

Yansi shrugged. "To apologize."

"Really?" I croaked. "Wow."

"Yeah, wow. She told me everything that happened at the party, that it was her fault, and that you ... you were drunk and ... you thought she was me?"

Her voice turned a corner at the end, becoming a question by accident.

"Is that true?"

I nodded slowly, my cheeks reddening with shame as the memory flooded behind my eyes.

"I was dreaming about you," I whispered, my voice hoarse. "I said your name, but then I realized it wasn't you and ... it was too late," I finished lamely.

Yansi frowned, and two parallel lines appeared between her eyebrows. "That's what Erin said."

"God, I'm so sorry, Yans. I've missed you so much."

"I've missed you, too," she said sadly. "I asked Papi how you were, but he wouldn't tell me anything."

"I guess he doesn't know why we split up then," I said quietly.

Yansi shook her head. "No."

Well, that was something.

"Your mom?"

"Yeah, she knows."

Crap.

"She was there when Erin came over, so I had to explain. I didn't tell her everything, but I think she probably guessed the rest..."

"So she hates me, too," I sighed, wearily.

"I don't hate you."

Yansi's voice was quiet, but I felt a flutter of hope as I looked up into her beautiful dark eyes.

"You don't?"

"I wanted to," she admitted. "I tried to, but I just couldn't."

My mouth was dry as I tried to swallow.

"God, if I could take it back, I would. I wish I'd never gone to that stupid party. I was just so angry after what Julia said and…"

Yansi's head snapped up. "What did Julia say?"

"Oh. Well, nothing really."

I didn't like remembering that night.

"It can't be nothing!" Yansi insisted.

I sighed again and lowered my eyes to the table, mindlessly peeling the label from a bottle of ketchup.

"The usual, you know. Going on about me being a fuckin' waste of space. I guess she was right."

Yansi shook her head briskly.

"That's not true. You can be a real idiot sometimes…"

"I'm sorry."

I didn't know how many times I could keep on saying that. Maybe as many as it took for Yansi to forgive me?

She sighed and stared out of the window.

"You know that me and Erin…" I took a deep breath. "You know that I don't like her that way?"

Yansi pulled a face and looked down at the glass of water.

"Yeah, I guess. She told me what you said to her."

I winced. "I was angry."

Yansi smiled, a sad lopsided smile. "Yeah, she said that, too."

"Um, I don't really get why she came to see you. You said she wanted to … apologize?"

Yansi frowned. "She really cares about you."

I shook my head. "I don't care about her."

"She's not all bad."

"Why are you defending her, Yans? She got what she wanted," I said bitterly.

"No, she didn't," Yansi said briskly. "She thought …

she thought that if you had sex with her you'd want to start dating her. I think she was pretty shocked when you blew her off. She said you'd always been nice to her, so she, well ... she blamed me for taking you away from her, I guess."

"She didn't take me away from you," I said impatiently. "I never wanted her. We went out one lousy time, and that was only because you weren't allowed to date until you were 17. I couldn't wait to get rid of her."

"She was really upset."

"I don't care!" I shouted, and Yansi flinched. "She fucked things up for us. What she did, it wasn't an accident! I want *you*, and now it's all ruined."

I swept my hand across the table, sending the pile of papers flying. Yansi stared at me, shocked. I didn't usually lose my temper around her, but I was having a really bad day.

"Sorry," I mumbled after a moment, then knelt down to start picking up the papers.

Yansi was quiet, and then she bent down beside me and began shuffling everything into a neat pile.

"What is all this?" she asked.

"Mom's stuff."

"Oh," she said quietly, stacking it back onto the table in a neat pile.

Then she pulled out a photo of me as a kid, flattening it on the table because it was curled with age.

"Aw, look at you. You're so cute."

I glanced across.

"That was my first boogie board. I think I was maybe five or six."

She smiled, then carefully pushed the photo back into the pile.

"I found my birth certificate," I said.

She paused, looking at me intently, but I couldn't hold her gaze. She saw too much—she always had.

"Did it tell you ... anything?"

"Yeah, it did." I took a deep breath. "My dad is some guy named 'Robert Alan Croften'. It's weird, seeing it written down like that. Makes it real, you know?"

"Are you going to try and find him?"

"I don't know. I haven't really thought about it. I mean, what's the point? His name is on the birth certificate so I guess that means he knows I exist, but the dude hasn't wanted anything to do with me in 17 years—why would he change now? Anyway, I don't think Mom wanted me to know him, or she would have said something, wouldn't she?"

Yansi looked doubtful. "Maybe. She obviously had her issues with him…"

I started shoving the papers back in the box, feeling confused and miserable.

"Why are you here, Yans?" I muttered without looking up.

"I want us to try again."

My hands stilled and the flare of hope was painful. When I dared to meet her eyes, she was watching me, a tiny smile on her face.

"Really?"

"Yes. Really."

I stared at her stunned. "You mean it?"

"Yes, you idiot!" she half laughed, half shouted.

She launched herself at me, and I could have cried with relief at the way her soft body molded against mine. I wrapped my arms around her, burying my face in her hair, breathing in the scent of warmth and spice.

"Don't ever do that to me again," she whispered.

"I won't. I promise," my voice stuttered. "Oh God, I promise."

"No more getting wasted at parties?" she asked carefully.

I hesitated, not wanting to lie to her. "I promise I'll try."

She sighed and shook her head slightly. "Good

enough, I guess. At least you're honest."

"I'd never lie to you, Yans."

She frowned. "No, you'd rather not tell me the truth."

I felt ashamed, because she was right.

"I'd rather know," she said softly. "I'd rather hear it from you. It hurt so badly when Megan told me. I didn't want to believe her."

"I'm sorry," I said again. "I'm so fucking sorry."

"Me, too. I'm sorry I didn't give you a chance to explain. Although I'm not sure I would have listened there and then."

I winced at the memory. "Probably not."

"But I missed you so much. When Erin came around, I was desperate to hear what she had to say. She felt bad for what happened, especially when she saw that you were never going to go out with her and that you were really miserable."

"I don't want to talk about Erin ever again," I said coldly.

Yansi paused. "Okay. We won't. Well, just one thing: at least now I know what I can't live without," and she pressed her soft lips against mine.

My girl always had to have the last word.

My girl.

The next few days were strange. Awkward. But it was getting easier.

Yansi was grounded. It was obvious that she got into a shit load of trouble for coming to see me when she did. She'd never had much freedom, but now her parents wouldn't let her leave the house unless one of them was with her, although she wouldn't tell me what they'd said when she went back home that day. I tried to ask her, but she just said it wasn't important. I wasn't sure how that squared with her insistence on complete honesty—from me—but I didn't want to push her either.

It was getting good again, and I wasn't going to risk that.

Mr. Alfaro wasn't happy. Not that he ever looked anything other than a Hispanic grim reaper—or maybe he was just constipated. Either way, the sight of me made him pissed, and I kept expecting to be fired, but he never did.

Although I wasn't allowed to sit in the truck's cab anymore, but I was used to that by now.

Yansi sent me at least a dozen text messages each day. Every time Mr. Alfaro saw me checking my phone, this weird vein throbbed in the side of his head. On the third day after we got back together, he made me leave my phone in the truck while we were working. But then I spent my whole lunchtime texting, just to piss him off some more. Well, that was part of it, but I really wanted to hear from her. Whatever, I think it worked. Not that I was trying to give my girlfriend's dad a coronary, but he was being a complete douche canoe about it.

I changed the password on my phone, because if any of my friends saw the messages I sent her, they'd take away my man-card; probably tear it up and burn it, too. But knowing that she was thinking about me and wanted to be with me … it felt damn fine. A lonely corner of my mind wondered if maybe Yansi was right: the time we'd been apart had shown us both how much we had to lose. Well, I'd already known that, but I was glad that Yansi did now. I hated that I'd put her through so much shit, but we'd gotten better at talking to each other—the important stuff.

I thought Sean was going to be a dick about it when I told him that me and Yansi were back together, but he wasn't.

"No, I get it," he said. "I don't get *her*, but what you guys have—that's real."

I had to let that register in my brain, and then check that the words really had come from Sean.

He gave me an irritated look and then shrugged.

"I can think deep shit just as much as you can, bro. You were turning into a cock-sucking emo bitch without the ole ball an' chain around." Then his voice turned serious. "If she's what you want, hang onto that. Because if there's nothing you want, life is shit."

I tried to ask him what he meant. He blew me off, making a joke of it. But I didn't forget what he'd said.

I was keeping my promise to Yansi, too. When I hung out with Sean or Rob and the guys, I kept the drinking to a couple of beers—enough to get a buzz, but not enough to be tanked. I still took a few hits if a blunt was doing the rounds, but I passed on it more times than I inhaled.

Sean was still partying hard, but it didn't seem to make him happy. In fact, the more he drank and smoked, the more miserable he seemed. I thought about what he said, about not wanting anything. The only thing that he seemed to care about was surfing, but even then he'd been too hung-over to make it to some of the dawn surfaris we planned.

He was hanging with Marcus and his crew a lot more, too. I'd been kind of avoiding Marcus since the thing with Julia. I saw him at the Sandbar when I was working, and sometimes we passed each other in the kitchen or on the way to the shower; but he was out a lot, and I didn't go down to the pier as much as I used to.

The worst thing about Yansi being grounded was that she was going to miss the Fourth of July. That seemed unconstitutional to me, but her parents weren't letting her off.

Panama's Independence Day was November 28th. Yansi said that she hoped she wouldn't still be grounded by then. I think that was a joke. Whatever. It meant that all the things we'd planned to do weren't going to happen.

There was a free concert in Riverfront Park in Cocoa Village a couple of miles away on the other side of the causeway, then we were coming back to the beach to see the firework display, which was always awesome.

Now she was going be at some family bonfire and cookout instead. So, I took the lunchtime shift at the Sandbar, just to keep myself busy more than anything else. And I promised to hang with Sean and Rob, so I came down to the pier after work. Plus, I'd have felt like a loser staying at home on the Fourth. Yeah, and Sean would have given me shit.

At least I knew Yansi would rather be with me. That was something. She was finding it harder to put up with her parents' rules. I can't really say I knew what that was like. Mom had always been cool about stuff. As long as I wasn't hung-over on a school day, I could pretty much do what I wanted.

But Yansi was on a short leash. I wanted to tell her that having her parents care so much was better than having ones who didn't care at all. But I wasn't good with words, so I didn't say anything.

I was running late because the Sandbar had been slammed and Steve had wanted me to stay on. I did an extra hour, but that was all. Then I went home and took the time to eat something before heading out again. The food choices were pretty limited, but partying and drinking on an empty stomach—well, I wasn't going to make that mistake again.

It was hotter than balls, and all week the sweat had been running into my eyes, making them sting. My body was losing so much moisture, I was drinking a bottle of water every half hour. One day I used the garden hose where we were working to cool myself down for a few minutes.

Today the air was thick and heavy, and the palm trees looked like they were drooping. I'd taken a shower when I got in from the Sandbar, but it hadn't made a whole lot of difference—I was sweating again and my t-shirt clung to my back.

The ocean was a steely gray, flat and lifeless, just like it had been for days, and all of us surfers were grouchy with the lack of wave action. Paddleboards just didn't cut it when what you really wanted was to work some bitchin' waves, catch air, or ride some tubes.

I weaved through the evening crowds of vacationers on my skateboard, watching families enjoying the holiday vibe: Cocoa Beach was doing what it was born to do.

Mom loved the big holidays. I tried not to think about it too much because it hurt so bad. But Julia was the same, ignoring what we couldn't change. She was hanging out with Ben and some of his work friends, so she must have been pretty desperate to have something, anything to distract her. I wished I did, too.

A few people were jogging on the wide, flat beach, and in the distance I could see a sailboat moving sluggishly across the horizon.

The pier was crowded, people already jostling for the best position to see the fireworks, but the usual suspects were hanging out below.

Sean was trashed already. I wondered where he was getting the money to buy booze so often. But then again, money had never been a problem for him.

He saw me and grinned, his lips slack like a punctured tire.

"Hey, bro! We've gotta add Cloud Nine on Siargo Island to the list. Marcus says it's got an awesome reef break that's just itchin' for us to shred. Total death rides, man! One slip and the coral will shred your skin." His eyes were glassy as he turned to Marcus and tried to coordinate a high-five. "The guy rocks! He's a legend!"

I noticed that Camille was sitting on the sand next to Marcus. She was studying Sean carefully and didn't crack a smile when Marcus laughed and returned the hand slap.

She was still watching him, a small frown wrinkling

her forehead, when Sean lurched to his feet.

"Back in a minute: I gotta piss so bad, my eyeballs are floatin'."

I watched him stagger off to use the gross public bathrooms up on the boardwalk. At least, I hoped that was where he was going, because if he went and pissed behind a dune in daylight where families were walking on the beach with their kids, he was going to end up getting arrested for public indecency. And, without passing judgment, the guy liked to wave his dick around if he thought girls would see him.

He'd been doing that since fourth grade so I didn't think he was going to stop now.

I'd seen Sean's dick more times than his doctor. That sounds bad, but the guy was obsessed, whipping it out at every opportunity—the back row of the lecture hall, in classrooms, behind the bleachers, at the football field, but especially the locker room.

Believe me, there's an etiquette when you're in the locker room. Sean's brother Aidan said it's like the New York subway after night; it should be safe, but you never know when someone's going to pull out a dick.

When you're 13, there's a lot of towel snapping, wedgies, and comparing of various body parts. There just is.

The length of your johnson becomes common knowledge: hung like a horse *versus* has a weenie.

But by tenth grade, the rules change, and they're pretty simple:

- Keep your eyes to yourself. (Although there's a school of thought that says you should keep your eyes on the floor, I think that makes you look like a weirdo loser. No, look at eye-level or above.)

- Don't get in the personal space of the guy next to you. And never, ever bend down to pick something up if you're close to someone's personal space. Leave that fucker on the floor, or you'll be leaving with a split lip.

- Keep your towel nearby and don't spend any more time naked than you really have to.
- Get in. Get out. It's not the time to check your phone for messages. Creepy. And don't start a conversation with naked people. Not cool.

Sean could never seem to remember that. You'd think he had a dick like a donkey the way he went on, but I'd checked, and it looked pretty average to me.

Rob passed me a beer and told me about some girl he'd met at a party and how she said she was going to hang with us tonight. Maybe she would, but Rob had been so stoned all summer, he admitted he couldn't really remember what she looked like.

Typical Rob. Guy was such an asshole sometimes.

Sean was back a few minutes later. I guess he'd used a dune after all.

He plopped down beside me and pulled a bottle of Jack toward him.

"We gotta do it, man. We gotta do our surf trip. Nothing else matters. That dude," and he pointed at Marcus, "that dude has surfed all around the world—I mean, just, like, everywhere—every continent."

I wondered briefly what the surf was like in Antarctica. Cold, probably.

"That's what I wanna do," Sean breathed, his eyes glassy and reverent, "I don't want to stay here in the ass-end of nowhere."

"Where are you going to go next?" I asked Marcus.

He smiled. "I'm thinking of French Polynesia."

Rob scratched his head. "Is that in France?"

There was a brief discussion of the merits of surfing Hossegor or Biarritz, which got pretty heated even though none of us had ever been there.

Marcus slung his arm around Camille and they shared

a secret smile.

"I hate to break it to you guys," said Marcus eventually, "but French Polynesia isn't in France; it's a group of islands in the Pacific. You've heard of the awesome surf breaks at Papeete, right? That's the capital."

"Oh yeah, part of Hawaii," said Trey.

Camille looked appalled.

"Yeah," laughed Marcus. "Right by Hawaii—just head south 2,000 miles."

I could see Sean squinting as he tried to work out the geography, but in the end he just shook his head and grinned.

"Whatever, man! Sounds good. I heard that the barrels at Papeete are brutal!"

Camille rolled her eyes. "Is this all you talk of? Ripping and cutting and brutal barrels!"

Sean smirked. "Sure. What else is there? You think we want to sit around talking about chicks?"

I couldn't work out why he was deliberately trying to piss her off. Marcus ignored him, but Camille looked annoyed.

"We are going there to create a life," she sneered, "not to waste our life."

Sean's smile dropped away.

"You're *moving* there, man?"

Marcus shrugged. "Yeah, maybe, why not?"

Camille pushed his shoulder. "Maybe? We have decided, haven't we? I will work as a nurse again, and you will set up a surf school while you write your music."

"Sure, baby," he said, kissing away her concerns.

A brief flash of some emotion flickered in Sean's eyes, then it was gone. He took a long slug of Jack Daniel's, then flicked me on the ear.

"Put Papeete on the list," he grinned.

Jeez, I was going to have to win the Mega Millions to be able to afford this surf trip.

Then Sean leaned toward me and pulled a scrunched

piece of saran wrap out of his pocket.

"Wanna see some good shit?" he whispered, unfolding the plastic to reveal a small, blue pill. "Molly, this bitch always shows you a good time. I can hook you up, if you want some?"

I was tempted. God, was I tempted. I was so tired, and the idea of taking something that would make me party … it seemed like an answer to a question I hadn't thought of asking.

I'd done Molly with Sean a couple of times before, although not for a while, and it had been good—hell, better than good—but for days after, it left me barely wanting to get out of bed. I'd tried to tell Mom I was sick, but she'd kicked my ass out and made me go to school anyway. That sucked.

"Nah, man," I said reluctantly, shaking my head. Not that I could afford it anyway.

He raised his eyebrows. "You sure? I know a guy who knows a guy. The fireworks will be something else— you'll feel like you're up there with them."

I shoved my hands in my pockets. "I'm good." Then I watched jealously as he tossed the pill into his mouth and washed it down with whiskey.

He licked his lips. "Like mommy's milk," he laughed.

The bottle got passed around a few times as people were spilling onto the beach, laughing and happy, all celebrating the holiday.

My phone vibrated and I smiled to see a text from Yansi.

* No fun celebrating without you.
Miss you. X *

I could tell the moment the Molly started to work. Sean was running sand through his fingers, like the texture of it fascinated him. Then he started talking real fast, some shit about girls and surfing and life in general, that made no fucking sense whatsoever. He was waving his arms around and the other guys were laughing at him.

He leapt to his feet and started going around our group that was spread out loosely under the pier, hitting on girls, even if they were with their boyfriends. He was laughing so hard as he staggered across the sand. I kept an eye on him, because he was likely to get the shit kicked out of him if he carried on like that.

The sun was sinking behind the town and an excited murmur ran through the crowd. As soon as the purple sky faded to black, a single rocket zoomed upward. Then the night exploded, the sound so loud you could feel the heavy thuds of exploding fireworks. The blackness was filled with color and light, and the flashes were caught and reflected in the glassy ocean, a warped mirror of the sky above.

Sean was gazing up, a huge grin spread over his face and he started spinning around, laughing loudly.

Then I saw him fall over. I thought maybe he'd tripped on something, but when he sat up, he looked dizzy.

"Hey," I said quietly, crouching down next to him. "You okay?"

His pupils were dilated when he looked at me. He was shivering uncontrollably and twitching, but his skin was burning.

"I don't feel so good, Nick. I'm really hot."

He almost never called me 'Nick'; it was always 'man' or 'bro', so I was immediately worried.

Sean was sweating bullets, even more than the rest of us in the high humidity, and he kept clenching his jaw like he was trying to grind his teeth flat.

People were beginning to stare, and their glances gave me a feeling of ants running across my back.

"Come on," I said, heaving him to his feet. "Try and, um, walk it off or something."

He was twitching so bad, he could barely stagger more than a few steps.

"It's all false," he started rambling. "It's just shit. Why can't anyone see it's shit? It's not real. Nobody's real."

"Anyone got any downers?" Rob asked, looking slightly concerned through the haze of scented smoke.

I shot him a look. Seriously? That was his way of helping?

Camille came hurrying over.

"Has he taken something?"

"Just some Molly," Rob slurred, opening another can of beer.

"Molly? What is this?"

Marcus spoke up. "Ecstasy."

I could see Camille translating in her head, and her eyes widened.

"He is having a bad reaction, I think. You must take him to hospital."

Everyone started looking nervous, and a few people began to leave. No one wanted to be around if shit was going down.

Hospitals + illegal drugs = no one wants to know you.

Sean looked really sick, and I was beginning to panic.

"We must drive him to hospital," Camille insisted, looking at Marcus.

He pulled a face.

"I can't drive him. I've been drinking."

"Then call an ambulance!" she hissed.

"They'll never make it through these crowds," I gritted out.

"Fuck," muttered Marcus. "Fine, we'll take him in the van."

We half dragged, half carried Sean through the crowds. Some people threw us disgusted looks, others looked concerned, but mostly people just stepped out of the way. We manhandled Sean into Marcus' van and

Camille stayed with him in the back while I gave Marcus directions to the causeway so we could get to the hospital.

"He'll be okay," Marcus said reassuringly. "It's nothing."

"I don't think it is nothing," Camille snapped. "He is so angry all the time."

I blinked, not sure what this had to do with Sean taking Molly.

"He's 17," said Marcus, sounding rattled.

Camille huffed disbelievingly.

"Why would that make him angry?"

Marcus concentrated on driving before he answered. Maybe he *was* kind of drunk. Shit. I braced against the dashboard with one hand.

"I was like that when I was 17," explained Marcus. "It's like, 'What are you rebelling against?', 'Whaddya got?' You know?"

"I don't understand," Camille said frowning.

I looked over my shoulder at her. Sean was lying on an old board bag and she'd covered him with a couple of beach towels that she'd soaked using a bottle of water. I guessed that was to try and cool him down. His skin looked clammy and he was still sweating and shaking.

"Didn't you ever feel angry ... with the world, when you were 17?"

Camille snorted.

"This boy—he drinks and smokes too much weed. It makes him crazy. So do you—but without the crazy. And now this Molly. He needs help."

"He's not that bad," Marcus disagreed. "All the kids do it, don't they, Nick?"

I turned back to look at Marcus.

"Maybe, I guess. I don't know. Not this much..."

"He is not healthy," said Camille softly. "He has nothing in his life. His eyes are empty."

I shivered at her words and wanted to ask what she meant, but she turned away and was holding Sean's wrist, counting his heart rate. It must have been going through the roof because her lips were moving rapidly as if she was trying to keep up.

She muttered something under her breath and shook her head.

My heart started to pound, the tempo almost matching Sean's racing pulse, and my mouth went dry.

I hated this hospital. I'd been here too many times. Too many times, and now with Sean.

Marcus pulled into the front of the ER area, next to a parked ambulance.

"Look, kid," he said, his voice quietly urgent. "You'll have to take him. I can't come in with you—I've been drinking. I can't afford to lose my license. It'll be cool. Just say you don't know where he got it, okay? In fact, don't tell them anything."

I stared at Camille, but she bit her lip and shook her head.

"Has he got any more?" asked Marcus.

"Fuck," I whispered. "I don't know."

"You find something, you toss it," snapped Marcus.

"No!" hissed Camille. "He must show it to the doctors so they can decide how to treat him."

Marcus looked at her coldly. "Yeah, if the kid wants to get arrested along with his fucktard friend."

He shook his head then jumped out and opened the van's doors. I hauled Sean to his feet, staggering under his weight as I tried to drag and carry him through the ER doors. I heard the van pull away before we were inside.

A nurse ran over as soon as she saw me, and called to an orderly to bring a wheelchair.

She started yelling questions at me.

What happened?

What has he taken?

How long has he been like this?

My hands were shaking and it was hard to concentrate on giving her answers.

Sean was wheeled away. I tried to go with him, but the nurse gave me a long, hard look.

"Have you taken anything?"

"What? No. I haven't had anything. Is he going to be okay?"

"You can help him by answering some questions at the registration desk," she snapped, hurrying away.

I stumbled to the desk she pointed at, and a clipboard was shoved into my hands.

"We need to call his parents," the registration clerk said, her voice softening as she looked at me.

I pulled my phone out to give her the number for Sean's mom and dad.

Oh shit. He was going to be in so much trouble. But I had no choice.

I filled in his name, address, and date of birth; but I couldn't answer any of the questions about insurance, allergies, or previous illnesses.

When I handed the clipboard back, the clerk looked at me sympathetically.

"They'll take real good care of your friend."

I stared at her numbly.

"Why don't you sit down to wait for him."

I sank onto a hard, plastic chair, my head in my hands.

I didn't want to believe this was happening. Not Sean, too. *It wasn't fucking fair.*

My phone beeped, making me jump.

> * Heard you are at hospital.
> What happened?
> Are you ok?
> Do you need me to come? Y x *

Before I could reply, Sean's parents rushed in. They were dressed up, like they'd just come from a fancy party. They didn't see me sitting in the corner. Mrs. Wallis was clutching at the pearls around her neck while Mr. Wallis strode up to the registration desk and demanded to see his son. When the clerk explained that he couldn't yet, his volume rose. *My rights*, blah blah; *my son*, blah, blah; *sue you*, blah blah.

She'd probably heard it all before, because she just handed him the same clipboard I'd written on and waved them both into a seat.

That's when they saw me.

"I might have known," barked Mr. Wallis, marching across to stand over me. "I've been telling Sean for years that he should find better friends. You'll regret fucking with my family!"

I stared at him. The guy really was a Grade-A asshole. No wonder Sean was so messed up.

He ranted on for a while, and I was kind of fascinated as the spit flew from his mouth while his face got redder and redder. It was like watching through a plate-glass window: I was aware of sounds, but none of it touched me.

By the time he got to shrieking pitch, one of the male orderlies told him to calm down or he'd be asked to leave. There was some more shouting and yelling, before Mrs. Wallis whispered something to him.

He looked around, realized he was causing a scene, and shut right up. Maybe he was worried that someone from the country club would see him.

They sat at the other end of the room, staring at me as if I was a walking disease.

When Mr. Wallis pulled out his phone and started shouting at someone else, I lost interest. Quietly, I walked over to the registration desk.

"Is there any news about my friend, Sean Wallis?"

The clerk gave me another sympathetic smile.

"Not yet, honey. But I'll let you know as soon as there is." Then she lowered her voice. "They'll only let his family in to see him…"

I had to swallow the rock choking me before I could

even try to speak.

"Yeah, but I just want to know he's okay."

She patted my hand. "I'll let you know."

I nodded and slumped into my seat again, avoiding Mrs. Wallis' eyes lasering into me, trying to burn me into dust. She didn't need to make so much effort, I was almost there already. My throat was Sahara dry even though my palms were sweating in the air-conditioned waiting room.

I thought I hated Sean's parents then, but it wasn't a fraction of the hatred I felt when two police officers walked in and Mr. Wallis pointed at me and roared, "That's the boy who gave my son drugs!"

My stomach lurched as everyone turned to stare at me, disapproval and disgust in their eyes.

"I didn't!" I stuttered, but Mr. Wallis shouted me down.

"You've always been a bad influence," he accused. "Every time Sean got into trouble, you were there. I've always known it would come to this, the drinking, and now drugs—God knows what else. You probably supply half the High School."

"That's bullshit!" I shouted back, standing up so fast my chair rocked dangerously before clattering to the floor.

"I want him arrested!" yelled Mr. Wallis. "And you can bet your ass I'll be pressing charges!"

"All right," said one of the police officers calmly, "I think we should take this down to the station."

"I'm not leaving my son," Mrs. Wallis said, speaking for the first time.

There was a pause, then the officer turned to me again.

"I'll need to see some ID."

My hands were shaking as I dug into my wallet and pulled out my driver's license.

The cop scanned it quickly then passed it to his colleague.

I think it would be best if you came with us to answer

some questions, Mr. Andrews."

"I didn't do anything!" I insisted, my voice coming out in a croak as I started to panic.

"We'll need to contact your parents," he said, as if I hadn't spoken.

My stomach was rolling so badly, I thought I was going to throw up.

"Mom's dead," I said.

The cops exchanged a look, then handed back my ID and told me to go with them.

Mr. Wallis didn't even look at me as I was escorted from the hospital—he was shouting at the woman at the registration desk again.

And it didn't matter how much I denied knowing anything about the drugs Sean had taken: when you're 17, wearing old clothes, and have 'no discernible parental authority', and the guy who's accusing you wears a fancy suit and drives a new Mercedes, you'll be the one sitting in a patrol car on your way to a police station for questioning.

I thought I was going to be arrested like Mr. Wallis wanted, but instead they made me give them Julia's number, even though she wasn't my legal guardian. Then I had to hand over my phone, wallet and house keys before they left me in an interview room. At least it wasn't a cell. Maybe that's because I was still a minor.

It seemed like forever before Julia arrived. She was with Ben, shocked as well as angry.

I looked up and met her eyes. She looked like she was going to cry.

"I didn't do it."

She bit her lip and shook her head slightly.

We were joined by a guy who introduced himself as Officer Flowers. I kind of wanted to laugh.

"Just tell the truth, Nicky," Julia said. "That's all you have to do."

So I did. And then she looked at me, and the police officer looked at me, and I could tell that neither one of them believed a single word.

"It'll go easier on you if you tell the truth, son," said Officer Flowers.

I stared at him. "I'm not your son."

My voice was bitter and cold. I wasn't anyone's son. I was a friend, a brother, a boyfriend, but I wasn't anyone's son.

He looked bored and irritated.

"Supplying is a felony," he snapped. "You're in a whole world of hurt here."

"I don't supply."

"Just tell the truth, Nicky," Julia begged.

I fisted my hands in my hair, frustration burning through the weird lethargy.

"I am!" I yelled, shooting to my feet. "But you won't fucking believe me!"

"Watch your mouth, kid," said Flowers. "Now sit your ass down."

I collapsed back into the chair, only half aware of what they were saying to me now.

I don't know how long we were in there. My throat was bone dry, and I was so thirsty I could have shit dust.

Eventually Flowers left, and I was moved into a waiting area with Julia and Ben. I guess they didn't consider me a flight risk.

At least she didn't look like she wanted to cry anymore. I hated when she was like that.

"How you holding up, bud?" asked Ben.

I raised my eyes to look at him, tiredness turning my limbs into ton weights.

"Can I get some water?"

He nodded and left me with Julia. We stared at each other in silence.

"Is Sean okay?" I croaked at last. "Have you heard from the hospital?"

She pulled a face. "No. I tried, but they wouldn't give any information to someone who isn't family."

"Do you think…?"

I couldn't get the words out.

"No, I don't," Julia said quickly.

I rested my head against the wall, my brain too exhausted to process anything else.

Julia nudged me.

"It's just us now … did you do what they say you did?"

I didn't even lift my head.

"No," I replied, my voice hoarse.

"You can tell me," she encouraged. "I won't be angry. Well, I will … but if you just tell me the truth…"

I started to laugh. I couldn't help it; the laughter just poured out of me in huge, whooping coughs until I was red in the face and gasping for air.

"This isn't funny!" she hissed, spitting out her words like bullets. "This is serious! This will affect your whole future, Nicky! I'm trying to do the right thing and look after you like I promised Mom, but you can't keep doing shit like this!"

The laughter left me as soon as she mentioned Mom.

"Fuck you!" I shouted. "Fuck you! You don't believe a word I say! I've told the truth over and over—to you, to them. I don't know who Sean got the Molly from. I don't know when he got it. He already had it when I got to the beach. Everyone saw. I was the last person there!"

But when I thought about it, I wasn't sure if anybody had seen Sean with the Molly before I got there. Fuck, it must have looked like 20 minutes after I arrived, Sean got sick. *Shit. It looked bad.*

My temper surged and snapped, heat shooting through my veins, all of it aimed at my sister.

"My best friend is lying in a fucking hospital bed, and I don't know if he's going to live or die and you're accusing me of all this shit. You're supposed to be my sister! I'm not a fucking drug dealer!"

I was breathing heavily now, fighting for breath, for

the slightest hold on my boiling temper.

"It's like you *want* to believe I did it. Like you *want* to think the worst of me. You're just like *them*, Sean's parents. Poor white trash—that's what they think I am." I sat back in my chair, panting. "That's what they think you are."

Julia looked stunned.

"I'm sorry," she whispered. "I…"

I couldn't look at her, but my voice was weary when I spoke.

"Fuck you."

She didn't say anything else, but stood up, straightened her skirt and left me alone.

All the fight had drained out of me and I was just tired. I lay my head back against the wall and my eyes closed.

Someone brought me a paper cup of water and I drank it down greedily.

There was no clock, so I couldn't tell how long I'd been there. I think I slept a little, but jerked awake when I had a nightmare. Well, more of a memory than a nightmare.

I was about three and I'd gotten separated from Mom in the mall. I was lost, and strangers kept trying to talk to me, and I was afraid, and I was looking for Mom everywhere but I couldn't find her.

God, I hadn't had that dream in so long. I rubbed my hands over my face, shocked to see that they were trembling slightly.

Then I looked up and saw Julia.

Dark rings framed her eyes, and she looked as exhausted as I felt.

"They're letting you go."

"What?"

I rubbed my eyes again.

"Sean's awake. I sent Ben to the hospital and he pretended to be one of his brothers. Apparently Sean told the police that it had nothing to do with you, so they're not filing charges."

I stared up at her, hope and disbelief waging war in my brain.

"Come on," she said softly. "I'm taking you home."

I stood up on wobbly legs and followed her to the front desk.

The police officer on duty returned my phone, wallet and keys, and I was allowed to leave.

Ben was waiting outside, leaning against his car. He took a step forward when he saw me, and I stiffened because I thought he might try and do the man-hug thing. But he draped an arm around Julia's shoulder and kissed her forehead, then he held out his hand toward me, so we did the fist-bump instead.

"Thanks for finding out about Sean," I mumbled, as we rode home along quiet streets.

The sun was just beginning to appear behind the ocean, burning away the cool gray of dawn.

Ben's eyes searched mine in the rear view mirror.

"He's going to be okay," he said quietly, "but if you ever do any of that shit yourself, I'll help Julia kick your ass. Okay?"

I'd never heard Ben say anything like that before.

"Okay," I muttered, and stared out of the window.

"I'm sorry I didn't believe you," Julia whispered.

I nodded, but didn't look at her.

When I got home, I trudged upstairs. I threw myself face onto the bed, and spiraled down into oblivion.

Chapter 8

I slept most of the next day, finally waking about three in the afternoon.

I plugged in my cellphone while I showered, and came back to find that Yansi had just about blown up my phone with texts and messages.

I sent her a quick reply saying that Sean was okay and asking if I could see her today.

She sent an unhappy smiley face with the words,

> * Can't : (Family time. Miss you.
> Glad you're ok. And Sean. x *

I wasn't surprised; she was rarely allowed out on a Sunday. Fuckin' family time.

My stomach rumbled loudly, so I pulled on shorts and a clean tee, irritated that the laundry seemed to have piled up again already. I could have sworn I'd just done a load. I preferred it when Julia had done all that sort of shit. I wondered if I could ask her if she'd start again—make some sort of deal, but I had the feeling she wouldn't be doing me favors anytime soon.

The kitchen was mercifully empty. I didn't think I could face talking to anyone right now.

I was surprised to see that my skateboard was propped up in the hall. Marcus must have gone back to the beach last night and saved it for me. I thought that was pretty cool of him.

I shoved some bread in the toaster and slumped at the table waiting for it to pop up. I was surprised when Aidan's name flashed on my cell.

"Yeah?"

But it was Sean's voice instead.

"Hey."

"Sean! Fuck! How are you? Are you okay?"

His voice was subdued.

"I'm okay. Back home. Look, I'm sorry about last night, man."

"Fuck that, bro, I'm just glad you're all right."

There was a long pause.

"I told the police it had nothing to do with you."

I swallowed, pushing back the memory of sitting in the cruiser on my way to the police station.

"Yeah, I know," I said quietly. "Julia told me. Thanks for that."

"Well, it's true. That was some bad shit. Got a killer headache," he laughed softly.

I grinned into the phone. "I bet it's bitchin'."

There was another long pause.

"So, the parentals are freaking out. And I'm grounded. They're saying it'll be for the rest of my life. Well, definitely for most of it. Weeks, for sure."

"Wow, that's harsh!" *Jeez, it was only the first week in July.* "They really gonna stop you surfing?"

"Yeah, they can try," he snorted. Then he sighed. *"But they've taken my car keys."*

"Shit!"

"Yeah."

"Well, um, I guess you're feeling pretty rough. But, uh, you're going to be okay, right?"

"Yeah, I'm fine," he said, although there was something off in his voice.

"I can come over, if you're up for some Xbox action. Or tomorrow after work."

He didn't reply right away, and I had the weirdest feeling, like someone had opened up my head and poured cold water in, filling my body with chills.

When he still didn't speak, I knew why.

"You're not allowed to see me," I said flatly. "They don't believe you—they think I gave you the drugs."

"I'm sorry," he said, his voice sounding choked. *"You're my best friend, man. You're my brother. But they're being real assholes about this. I told them it had nothing to do with you, but yeah—they don't believe me."*

I understood, I really did. They wanted someone to blame, and I was first in line. *Blame the kid from the poor side of town. He must be selling drugs, right?*

"It's okay," I said stiffly.

"Nick, I'm so sorry. I…"

I shrugged, even though he couldn't see me.

"It's not your fault," I said tiredly. "They really going to ground you for the rest of the summer?"

"Yeah, I think so. They're pretty mad. I'm only allowed to leave the house if I'm with one of my brothers. That would be okay if it was Aidan, but he's going north tomorrow to start his new job. I'll be stuck with fucking Patrick. He's such a prick."

"Shit. That sucks."

Sean gave a small laugh. *"Yeah, but he hates me just as much, so he hasn't stopped bitchin' about it since Mom and Dad handed out the jail sentence."* He sighed. *"They've taken my phone and my laptop. That's why I'm using Aidan's. I needed to tell you, man. I'm so fuckin' sorry."*

Something tightened inside my chest.

"Yeah, me too." I took a deep breath. "This is so fucked up."

The silence stretched out before he replied. *"Yeah, really fucked up. Look, I gotta go, man. I'll call you when I can, okay?"*

"'Kay."

The call ended.

My toast was cold.

I texted Yansi all Sunday, but there was no reply. The silence made my skin prickle.

And when I showed up for work on Monday morning, Mr. Alfaro fired me.

I already knew he didn't like me much; I never had been allowed back in the truck's cab, and I was cool with that.

But today he was waiting for me with his arms folded across his chest, a look on his face that told me he wanted to chew me up and spit me out. He always looked pissed, but today it seemed like the supersized version, and all aimed at me. I guessed he'd heard about Sean, although it could have been about Erin. Shit, I hoped he didn't know *all* the details. I didn't know which one would make him more pissed. I had a feeling I was going to find out.

His eyes narrowed as I got closer. Yep, this was definitely more than just his usual pissiness. I jumped off my skateboard and flipped it up so I could catch it under my arm. Yeah, a bit of a showy move, but he looked so mad, and it was all I had.

He didn't speak, so I wondered if maybe I'd got it wrong and it was okay. I went to climb up into the truck as usual. I already had one foot on the flatbed when he grabbed my shoulder and spun me around, making me lose my footing. I nearly fell, and it was only years of keeping my balance on a surfboard that stopped me from hitting the ground.

Now I was the one who was pissed. He may have been my boss, but that didn't mean I was going to let him lay his hands on me.

I shoved his arm off, breathing hard, and met his eyes.

"No!" he barked out. "You will not work with me today. You are fired. And you will stay away from Anayansi. I have forbidden her from seeing you. No more!"

What the fuck?

He turned away.

"Hey!" I called after him. "Hey! Why are you firing me? I've done every damn thing you wanted!"

He pulled some dollar bills out of his wallet, balled them up and threw them at my chest.

"Aléjate, muchacho! Manten tu distancia, niño! Go and never come back. Stay away from my daughter!"

Then he grabbed my skateboard and threw it into the road.

Fucker!

I sprinted after it, but was one damn second too late—a van ran over it, and I heard the crunch that meant instant destruction.

The driver yelled something at me, but I was staring down at my ruined skateboard. The wheels had snapped off and the deck had a huge crack running the length of it.

I was burning with rage. My Mom had given me that board for my fifteenth birthday. It was *mine*.

"What the fuck is wrong with you, man?" I yelled.

I picked up the broken pieces. My board was dead. There was no coming back from that massacre. I was so furious, my vision went red and I threw the remains of my skateboard at Mr. Alfaro's truck, taking satisfaction in the thud as it bounced off the driver's door.

He took a step toward me, his face threatening. But I wasn't backing down.

Then Yansi came running out the house, screaming at her father in rapid Spanish. I couldn't catch all of it, but heard enough to know that she was angry with him and not me. Thank fuck.

He caught her shoulders and dragged her back into the house, shouting angrily, drowning out her cries. Sean's name was shouted several times, and a cold feeling swept through me, chasing away the burn of anger.

I'd wondered if Mr. Alfaro had found out about Erin—but now it looked like he'd heard about my night in the ER and … and what? Assumed that I'd given Sean the drugs. Just like everyone else. So what was new?

Goddamn it! No wonder he didn't want Yansi near me—he was probably thinking I was a freakin' drug dealer or stoner or … jeez, any-fucking-thing.

I knew I wasn't thinking clearly, but I was so fucking angry. I marched up to the door and hammered on it, yelling Yansi's name. I heard more shouting and the twins were crying and screaming. Mrs. Alfaro was wailing, a high-pitched keening sound. Yansi's furious words punched through the chaos of sound. She yelled "no" over and over again.

I pounded on the door repeatedly, and the noise seemed to escalate.

Eventually, Mrs. Alfaro opened the door a crack.

"You go now, Nico," she hissed, her mouth turned down, her face tense.

"Please, por favor!" I begged. "I just need to talk to Yansi."

"Go! Vete!"

And she slammed the door.

I sat on the doorstep and texted Yansi again. I hoped like hell that her cell hadn't been confiscated, too. I waited a couple of minutes, but she didn't reply and nobody left the house.

Defeated, I scooped up the pieces of my skateboard, kicking the door of Mr. Alfaro's truck, before I started walking home.

I couldn't fix my board, but Mom had given it to me. I wasn't going to leave it in that old bastard's driveway.

I couldn't take the loss of one more thing that I cared about.

My legs were weak and my whole body ached. Every step felt like I was weighted down by a gravity heavier than Earth's.

Sean gone. Yansi gone. Mom gone forever. And I realized something else: I wasn't technically an adult, but I'd stopped being a child the day Mom told me she had cancer.

Yeah, not a day I'd ever forget.

I'd been surfing with Sean, and even though I said I'd be home early, I'd stayed to hang out at the pier.

When I walked in, I thought she was pissed because I was late. But she was pissed that the doctors had told her she'd be dead at 42, and because she'd promised to be there for me. And now she was dying and couldn't keep that promise.

"Sit down, Nicky," she said, her voice soft and ragged. "It's bad news, baby."

And then she told me.

I said all the usual things.

Are you sure?

The doctors must be wrong!

There must be something they can do? Some different medicine?

New treatments are being discovered all the time, maybe…

And she'd said all the usual things too, the answers someone gives when the answer is no, but no one wants to say it. Or hear it.

Maybe.

Maybe.

Maybe.

And then finally she was tired of saying maybe, and she said, "No, baby. There's no hope. They've tried everything."

I didn't want to believe it. Of course I fucking didn't. But over the next few days, it started to sink in.

I'd be sitting in a classroom at school, trying to pay attention to a lesson in Trig or American History, and I'd suddenly think, *Mom is dying. She's going to be dead. She won't be coming to anymore parent-teacher conferences. She won't see me graduate or win any more surfing trophies. She lied. She won't be there for me.*

So you start making deals.

"God, if you let her live, I'll stop drinking and smoking weed; I'll study hard; I'll do any fucking thing you want, but don't let my mom die. Please, God."

But she got sicker.

And sicker.

And then she died.

And I wanted to stop believing in God, but I couldn't. So I just hated him instead.

And he hated me right back.

So now I was losing Yansi for the second time.

Walking felt really slow compared to how I usually traveled. I could have jogged home, but I was too depressed to have the energy. And I was wearing a pair of old hiking boots instead of sneakers. They weren't really made for running.

I'd started wearing them to work after nearly losing a foot because I wasn't paying attention while I was using a really sharp edging tool. Mr. Alfaro wore steel-toe work boots every day. I'd thought about getting a pair, but they cost like seventy bucks.

It's weird the things you think about when there's too much important shit going on. It's like your brain takes a vacation because it knows you can't cope with one more thing.

But once you think you can breathe again, your brain snaps, and you're right back where you were: at the bottom of the heap, totally fucked.

My heart still beat, but each time it thumped in my

chest, it brought a fresh wave of pain.

Bad friend. Bad son. Bad boyfriend. Loser. Loser. Loser.

I kept checking my phone, but there was nothing from Yansi. Nothing from Sean. Of course not.

It was so fucking unfair. I wasn't the one who'd used Molly and ended up in ER. I hadn't done anything!

But that bastard voice at the back of my brain that went by the dickwad name of 'conscience' was sneering. *You've taken Molly before. You drink till you pass out and you smoke everything going. You even fucked a girl you can't stand because you were so wasted. What makes you so fucking special? It could have been you in the ER. You got lucky, fucktard.*

And the fact was, if I was Yansi's dad, I'd kick my ass out, too.

I really hated having a conscience.

Marcus' van was still parked outside the house when I got home. He didn't start work till either ten or two, depending which shift he was on, but he usually headed out to find somewhere the waves were working, or the paddleboard as a last resort.

I was going to knock on his door to see if he wanted to hit up some surf spots, but when I heard the sounds of a woman's voice moaning, I headed to the kitchen instead.

It was weird not having anything to do. I'd gotten so used to being crazy busy all summer, just having time to sit around was strange. Last summer I'd been the master of lounging around. Mom complained non-stop that I was wearing out the couch by lying on it watching TV, unless there were waves, of course.

But somehow I'd lost the habit of doing nothing. If that was part of being an adult too, it sucked majorly.

I could have gone down to the pier to find someone

to hang with. I could have called Rob. Instead, I trailed up to my room and collected all the clothes that needed washing, and yanked the sheets off my bed, too.

I washed the breakfast dishes and made myself some lunch.

It was 10AM.

How freakin' depressing was that?

I was finishing up a plate of eggs that had somehow got a little charred where they'd stuck to the pan, when Marcus walked in.

"'Sup, Nick. How you doin'?"

I nodded, my mouth full.

"How's that friend of yours? Um, Sean?"

I swallowed down the eggs. "Okay. Got grounded."

Marcus laughed. "You bet your ass he did!" Then he looked at me quizzically. "Your sister ground you, too?"

I shook my head. "Nah. My boss fired me."

"The hell you say? What for?"

I looked at him evenly. "For the same reason everyone else is mad at me—they all think I gave Sean the drugs."

He looked sympathetic for a moment. "Wow, tough break."

I heard Camille walk into the kitchen behind us and I opened my mouth ready to say hi, but it wasn't her. Instead, Cheyenne who was one of the bartenders at the Sandbar, was yawning and rubbing her eyes, wearing nothing more than Marcus' Quiksilver t-shirt.

It was pretty damn obvious that she wasn't wearing a bra, and she was seriously hot.

My cheeks flushed when Marcus caught me checking her out.

"Hi, Nick," Cheyenne yawned.

"Hey," I mumbled, dropping my eyes to my plate and vaguely waving my fork at her.

"What's for breakfast?" she asked.

She turned to Marcus, wrapping her arms around his

neck and plastering her body up against him.

I nearly choked on a mouthful of eggs when Marcus slid his hands down from her waist and started kneading her ass. Cheyenne wasn't wearing anything under the shirt *at all*.

I remembered Marcus' comment about *little brother likes to watch*. Was this some kind of weird test? I dropped my fork and almost kicked over my chair as I ran to get the hell out of there, leaving my untouched coffee cooling on the table.

I heard a low chuckle as I slammed the front door behind me.

Well, this day was sure turning out to be shitty.

I decided I was going to see Sean, no matter what his parents said. We'd snuck in and out of his house enough times for it not to be a huge problem. Unless his parents were in the backyard, but I figured Mr. Wallis would be at work on a Monday, and his mom was always busy with her book club and charity work.

It was fuck hot again, but the sky was a dull, metallic gray and threatening—weighing down the air, so you could feel the pressure falling one isobar at a time.

A storm was coming.

By morning the swell would be topping eight or nine feet. Buoys in the Atlantic had sent out warning spikes during the night, and every surf-dog was waxing down his board, getting ready to ride.

But I'd be riding without Sean, and that just didn't seem right.

I trudged along the road, feeling the heat burning up through my sneakers.

Walking sucked. I was so used to getting places relatively fast on my skateboard. It took 15 minutes to get to Sean's place on my board, but nearly an hour to walk. I could have jogged, but it was just too damn hot.

What I hadn't counted on was Dylan and Patrick seeing me at the roadside along Orlando Avenue.

Patrick blasted the horn on his BMW as he made an illegal U-turn and skidded to a halt next to me, kicking up a swirl of dust that threw sand into my eyes and made me cough.

Dylan pushed a button and the window wound down. A gust of cooler air rolled out, making me feel sweaty and dumb as I took in their matching polo shirts. They must have been going to play golf.

I'd never played golf. Sean told me once how much green fees cost for a day: it was more than the monthly allowance Mom used to give me. Annual membership would have bought a brand new car. Sometimes I forgot how much money Sean's family had—he'd never made me feel it. Even when he got something new, he always shared it.

"Hey, Nick," Dylan said, his voice aiming for neutral but sounding tense.

"Hey," I said sourly, wiping the grit and dust from my streaming eyes.

"Where are you going?" he asked, his voice struggling to stay calm.

I didn't reply because it must have been damn obvious where I was headed.

He sighed and shook his head.

Dylan wasn't a bad guy. I didn't know him that well because he was older, but he wasn't a prick.

"You can't see him," he said. "Not just because Mom and Dad grounded him; he's been pretty sick. That shit could have killed him."

He was still staring at me. Maybe he was waiting for me to fall to my knees and confess my sins. He'd wait a long fucking time.

I folded my arms across my chest and stared back.

Patrick must have had enough of keeping his mouth shut, because he decided it was his turn.

"Listen you, little shit," he shouted. "Stay away from my brother. You're a fuckin' coward, letting him take the fall like that."

Out of all the Wallis brothers, the only one I couldn't stand was Patrick. He made it so easy to hate him.

"You don't know shit," I said, walking away.

When I heard a car door slam behind me, I guessed what was coming.

Patrick swung at me as I was turning around, but his fist missed my face, thudding against my shoulder instead. It stung, but it would have been worse if he'd connected with my jaw. That would have meant game over.

But now he was off balance and he'd left himself wide open. I landed two solid punches into his gut.

He folded, stumbling backwards, almost tripping over his own feet. He looked shocked, surprised that I'd taken him down so easily.

Dylan was close behind, but instead of heading my way, he locked his arms around Patrick, hissing at his brother.

"Leave it! He's not worth it."

Patrick was cussing me out, calling me all kinds of shit, but Dylan hustled him back towards the car without saying another word to me. The car screeched off, burning rubber onto the boiling hot road.

I shook out my fists as they drove away, rubbing the knuckles and massaging my fingers.

It's not like in the movies where the actors go around slugging it out. You hit someone with a fist, it fucking hurts.

My knuckles were red and I suspected they were going to start swelling. I probably needed to ice them.

I worked my fingers some more. At least nothing was sprained or broken. Hitting someone in the gut, you can pull muscles, or, if you're really unlucky, get them at the wrong angle and break your wrist.

The worst is hitting someone in the face. Human saliva has more bacteria than a dog bite, and a friend of Aidan knew a guy who cut his knuckles on someone's teeth, got an infection and had to have his hand amputated. True story.

I wished I'd hit Patrick on his nose, because that really hurts. Your nose swells up making it hard to breathe, and it bleeds like a mofo. But I would have got off on hearing his nose crunch. That's the only bit Hollywood ever gets right.

The brief shot of pleasure at landing one on that self-righteous pile of crap didn't last. Dylan's car had disappeared in the direction of their house, so unless I wanted another confrontation O.K. Corral-style, I'd have to stay away from Sean. For now, at least.

Depressed, and with aching hands, I squatted on the ground, staring down at the roadside.

The dust in the gutter was a light brown that blossomed into the air every time a car passed.

I heard a couple of vehicles slow down as they approached me, but nobody stopped. Just another dumb kid sitting at the side of the road. *Stoned*, they would think. *Drunk at this time in the morning.* Or maybe, *Dangerous—call the cops.*

It was that last thought that made me drag myself upright; I really didn't need another run in with Cocoa Beach's finest.

I turned around and headed in the direction I'd come from. I wasn't really looking for company, but I was sick of my own depressing thoughts.

So, I went to the pier.

Rob was there with some of the other guys, but I was more than surprised to see Marcus. With Camille.

He shot me an amused look, but didn't speak. Camille said hi, and I muttered something unintelligible back.

I knew what Sean would have said, *The guy's a legend*, and if it had been before I'd met Yansi, it probably wouldn't have bothered me so much.

Nothing in life was black and white, but cheating

didn't seem like much of a gray area to me. But at the same time, ever since the night with Erin, the familiar prickle of guilt haunted me. Who the hell was I to judge anyone else?

"How's Sean doing?" Rob asked, his eyes slightly unfocussed.

I could smell the weed before I'd walked over, so I wasn't surprised.

"He's out of the hospital. He's okay, I guess, but his parents grounded him."

There were mutters around the group, and then some trash-talking about Sean's folks.

Nobody asked for more details, and the discussion moved to the batch of bad drugs that had been going around town. Rob said that two other kids had been hospitalized.

I could see the glances that were thrown my way. Even though these guys knew I didn't deal, bad news spread like fungus.

When Rob tried to pass the blunt my way, I shook my head.

Instead, I walked down to the water's edge and soaked my sore hands in the ripples at my feet. It helped. A bit.

I turned around to look at my friends, the people I hung out with, sitting in a loose circle on the sand. I missed Sean. Despite all his shit, he was the one person I could talk to. When he was sober.

Feeling more isolated among my friends than if I'd been alone, I flopped down onto the sand, a little away from the others, staring at the sullen gray waves that mirrored how I felt.

I must have been giving off serious keep-the-fuck-away vibes, because no one tried to talk to me. I wrapped my arms around my knees, and wondered what the fuck I was going to do now. Everything had gone to shit, in every possible direction.

I looked up when someone sat down next to me.

"Hey, Erin," I said tiredly.

"Mind if I sit here."

You already are. I shook my head.

She pulled her knees to her chest, matching the way I was sitting. For nearly half a minute, neither of us spoke, but it was making me tense having her so close by. I didn't want to give her the wrong idea. Again.

"Did you … are you back with Yansi?" she asked at last.

I let out a long sigh. Was I? I had no idea. Probably not. Not after this morning. I couldn't imagine her parents letting her anywhere near me. Maybe when we were back in school…

I realized it must have looked like I was thinking about ignoring her, because Erin was still looking at me, waiting for a reply.

"Thanks," I said. "For talking to her."

Her lips curved upward in a tiny smile. "Yeah," she said, with a low chuckle, "that was interesting."

I couldn't help smiling back at her. "I bet!"

Her smile slipped away. "So, you guys are good now?"

"We were, but…"

"But what?"

I wasn't sure I wanted to talk to Erin of all people about this, but I couldn't talk to Sean. And Rob, hell he wouldn't care even if he wasn't stoned.

"Her parents won't let her see me."

"Wow, sucks," she muttered. "Why?"

I shrugged. "They think what happened to Sean was my fault." I laughed without any humor whatsoever. "They think I'm a freakin' drug dealer."

She took in a surprised breath.

"Jeez! That's random. Why do they think that?"

I couldn't help smiling at her again. So far she was the only person who *didn't* think I'd given Sean the Molly.

"Because he's my friend. Because we hang out." And

then I was hit by a deeper truth. "I guess because they've sort of been expecting something like that. For me to fuck up, I mean. They never wanted me to date her anyway."

She nodded and raised her eyebrows. "Well, you are a guy." She laughed coldly. "And you all want the same thing, right?"

I wanted to deny it, but I couldn't. I did want to sleep with Yansi. I wanted it really badly. But it wasn't all I wanted. I just wanted *her*.

Erin's accusing stare softened. "Except you. So maybe you're not like that."

"Yeah, I am," I contradicted her, tired of pretending.

Erin shook her head. "No, you're really not. Trust me on that."

I frowned, but she carried on.

"Most guys are total horn dogs. All they want is fresh pussy, and as much of it as they can get. At least you want it with someone you care about."

I glanced at her in surprise.

That summed it up pretty good.

She sighed and studied her fingernails. "I wish some guy cared about me like that."

I twisted around to look at her—really look at her.

Erin had long tan legs, great tits, and her face would have been kind of pretty if it hadn't been covered in all that gunk and those scary stuck-on eyelashes that reminded me of spiders. A lot of guys thought she was hot, but they also thought she was the school bike. I knew that wasn't true exactly, but she'd been with a lot of guys. Including me.

"Erin, you're a really nice person. What you did for me and Yans ... you didn't have to do that, and I know it couldn't have been easy. You *will* find a guy to care about you, but you make it kind of hard when you do the stuff you do."

Her eyes widened and her mouth dropped open. I didn't really talk that much, so she was probably shocked by the whole sentences as much as anything else.

She swallowed several times before she spoke.

"You think I'm nice?"

"Yeah." I gave her a small smile. "And you're pretty. All the guys think you're hot. But that doesn't mean you have to sleep with them."

She looked down, and I could see that her eyes were filling with tears.

If it had been Yansi, I'd have pulled her into a hug and squeezed the shit out of her. But it wasn't, so I sat there feeling as useful as tits on a bull, hoping she didn't cry.

"Okay. Thanks, Nick." Her voice was so quiet, I almost missed it. "Yansi's really lucky."

She gave me another small tentative smile, then stood up and walked away. I was left staring out at the waves by myself.

Suddenly lightning flashed across the sky.

"Whoa! Electric storm!" Rob yelled.

I realized that the clouds had gotten darker while I'd been sitting there, and I could see a squall line edging closer. Thunder rumbled and shuddered above us, and I found myself counting instinctively. Ten seconds: that meant the storm was only a couple of miles away.

We were all used to electric storms living where we did, and we knew that they could be dangerous, especially if you got caught out in the open.

The beach was clearing quickly, people hurrying back to their cars. Some of the guys decided to head out and I wondered about getting a ride with them, but as I didn't have anything to go home for, I decided to stay. Besides, I liked watching the lightning, just so long as I wasn't out in it. I could feel that strange sensation as electricity crackled across my skin, making the hairs on my arms stand up.

Sometimes I used to sit on the back porch with Mom; we'd stare up, and Mom called it 'God's free light show'.

A couple of minutes later the sky turned black. Thick, heavy drops of rain began to sheet down, turning the road into a river in seconds.

I scrambled to my feet and ran to wait under the pier with everyone else.

We'd all seen the same thing a hundred times before, but we were silent, mesmerized as the ocean churned and the clouds hung low and hungry above us.

We stood staring into the rain, but after a few minutes Rob nudged my arm.

"You heard from our boy?"

I shook my head. "Not really. He got in one quick call, but his folks confiscated his cell and laptop."

Rob blew out a circle of scented smoke. "Harsh." Then he surprised me. "It might not be so bad—guy seriously needed to chill out."

He was right; Sean was wound tighter than I'd ever seen him.

"He's better when you're around—less of the crazy. But you haven't been around this summer."

I bristled immediately. "Yeah? Well some of us have to fuckin' work."

He nodded sagely. "No judgment, bro, just saying how it is." Then a puzzled expression drifted across his face. "It's Monday."

"Yeah, and…?"

"So how come you're not at work?"

"Oh. I got fired."

"Huh?"

"Fired. Canned. Let go. Services no longer fucking required!"

"Harsh," he repeated, then passed the blunt.

Before I could take a hit, I realized Lacey was standing next to me.

"Have you seen Sean?" she asked.

She was biting her lip and looked upset.

"No, but I spoke to him. He's okay."

"Good," she muttered, sounding distracted. "That's good." Then she looked around, as if embarrassed being seen talking to me. "Can you give him a message for me? He's not answering his phone…"

"Yeah, his parents confiscated it because of … you know."

She looked relieved. "Oh, I thought … never mind. Well, if you see him, can you say that … just tell him to call me, okay?"

I nodded and she walked back to her friends.

That was weird—maybe they'd gotten closer than I realized. Were they dating now?

Rob nudged me again.

"Your girl's up there."

I peered through the curtain of rain, my eyes following the raindrops hammering and bouncing onto the street. And then I saw her.

Yansi was standing shivering, soaked to the skin, her long black hair plastered across her face and shoulders.

She was here. She'd come to find me.

I dropped the blunt, ignoring Rob's irritated shout, and was up and sprinting toward her. Lightning flashed again, closer now, and I shouted at her to move, but her eyes were still searching for me.

She jumped when the loud crack of thunder split the sky above our heads.

I almost crashed into her, wrapping my arms around her at the last minute then towing us toward the boardwalk where we could find shelter.

"Shit, Yans! What are you doing? You could have been fucking killed out there!"

"I had t-t-to see y-y-you," she stuttered, pressing herself against me.

"You're soaking wet," I said, stating the obvious.

Her skin was cold too, so I rubbed my hands up and down her arms, trying to drive some warmth into them, but it wasn't doing much good.

She needed to get inside and drink something hot. She also needed to get out of her soaked clothes, but that thought took my brain in a direction that wasn't helpful.

Not at all.

Bad, bad idea.

Fucking wonderful idea.

My hands slowed on her arms, and I lowered my head to her lips. Her breath caught in her throat and her eyes widened. Then our lips were touching; hers cool and soft, her tongue warm when it met mine.

That kiss superheated me from the inside, making me forget that we were standing in a shop's doorway while a storm raged around us.

Too soon, Yansi pushed me away, her dark eyes sparkling even as she shivered uncontrollably.

"Come on," I said, gripping her tightly. "We need to get you inside."

There was a coffee shop across the street, but even though that meant heading out into the downpour again, it seemed preferable to waiting here.

We stumbled into the road, laughing as the rain pelted our bodies, running off our faces and drenching us again. And I couldn't stop smiling.

Breathless, we fell through the door of the coffee shop, startling the people already inside. But my eyes were on her, and the way her white t-shirt had turned transparent. I could see her bra and it was pink. *Jee-zus.*

She threw me a look that said, *I know what you're thinking,* and then her cheeks reddened.

While Yansi slid into a chair, I stood in the short line to buy drinks. She'd asked me to order her a skinny chai latte, whatever the hell that was: some weird, perfumed shit. I ordered a hot chocolate with extra whipped cream on top. I was a bit startled when the two drinks came to $11. Café prices always went up in the summer. I'd have to be careful with my money now I only had the part-time job at the Sandbar. But what the hell, she was worth it.

I couldn't help staring across the café at her. Even soaking wet, she looked stunning. Although it was hard to keep my eyes on her face and away from her chest, the way her t-shirt clung to her.

She caught me checking her out and raised her eyebrows. I grinned guiltily and she pretended to pout, but it ended up in a huge smile a few seconds later.

She pulled a Chapstick out of her pocket and rolled it over her lips. Watching her do that was warming me right across the room. God, I loved the way she tasted with that stuff on.

She knew what she was doing to me. I had to turn away again.

As soon as the drinks were ready, I carried them over to our table, and Yansi wrapped her shaking hands around the mug.

"Thanks."

I sipped at my chocolate, drinking in her face, memorizing the soft planes of her cheeks, the dark pink of her lips, her high cheekbones, the curve of her eyelashes— I wanted to memorize every part of her. Remember her just as she was right now, glowing from the rain and our kiss, her skin flushed with the warmth of the café and the intense energy heating the air between us.

"I didn't think I'd see you till school started again after what happened at your place," I said, laying it out for her.

She wrinkled her nose and shook her head. "I had to see you."

"I'm really glad you came," I said quietly. "But I'm guessing your mami and papi won't be too pleased."

"Screw 'em!" she snapped.

I was surprised. Yansi didn't cuss much, and she didn't like it when I did, although I could never seem to shake the habit.

"I can't believe Papi fired you!" she hissed. "That is *so* unfair."

I sighed and leaned back in my seat.

"Tell me about it."

"I told him he was wrong and that you didn't have anything to do with … to do with what happened to Sean." She bit her lip. "How is he?"

"Okay, I guess. His folks grounded him. Took his phone." My voice dropped. "They blame me, too."

"What! Why?"

"Same reason as your papi. They think the drugs came from me."

"But that's ridiculous! Everyone knows that Sean is the biggest stoner around."

"Not his parents," I said, with a bitter smile. "According to them, I'm an all-around bad influence … they've banned him from seeing me, too."

Yansi's hand shot to her mouth. "Oh God, I'm so sorry, baby. That is so … it's just so…"

"Yeah."

She reached out to touch the back of my hand, her fingers warmed by the mug she'd been clutching.

"What happened to your hands?" she asked suddenly.

I tried to pull away, but she held my wrists firmly.

"Baby, what happened?"

I sighed. "I ran into Sean's brothers. They weren't too happy that I was on my way to see him."

"Oh my God! Are you hurt? Did they hurt you?"

"Nah, it was kind of a one punch thing. Well … two. No biggie."

As she traced her fingers over my knuckles, tingles of desire raced across the back of my hand, shooting up my arm like an electric charge.

"Don't look at me like that," she whispered.

"Sorry," I muttered, dropping my eyes to the table.

"Don't be sorry. Just … not here." She paused. "Take me home?"

She phrased it like a question.

I nodded and tried to check my wallet without her

seeing. I wasn't sure how much money I had—probably not enough for a cab to her place.

But then, hidden by the table, I felt her bare foot slide up my calf to my knee. I stopped breathing and stared up at her.

"Your home," she said.

Chapter 9

I was pretty certain what was going to happen.

I was too excited to be nervous, but every now and again, little ticks of anxiety jittered through me.

The moment the rain stopped, we started walking back to my house. The temperature was rising rapidly, although I couldn't tell if that was from the storm passing, or because my blood was slowly being brought to a boil every time her thumb stroked over my hand, or our arms brushed against each other as we walked.

It seemed to take forever to get to my house, and my hands shook slightly as I slid the key into the lock.

"Um … do you want a drink or anything?"

She shook her head. "No. I want you."

Holy fuck.

Walking up the stairs together took half a lifetime.

My room was stifling hot, humidity weighing me down like a thick blanket. My limbs felt heavy and sun drunk.

"Are you sure?"

I asked the question again, needing to hear it, needing

to know that it wasn't just me who wanted this.

"Yes, I'm sure."

Her voice was strong and clear, but I could see fear lurking behind the certainty in her eyes.

She pulled me toward my bed and I followed like a puppy, desperate for her affection, for any scrap of love that she would give me. But it wasn't just scraps she was giving me—it was huge and substantial and everything, and I was the man she was going to give it to. And fuck, if that thought didn't suddenly make me as nervous as all hell.

Yansi knelt on the bed and tugged me toward her and we kissed for the longest time until my body felt liquid. Her lips were sticky and tasted of mangoes and I laughed because it was crazy, and she laughed too, her small body vibrating and humming against mine.

Then she pulled hard and my knees hit the bed so I crashed down on top of her, bracing myself with my hands at the last second.

Sweat broke out all over me as the spicy heat of her body was pressed under me. I lowered my head and kissed her slowly, drawing out every touch and every taste of her lips, her tongue, the salty skin of her cheeks and neck.

I was trying so hard to stay in control, even though her scent and touch drove me crazy. Her fingers danced down my spine and pushed up under my t-shirt.

I pulled back to look at her, only half believing that she was here with me after wanting it and imagining it for so long. I stroked my thumb across the smooth silky skin of her cheek, then gently holding her head while I kissed her again.

Kissing her like this, in my room, on my bed … it was like diving into a pool of warm water. I felt her everywhere, over and in and on every part of my body, and my senses were overwhelmed and drowning in pleasure.

And it was *nothing* like when I'd been with Erin, the awkward fumbling and hurried, humiliated, heated thrusting; quick release and rough hands in the dark.

And I knew the difference, and was glad and sad, elated and miserable.

"God, Yansi, I don't even know why you're with me. I'm such a fuck up."

Her hands stilled, resting feather light on my shoulder blades.

"We're 17—we're allowed to fuck up. But I'm with you because I see your soul. You've got a beautiful soul, you just don't know it."

I sighed, wishing it were true. But she'd seen the worst of me, and hadn't pushed me away. Maybe, for once, I could let her see the best of me.

"I love you," I whispered, the words tearing out of me like steam, visible for a moment then disappearing into the evening air.

I'd only said those words once before, to a dying woman. Then it had been about saying goodbye; now it was about living.

Yansi gasped, then smiled.

"Te amo demasiado," she murmured against my lips. "I love you too much."

Then she cupped her hands around my face and pressed soft, closed-mouth kisses to my lips, my cheeks, my chin, each eyelid.

"Mi vida," she said.

And then I didn't have the words because it was like she'd ripped open my chest and stolen everything I could ever say, and maybe she hadn't stolen it, maybe I'd given it.

She pushed up my t-shirt until it was bunched under my arms and we were laughing, because neither of us wanted to stop kissing, because it seemed impossible to stop, and I didn't want to stop, but then she was tugging at the material, and I cursed and she laughed, and I ripped it over my head.

She sighed as her hands stroked across my waist and

along my hips, then she pushed on my shoulder and I rolled onto my back, my hands above my head, surrendering, taking what she'd give, giving what she'd take.

She murmured something in Spanish that I couldn't catch and I knew she didn't want me to, and that made my heart burn, but it didn't matter because some words are private.

Her head dipped toward me, the black waterfall of her hair sweeping across my chest. I shivered with longing and hope. Her hands brushed across my stomach and up to my chest, drawing patterns I couldn't see, her lips murmuring and soothing.

"Undress for me?" she whispered, and I could hear the shyness creep back into her voice.

I'd never been naked in front of her before, but I knew she needed this, for me to go first, to show her the way, the way we could be together. Let her look, let her touch, let her take me inside her with her eyes.

I pushed my shorts down and kicked them free, letting her see all of me. The parts she knew, the paler skin from my hips to the middle of my thighs, the hard center that was crying for her touch.

"You're so white!" she gasped, and I laughed, because yeah, wasn't expecting that, and then she laughed, because neither was she.

And I'm lying there, buck naked and we're both laughing, because it's ridiculous, and it's love, and I don't care.

She's touched me before, but not bare, not with nothing between us, and when her small hand, damp with heat and sweat and desire touches me, I'm a little lost and a little found and a lot crazy.

"So many colors," she said. "White and golden and light brown and your dick is pink and purple."

"I'm a fucking rainbow," I said, and she laughed again.

"I'm going to kiss it," she said, and I forgot how to breathe, and my lungs burned and I gasped.

"It's hot!" she said, like she'd just discovered gravity.

"Yeah," I sighed with happiness. "That's what you do to me."

"Uh-uh! That's how you wake up every morning, you told me!" she accused, her lips sliding across her teeth.

"Yeah," I said again, "but dreaming of you."

And it's true, but it made her shake her head, and her eyes danced like wildfire.

I want to make love to her, to be inside her, but maybe that's not going to happen, because if she touched me like that again, I was going to explode. Don't ask me to control that. I can't uninvent gravity or the laws of motion. I'm going to come, I'm going to be a fucking freight train and the roaring in my ears is getting louder, and I squeeze my eyes shut because it's too soon, but she knows, I think she knows, and she doesn't care because her hands are on me and her lips and her hair tickle across me and that's when I lose it, and I care but I don't.

Yansi jerked back and I would have laughed at the look of surprise on her face, but I was gasping for breath, my blood shooting through me so fast it felt like I'd dropped down the face of a 30 foot wave.

Holy shit!

And maybe I said that out loud, because she's laughing again.

"Holy something!" she said, covering her mouth with her hand, her shoulders shaking, her eyes laughing.

I leaned over the bed and picked up my t-shit to wipe myself off, and my dick gives up and deflates a little, but not all the way because hell, my girl's eyes are still fixed on me like she can't believe that piece of me, the sideshow she just saw, like she's waiting for my dick to leap up and bite her, and hell it wants to.

"We don't have to do anything else," I said, and I'm lying and lying and lying, because I *have* to know what we're like together. It'll be a little piece of heaven, or the stars, or the galaxy, and I know I'm a little crazy but she's a drug, she's my love heroin, and I need another fix.

"I want to," she said. "I'm ready."

And she pressed her hand onto my chest, dark brown against my tan. And her hand slid down below my stomach, rising and dipping as I took a deep breath.

And I think she knows I need her to show me, because she pulled off her t-shirt.

I leaned up on my elbows to get closer to her without touching her. I'm careful, like I've found an injured bird, the wings are beating, but it can't fly, and maybe if I can just calm it down, it'll be okay, it'll fly again.

I reached out with just one, trembling finger, and drew a line down between her breasts, snagging on her bra, down to her bellybutton, playing there for a moment before I brushed the waistband of her shorts.

"Take your bra off," I said, but my voice turned up at the end, like the hook of a question mark. "Take your bra off?"

"You take it off."

Bold and sure and oh God, I wanted to hear that.

I sat up and unhooked her bra, fumbling deliberately and maybe accidentally, I'm not sure, but it made her laugh. And that's us—laughing while we love, and what can be better?

But then I stopped laughing because damn, she was perfect. I knew she'd be perfect, but this is *perfect*.

"You feel me," she said, and maybe that was ironic and maybe it was an order, but I did it anyway.

My hands reached up to touch her, my thumbs brushing over those dark chocolate nipples. And touching them isn't enough. I wanted to taste them.

"Can I?" I said.

"Please! Please!" and her head was nodding so fast it made me smile, but then my mouth fastened over that pebble and I sucked it, so sweet, like hard candy, and the sound that comes out of her mouth, I'd never heard that before.

And the harder I sucked, the more she moaned and I was more turned on than I'd been in my entire life.

We've barely started, I thought to myself. *This girl is going to kill me*, and I couldn't be happier.

A bead of sweat ran down between those beautiful breasts and I was jealous. I followed it with my tongue, chasing it all the way down, but losing because I was lost in the spicy scent of her skin.

Want, want, want and *need, need, need*, and no one ever told me it would feel this good.

My hands are making love to her body and I'm greedy for her, and jealous of my hands. How can I be jealous of my hands? I don't understand, but every part of me wants her.

My dick twitches, trying to reach up to her and she laughs, because it is kind of ridiculous, but her eyes are wide too, wondering how and when and *will it hurt?*

She lay down beside me and we kissed again and her legs tangled with mine and I was drowning in her kisses, but a lazy failure of lungs, happy drowning, I guess. Like a warm bath and slit wrists, and dying a little because no one ever told me it would feel this good.

My body thrusts against her and she says, "Oh!" like she hadn't realized what it was there for, and I'm kind of surprised too, because I didn't give it permission. I'm trying so hard to make this about her, and her body is fighting me, because damn, if it doesn't feel like it's trying to make it about me, not her. *Not fair!* I want to yell, and *Give me a break here, I'm trying!* But no one is listening and I'm thrusting against her, against her shorts.

Then she pushed away from me, and my lips parted because she kicked off her shorts and then slowly, so slowly, peeled away those little panties.

Boy, they're small. Do they do anything useful? Cover anything? They're so small, but perfect, too, like the frame on a favorite photograph.

And she lay down for me, moving in slow motion, a film with no soundtrack.

I kissed a trail of salt and promises down her belly, and it fluttered like a butterfly wing, but then I parted her legs and licked upward, and I thought my head would explode with the taste and the way her hips rocked into my mouth like *more, more, more*. And she's pulsing against me, fighting my slowness, because *now, now, now*.

"Condom!" she said, it was a plea and an order.

My hands shook and I cursed them because, you know, shaky hands and thin rubber, and I fucked up the first one, so I took another, and prayed, *please let me get this fucking condom on before I die*.

And then I'm wrapped and ready and her hips are doing little pivots across the bed and fuck, if that isn't the sexiest thing I've ever seen.

I touched her, my fingers soaking in her warm, wet flesh, and maybe *that's* the sexiest thing I've ever seen.

And I'm poised above her, but want to be inside, and I know it'll hurt her, I know it will, and I can't do it, I can't hurt this girl. *Precious, precious, precious.*

And she knows. She knows it's a massive fail but *no, no, no*, she won't let that happen.

So she gripped my ass and raised her hips up and pulled me into her.

Inside ... then a pause, then she pulls again and God, I'm sheathed inside her and no one told me it would feel this good, and I didn't know I could feel this good and holy shit, I'll die a happy man.

"Ow," she said softly, and I'm back with her and ashamed. I waited in the heavy silence, afraid to breathe. "I'm okay," she said, gasping softly. "Really. Hey, aren't you supposed to be moving or something?" And we're laughing again because, yeah, I'm supposed to be moving, so I do.

Slowly pull out then push in again, and die a little

more. And I know I should go slow, but fuck that, my body wants *now, now, now*. And I lose it a little and then a lot, and I can't stop and I'm swearing and apologizing and she's making little noises like *oh, oh, oh* and suddenly she screams and fuck! That was unexpected. Guess I was doing something right, and then I stop thinking because I can't see, I can only feel, and my balls are fireworks, and Fourth of July and fucking Thanksgiving, and I'm thanking someone, and maybe it's her and maybe it's God, and maybe it's the Easter Bunny.

And when I could breathe again, she kissed my shoulder.

"Te amo demasiado."

"I love you more than that," I said, and we laugh, because yeah, because we can.

Our bodies were glued together with sweat, and the air smelled like sex.

We lay there, not asleep, not awake and I couldn't think of anything more perfect, skin on skin, hand in hand.

"Does this change everything?" asked Yansi, her voice a little sad.

I thought about that. *Did it? Did it change everything?*

"Yeah. It changes everything, and it changes nothing."

She laughed a little.

"Spoken like a philosopher. Who are you and what have you done with my boyfriend? But seriously, do you … do you feel the same about me?"

"No."

I woke up enough to realize she'd taken that the wrong way and I had about two seconds to fix it.

"I don't feel the same way, Yans. I didn't think I could *feel* like this. It's just so much, you know? I can't even sort out in words what I feel. It's just … more."

She sighed softly. "I know exactly what you mean."

I looked out of the window and saw stars appearing

like happy thoughts in the purple-black sky.

"You're going to have to go home eventually, Yans."

Her body tensed.

"Are you trying to get rid of me?"

"Of course not," I said, pulling her toward me more tightly. "But your parents will be worried."

"I don't care!"

"Yeah, you do."

She sighed again. "Yes, I do. But I'm so mad at them. Papi was wrong: he had no right to treat you like that, but it's not just this ... they treat me like a child, and then I'm supposed to be an adult who looks after my brother and sisters."

"Parents make mistakes, too."

"When did you get to be so wise?"

I laughed quietly. "No idea. You must be rubbing off on me."

"I enjoyed the rubbing off," she said, almost shyly.

"Are you talking dirty to me? Because I've gotta say, that's hot!"

She slapped my stomach.

I caught her hand and brought it to my mouth, kissing her slowly.

She sighed happily and her fingers traced a line down from my shoulder to the crook of my elbow, and even though the humidity had turned the air to water, I shivered.

"What?"

"Just ... every time you touch me, Yans. It feels like the first time."

"It *was* the first time. I'm officially devirginized."

"No ... that's not what I meant. Never mind."

I rolled away from her, slightly embarrassed by the overwhelming emotions flowing through me, but she pressed her body against my back.

"I'm sorry, Nick. I was trying to be funny because ... it's scary ... feeling so much. I *do* know how you feel. I feel the same."

She kissed my back and wrapped her hand around my waist, stroking gently.

"It's getting really late. Your parents will be going crazy."

She shook her head. "They'll guess I came here."

That got my attention, and I sat up suddenly.

"Shit! Your dad isn't going to come beating down my door, is he? Because I'd hate to have to punch my boss—I'm pretty certain I'd get fired for that."

She gave a dark laugh. "He fired you already, remember?"

I flopped back. "Oh, yeah."

"But he could be sitting outside in his truck right now," she teased. "Oh wait, probably not. We'd have heard it drive up."

"Um, I don't think so. A fucking tank could have run over the house and I wouldn't have heard it when I'm with you."

But her words had struck home, so I sat up and shifted to the edge of the bed, standing reluctantly. "Come on, I should take you back."

But Yansi stretched out on the sheets, and smiled seductively.

"You have such a sexy ass!"

"Distraction tactics won't work," I insisted.

"Are you sure about that?" she purred, then knelt up in bed, the sheet falling away from her.

I groaned.

"Yansi! You're killing me here. I'm trying to do the right thing for once."

"I know, and I love that about you. Now come back to bed; I want to cuddle some more."

I was caving and she knew it, but then my phone rang. I'd been ignoring calls all afternoon. I picked it up from my bedside table.

"It's your mom again. You want to take the call?" As

I held out the cell toward her, she shook her head furiously. "You want me to take it?"

She bit her lip and nodded slowly.

Sighing, I pressed 'accept'.

"Hola, Mrs. Alfaro. Yes, she's here. Um, I don't think she … yeah, okay. I'm going to drive her home now. No. No, my sister's car. Yeah. About 20 minutes. Okay. Bye."

"What did she say?"

"She wanted to know if you were all right and when you'd be home."

"Is that all? How did she sound?"

"Worried, mostly. Upset. Relieved, I guess. We'd better get going. You want to take a shower first?"

"Is that okay?"

"Sure. I'll get you a fresh towel."

"That's okay, I'll use yours."

I frowned, trying to remember how many times I'd used it.

"No, you really don't want to do that. I'll get you a fresh one."

I pulled on a pair of jeans from the top of the heap of clothes on my desk chair. I didn't know where my boardshorts had gone—under the bed, maybe.

I glanced down at my sheets and winced when I saw the blood. I guess it was proof that our lives were changing, that we were adults now.

Yansi followed my gaze and blushed, her cheeks darkening.

"It's okay," I said, sitting down and wrapping my arm around her.

"Yeah, I'm just a little embarrassed."

"Do you feel okay? Does it hurt?"

"A bit. Not much."

"Sure?"

She smiled. "I'm sure. If it had hurt much more though, I'd have kicked you in the balls."

"One way to get rid of a hard on," I muttered under

my breath, passing her a fresh towel and watching as she wrapped it around her body.

While Yansi was showering, I pulled the sheets off the bed and ran downstairs to the garage, shoving everything in the washing machine. I even remembered to put detergent in this time.

I remade the bed with fresh sheets, making a mental note to thank Julia for washing them, otherwise I'd have been sleeping on a bare mattress tonight. Well, they were her sheets, but I'd make it up to her … or remember to do more laundry.

I even tidied up my clothes and got things ready for an early morning surf. The swell was now being predicted to be 12 feet plus: it was going to be epic.

Yansi smelled amazing when she came out of the shower. I got hard all over again seeing droplets of water on her chest, and her long hair in a damp knot at the nape of her neck.

I turned around to give her some privacy, even though I wanted to look at her and never look away again. I could hear the soft rustle of material moving over her body and I really, really wanted to watch.

"Ready," she said softly.

"You, um, you want a drink, some juice or something?"

"Water's fine."

I nodded and held her hand as we walked down the stairs to the kitchen.

Julia was sitting out on the back porch with a can of beer in her hand. She didn't look surprised when she saw us, and I wondered how loud we'd been.

"Hello, Yansi," she said, with a smile. "You're here late."

"Um, hi, Julia."

"She had a fight with her parents," I said, filling a glass with water and putting my arm around Yansi. "Can I borrow your car to take her home?"

215

Julia blinked a couple of times, her gaze shifting to Yansi. "Are you okay?"

Yansi looked worried. "Sort of, I guess."

Julia smiled reassuringly. "Mom and I used to fight like cat and dog all the time. I'm sure it'll be fine. My keys are on the kitchen table, Nicky."

I was surprised. I'd expected Julia to chew me out or give me a hard time, but she was being pretty cool about it.

"Thanks."

Julia surprised me again when she stood up and hugged Yansi, whispering something in her ear. Yansi nodded and smiled tightly, then looked at me.

"Okay, I'm ready."

As we walked to the car, I couldn't help asking, "What did she say to you?"

Yansi's eyes were soft as she spoke. "She said you'd look after me—that you were good at looking after people."

Well, fuck.

I didn't know what to think about that. My head was spinning with so many thoughts, and my body was like an electric cable that kept shorting, sending sparks rushing through my blood, threatening to detonate every second I was with her. I didn't want Yansi to go home; I didn't want her to be away from me ever again.

The short drive to Yansi's house was made in silence. I turned the radio on low, but neither of us were listening to the music. I could see Yansi's profile as she stared out of the window, white, black, white, black as we drove past the streetlights, her fingers drumming nervously on her thigh.

I put my hand over hers and she looked at me.

"Yans, we're in this together, okay? If they give you a hard time, you're coming home with me."

She gave a small, worried smile, her gaze shifting subtly under the flickering light.

Mr. Alfaro was waiting in the driveway, and I heard

Yansi's sharp intake of breath as we drove up.

Her expression was terrified and defiant all at the same time.

I cut the engine and climbed out while Yansi sat frozen in the passenger seat, staring at her father through the windshield.

I opened her door and leaned in. "Together," I whispered.

She nodded stiffly and held my hand as she let me help her out of the car.

"Anayansi," he said, his voice gruff.

"Papi?"

He held out his arms and Yansi gasped, then ran toward him and buried herself in his chest. His arms wrapped around her and he whispered something to her, making her nod frantically. I could see that she was crying again, and I wanted to go to her and take her in *my* arms, but I couldn't. It wasn't the right time; this was about Yansi and her dad, and no matter how much I hated it, I had to stay out of it.

Mr. Alfaro looked at me over the top of his daughter's head, unblinking, his face impassive again.

I stood up straighter and stared right back.

He nodded once slowly, then turned and steered Yansi inside the house where Mrs. Alfaro was waiting anxiously in the doorway.

I shoved my hands in my pockets and looked away as the door closed, but a second later the front door flew open again and Yansi came running out, throwing herself into my arms.

"I love you," she said, kissing my lips firmly.

I only had time to kiss her back before she turned and ran inside the house again.

I drove home happy-sad or sad-happy, but not quite either, and not quite whole, because Yansi had taken part of my heart with her, and that sucked.

Chapter 10

I lay in bed unable to sleep.

Even though I'd changed the sheets, my room still smelled of Yansi. My brain and body were reliving the afternoon, and when I closed my eyes, I imagined her moving under me and on me and around me.

I was painfully hard again, and the smart thing would have been to think of something else—anything else. But at the same time, I didn't want to let this moment go.

The wind was beginning to pick up, and I could hear the surf crashing onto the beach, making me restless. In a few hours it would be light, and I'd be heading to check out the waves.

But until then, my mind was with Yansi. I didn't know what was going to happen between us, but I knew I wasn't going to let her go. I'd fight her parents every step of the way, if that's what it took.

It would be harder on her because I knew she loved them. I wished again that I'd taken her to meet Mom. I wanted to go back in time. I'd say, "Mom, I met a girl. She's special. She's so fucking beautiful. She's funny and smart and she's totally kick-ass."

But you don't get do-overs in life, no matter how much you want them. Life is too short to wait for the perfect moment: take what you can get and get what you can take, and then work your ass off to make a perfect moment, because sometimes one chance is all there is.

I lay awake listening to surf pounding the shore, my brain pounding with too many thoughts, blood pounding in my body, and my cock pointing north like a freakin' compass needle. God, Yansi—my beautiful addiction.

I knew I had no chance of sleeping while my body was vibrating with memories, the sounds and tastes and colors of her body spread out beneath me.

I could get myself off or...

I sat up suddenly, checking my phone: 2AM. Yeah, this might be the only chance I had.

I jumped out of bed and dressed quickly, stuffing the boner into my jeans, which was just as uncomfortable as it sounds. Moving quietly, I crept down the stairs, scooped up Julia's car keys from where I'd left them on the kitchen table and headed out via the backdoor before she heard me.

Marcus' van was parked outside and his bedroom light was off. That meant he was home, but I had no idea if he was alone or had company. None of my business.

The roads were empty as I drove, but I was nervous. If the police stopped me at this time of night, I was pretty damn sure they'd run the plates. If they woke Julia and asked about her car, she'd find an empty space where she usually left it—and she wouldn't be too worried about leaving my ass in a police cell over night for taking it without asking. Plus, I was still jumpy from my run-in with the cops the other night.

But there was no one around, and when I arrived without being stopped, relief washed over me.

I parked a short distance from the house and made the rest of my way on foot. It was a one-story house, so at least I wasn't risking my neck breaking in.

I was hoping the windows would be open, but I wasn't that lucky. A/C, of course. I'd gotten so used to living without it, I forgot that 90% of Floridians thought it was something written into the Constitution.

I tapped on the window and waited. And waited.

Getting impatient, I kept up a low level tapping until I saw a light snap on.

"Open the fucking window!" I hissed.

After a moment, I saw the curtains pulled back and the window slid open.

"What the fuck, man?" said Sean sleepily, squinting from the dim light on his bedside table.

He stepped back to let me in, and I swung a leg over the window sill and jumped inside, catching the faint smell of tobacco and weed.

"Thought I'd drop in," I grinned.

A pale smile flashed across his face.

"You're crazy! How the hell did you get here?"

"Borrowed Julia's car."

He raised his eyebrows.

"Borrowed? Sure you did."

"Whatever. How's life in jail?"

He frowned and flopped back onto his bed while I made myself comfortable on the couch.

Sean's room was three times the size of mine, and tricked out like one of those fancy hotel rooms that you see in online ads.

He shrugged. "Sucks. I can't even take a piss without someone breathing down my neck."

My smile faded. "You still grounded for life?"

"I don't know. Probably the rest of the fucking summer? They don't tell me shit. They don't speak to me—we just have uncomfortable silences all through dinner. It's like they can't believe Son Number Four is such a fuck up, like they don't know where the hell I came from. If I didn't look like my asshole of a father, I'd be searching for an adoption certificate."

He caught my expression but didn't look away.

"Having a dad isn't all it's cracked up to be."

"At least he cares," I said.

Sean shook his head. "Not about me: he cares about his reputation. He keeps going on about how much I've embarrassed him. That's all he fucking cares about. Mom's just as bad—half the time she looks straight through me."

I was silent, trying to imagine how that felt. Mom might have kicked my ass sometimes or scared the crap out of me when she yelled because she was pissed about something, but she always saw me.

"I hate it here," he said, his voice dropping to a whisper. "You don't know what it's like. Dylan graduated magna cum laude; Aidan was in the top 2% of his class; even Patrick's going to be a fucking rocket scientist. But I'm not like them. The only thing I've ever been good at is screwing and surfing—and in the ocean you can whip my ass any day of the week with one hand tied behind your back. Have you any idea how much that sucks? Being a huge fucking disappointment all the time?"

Sean shook his head.

"Sometimes I think I can't take it much more. I just want to check out, you know?"

I nodded slowly. "Yeah, take a vacation from your life. I get that. When Mom ... I just wanted the world to stop turning for one freakin' minute. Just get all the noise out of my head."

I knew Sean understood. Because that's what it means to paddle through a swell, turn your board around and catch that mofo wave coming towards you. All the noise, all the voices, all the questions go away. It's just you and the wave moving together, like you've got a purpose.

"I can't get away from any of that now," he said moodily. "I can't get away from all the shit in here," and he pointed at his head.

We sat there in silence as I tried to think of

something to say. But what could I say? I understood what he meant, and it explained all the drinking and drugs and partying, because it's a quick and easy way to stop yourself from feeling or thinking. But I'd also learned that actions have consequences, and what looks like quick and easy just isn't.

"I can't get away from *them* even for one freakin' second," he groaned, flopping back on his bed.

"Is Patrick still being a prick?"

Sean smirked, easing some of the tension in the room. "He was born a prick and just got bigger." Then his smile slipped and he sat up, looking serious. "What happened with you and him? I'm not supposed to know, but I heard Dylan talking to Dad."

"Oh, yeah. I was coming to see you. They were driving past and figured out where I was going. Patrick, he kind of said what happened at the pier was my fault. I was walking away, but he tried to sucker punch me. He missed, and I got him in the gut. Twice."

Sean smiled, the first real smile I'd seen since I'd climbed through his window.

"Nice," he said.

"Yeah! Felt good."

I rubbed my sore knuckles, enjoying the memory. Then I remembered I had a message to deliver.

"Hey, when were you going to tell me about you and Lacey?"

Sean looked confused. "What about her?"

"She was down at the pier today. She was pissed because you weren't answering your cell. She probably thought you were blowing her off, but I told her you were grounded. She said she wants to speak to you." I raised my eyebrows and grinned at him. "So ... are you guys dating now?"

He shook his head. "That's a hell no! I hit that when I want to get some, but we're not dating."

"Oh, okay. She just looked ... I dunno, upset."

He shrugged. "What can I say? She's missing the action. I'm an animal in the sack. When a woman's been with me, she knows she's been rode hard and hung up to dry."

"Except you keeping going back to tap that," I reminded him.

He laughed, and it was like having the old Sean back. I'd missed him being an asshole.

"How's it going with you and Yansi, stud?"

I didn't answer, but I guess my grin said everything.

His eyes widened.

"Outstanding, my friend! About time! How was it? Worth waiting for?"

I shook my head. "Fuck you! I'm not telling you that!"

He laughed again. "That good, huh?"

We were silent for a moment, then he slapped my leg. "I'm stoked for you, man. The look on your face—like Thanksgiving and Christmas just showed up in July!"

"Yeah," I agreed. "She's pretty amazing."

"Was she screaming your name or mine? Because I taught you everything I know."

I threw a cushion at him and he ducked, laughing his ass off. But then his expression turned serious again.

"You really love her, huh?"

I dipped my head, embarrassed by the emotion I knew he'd see on my face. "Yeah," I muttered.

He nodded slowly. "Thought so." Then he paused. "What's it like?"

I looked up, confused. "What's *what* like?"

He shrugged. "Love. Being in love."

How do you answer a question like that? Even if I had the words, if you've never been in love, it's impossible to understand.

"When she's not there … it's like part of me is missing," I tried to explain. "When we're together, I can breathe again and it's … right."

I screwed up my face, searching for the words.

Sean looked away. "I've never felt anything like that."

Yeah, I wanted to say, *I know, but you will.* I didn't say it, because I would have sounded like a pussy. Or like I was patronizing him.

"I envy you," he said, so quietly I wasn't sure I'd heard him. "I'm not being funny, bro, but how fucked up is that? You don't know your dad, your mom died, you're working two shit jobs all summer, and you've got some ball-buster for a girlfriend." He gave a hollow laugh. "And I envy the fuck out of you."

"Sean, I…"

I don't know what I would have said, but Sean interrupted anyway.

"Oh man, I've got a one-way ticket on the crazy train!" and he shook his head as if to clear it. "Hey, how come you were walking when Patrick and Dylan saw you and not riding your skateboard?"

"Oh, yeah." I grimaced. I hadn't wanted to tell him about that, but he was still staring at me, impatient now. "Um, I kind of got fired."

"Fuck! Yansi's old man fired you? He figure you nailed her?" I didn't want to reply to that, but then he answered his own question. "Nah, he'd have done more than fire you … so what was it?" I looked up at him, meeting his gaze. "Oh shit. Because of me … because he thought you gave me the drugs. Ah fuck, man!" His head thudded against the wall. "I never realized … this has really fucked things up for you." He laughed bitterly. "Almost as much as it has for me. Life sure gets shitty fast." He paused. "So where does the Tony Hawk come into it?"

"That was the other crappy bit: ole man Alfaro tossed it into the road just as this van was coming. Totaled it."

"That bastard!"

And then I told him that I threw the broken deck at

Mr. Alfaro's truck, leaving a good size ding in the door.

"He deserved it. Oh man, your wheels!"

"Yeah, it sucks having to walk everywhere."

"At least you're allowed out," he stated sourly.

I couldn't disagree with that.

Sean chewed his lip for a moment then looked at me intently.

"Can I ask you something? Something important."

I was surprised by his tone. Sean was rarely serious—tonight was sure turning out different from how I'd expected. "Sure. What's up?"

He took a deep breath. "Do you ever think about your mom?" My stomach clenched as he hurried on. "I mean, do you ever wonder about … where she's gone?"

I swallowed several times before I could speak. "Yeah, I think about her. Sometimes I wake up and I've forgotten that she … I think I can smell those cinnamon rolls she used to make. But then I remember."

His eyes were fixed on mine, so I had to look away.

"I don't know if I believe in Heaven and all that shit. I used to, I think. I prayed … a lot. But it didn't make any difference. She died anyway, so I don't know."

It was weird having this conversation with Sean. I'd never said any of it to him before. He hadn't asked. Later, I thought we'd never really talked before that night.

"Sorry, bro," he said.

"Yeah."

We were both quiet for a moment, somewhere else, inside our heads. I realized that I'd never talked to Julia about stuff like this either. For the first time, I thought maybe I wanted to.

"Dad's talking about sending me to live with my grandparents," Sean said suddenly, his voice bitter.

"Shit! For real?"

"Maybe." He shook his head. "Fuck, I can't imagine living where I couldn't surf. I'd go crazy. Crazier."

I felt the same, and the thought of Sean going away

hit me hard.

"For how long?"

"I dunno. But I'll be away for my birthday next month. For all I know, he'll get rid of me until college. He wants me out of here, I know that. Too much of an embarrassment."

When he couldn't meet my eyes, I finally understood.

"To keep you away from bad influences like me, right?" I laughed sourly.

"I'm sorry, man."

"Yeah." I looked away from him. "It was some scary shit seeing you like that. I thought ... I don't know, but it looked really bad. Maybe you should ... cut back or something."

Sean looked irritated. "For fuck's sake, not you, too! I've got my whole family crawling up my ass giving me grief, I don't fucking need it from you."

I met his eyes. "Just sayin', man."

He sighed. "Yeah, yeah. I know. It just ... it takes the edge off of living ... with *them*. It's a total mind-fuck living here. Your mom was always so cool. And now I'm stuck here 24/7—can't see my friends, can't even *talk* to them. I hate it. I really fucking hate living here." He glanced across at me. "I told them it had nothing to do with you. I told them; I told the police…"

"But you didn't tell them who sold you the Molly?"

Sean shook his head, his eyes pained. "I couldn't. I get the weed from ... some guys I know, but the other stuff ... those dudes are whacked—seriously scary." Then his voice broke a little. "I hate this fucking shit: you're my best friend, man."

I didn't know what to do. I opened my mouth, trying to think of something to say, but suddenly a light flicked on in the hall, the beam filtering under the door.

"Shit! Someone's awake—they must have heard you!"

I leapt up, scrambling out of the window, keeping low and hiding in the shadows. I held my breath when I heard Mr. Wallis' voice.

"Who are you talking to?"

"No one," Sean mumbled, sounding like he'd just woken up. "Must have been dreaming."

"Do you have a phone in there?"

Sean's protest went unheard, and his main bedroom light snapped on. From what I could hear, his room was being searched and then the window was slammed shut.

Too fucking close.

I slunk away, keeping to the darkest parts of the shadows, until I reached Julia's car.

I drove home slowly. Seeing Sean hadn't fixed anything. My life wasn't always great, but I had Yansi, and I even had Julia, sometimes. Sean didn't have anyone, except me.

Which meant he was really fucked.

I managed to sleep for a couple of hours when I got home, but I'd set my alarm early, intent on hitting the beach at dawn.

For the last nine hours, the surf had been building gradually, a wall of white sound that washed over the whole town during the night. The beach was going to be busy today so I wanted to get there early, determined to get my ride before the waves were crowded out.

The air was cooler now, and I knew the storm would have churned up the ocean, drawing colder water from deep down. It rarely got cold enough to need a wetsuit, even a shortie, but I threw a rash vest into my backpack just in case.

I was heading out the front door when I saw a light on in Marcus' room. I stood outside for a moment, wondering if he was with someone, or intending to go surfing. But then his door opened and he saw me.

"Great minds think alike. You need a ride, kid?"

"Yeah, that would be awesome. Thanks."

He grinned, and I could see the same excitement in his eyes that all surfers had when a big swell came in. A real surfer never lost that, no matter how old you got. I heard them all the time in the Sandbar, reliving their glory days back in the last century: *remember the winter of '87?* Or, *did you see that epic ride Pete Lopez caught in '92*, or, *Hey, don't forget that 25 foot monster that Yancy Spencer shred back in '67*. It was hard to imagine anyone that old being a surfer.

But we all had that look, and I saw it in Marcus now. For the first time I knew exactly how he felt without any of the bullshit.

"Where should we go to catch the best waves? Jetty or further north?"

"Jetty will be good, but it'll be crowded. Nah, drive south toward Tables Beach, and we can park near 32nd Street. I know an access point—there won't be so many people."

He nodded and smiled. "Can't beat local knowledge."

I tossed my backpack into Marcus' van, carefully lying my board on top—a 7' semi-gun with FCS fins.

The surf was pumping, and I swear salt water was shooting through my veins as I stared out. I just wished Sean could have been here. He'd have been like a kid at Christmas, hyped up on sugar and the rush.

From the van's window, I could see clean, glassy lines of surf rolling in from the Atlantic, heaping foam onto the sand. The wind was offshore, holding the waves upright, making the rides long and smooth. The swell was even higher than predicted, topping out at 15, maybe 18 feet. I hadn't ridden anything that big in a while. Adrenaline started surging through me. I was fitter, stronger than I'd ever been. It was going to be intense.

The street was lined with cars, vans, vee-dubs and trucks when we got there. So much for it being less busy, but I knew Jetty would be worse. Guys who didn't know the area well would head over there—people would be dropping in all over the place, making it impossible to catch a clean ride. This was still better.

Marcus leapt out of the van and started waxing his board, covering the older, dirty crust with a fresh layer. You needed it for traction: these weren't the kind of waves where you wanted to lose your footing, or you'd be picking your teeth with your surfboard.

He tossed the cake of Sex Wax to me, and I rubbed it on my board, paying attention to the area my back foot would rest on.

When I was finished, Marcus was waiting impatiently. He locked the van and tucked the key into a waterproof ziplock around his waist. He usually hid the key under the wheel well, but with the number of people out this morning, it would be dumb to do that. They weren't all locals, and he wasn't going to risk coming back to find that someone had stolen his clothes and spare boards. That happened a lot—more in the summer. You had to look after your shit.

We jogged down to the shore, joining a bunch of guys who were warming up on the sand and planning their paddle-out. You couldn't just run into the sea and start paddling when the surf was this big—not unless you were itching to get pounded by a ton of water closing out on top of you. I was looking for smoother water, a channel that would give an easier ride out to the line-up, the area behind where the waves were breaking. Surfers really liked riptides, because if you knew what you were doing, those would pick you up and suck you out like a conveyor belt and drop you at the line-up. Swimmers hated rips, but they saved surfers a lot of energy.

Marcus was studying the sets coming in. In every group of waves, one would be bigger than the others: usually about the third or fourth one in. So although most of these waves were double-overhead, every now and then, you'd get a 18 footer or more. Not everyone wanted to ride a wave that big, but if you caught the wave in front of it and you didn't make it, you were going to get slammed by the biggest motherfucking wave that was rolling in behind.

That's why the smart surfers would take their time, studying the sets, picking their spot.

I found mine, and I was gone.

I ran into the waves, then leapt onto my board, belly down, stroking out through the froth and foam. The water was definitely cooler now, cold enough to take my breath away. I got maybe fifty yards before I had to duck-dive the first wave. I took a lungful of air, then forced my board under the wave, paddling through the wall of energy, popping up on the other side and hearing it break behind me. My eyes stung a little from the salt, and the wind whipped my hair across my face. I shook my head like a dog, and paddled to the line-up.

I nodded to a couple of guys I'd seen around, then sat up, paying attention, watching the sets roll in, waiting for my wave.

I let a couple go, and two of the guys in the line-up paddled for them. I waited.

Another guy took off on the next wave, and I waited.

Then the horizon disappeared, and a huge, dark wave started rising up. Fuck, it was massive! That wave had my name on it. I turned the board around and started paddling hard for the peak, powering through the water. Two other guys were paddling with me, but I was ahead of them. This was *my* wave.

The wave lifted me, roaring like a jet taking off. One more stroke. One more, and then I leapt to my feet, the wave tipping forward, my stomach dropping. The board bounced and shivered down the face of the wave, and I bent into it, crouching down, lowering my center of gravity. The wave was glassy on my left, my fingers trailing along its front, my right hand reaching out for balance.

The spray misted in my face as I stared straight ahead, my hips, knees and feet flexing and moving automatically, tiny adjustments that meant I'd ride this monster and not get chewed up and spat out.

The wave started curling above me, and I wondered for a heartbeat if it was going to close out and crush me down toward the ocean floor, but it held up, creating a perfect tube, a roaring tunnel of green light. I surged forward, the rail gripping the wave, the fin anchoring me to the water so I didn't side-slip.

My heart was hammering, blood singing, eyes focused, concentration like iron. Adrenaline poured through me—every microdot of negative energy, every bad thought washed out of me, suspending time. I felt all powerful, invincible, weightless, flying, a guru.

And then the water's energy began to ebb and the wave dropped, spitting me out of the tube like a dart.

The board slowed and I let it slip over the back of the dying wave.

A huge grin split my face as Marcus paddled over to me.

"Holy shit, man! That was fucking insane!" he yelled. "That must have been over 20 feet! You're crazy, kid, but you are one helluva surfer!"

He slapped his hand against mine, and I felt like I'd gone into battle and come out on the other side. A survivor.

"You'd love Maui," he grinned, excitement and approval in his voice as he jerked his chin at me. "You rock, kid."

I watched him paddle away, the smile threatening to send my jaw into a cramp.

This was why I surfed. For moments like this.

When I'm waiting for a wave, the noise of a thousand different thoughts makes it hard to think just one thing, to focus on anything. But when I paddle for a wave, I'm thinking about whether I'm paddling at the right speed; am

I going to get to the peak in time to take off? But once I catch that wave, when I ride that wave, I'm in the moment, really there, and there's only one thing—sheer fucking joy.

I turned my board around, and paddled back out.

Two hours later, the waves began to drop. There was still a steady six foot swell, but nothing like the epic waves we'd been catching. Which meant a lot more guys were heading out and the line-up was getting crowded.

I looked over at Marcus and signaled a time-out. I caught a wave to the beach and walked across the sand with him. We were both hyped up, totally stoked from the awesome session. But the high began to drain away, leaving us peaceful.

We drove home in a contented silence, but Marcus broke it first.

"Hey, so I was supposed to tell you, Camille wants to cook for you guys tonight."

I stared at him in surprise and the corner of his mouth rose in a half smile as he glanced across at me.

"She's a great cook."

"Okay, I guess," I muttered.

"Relax. Your sis and that Ben guy will be there, too. You want to bring a date?"

My face fell. I couldn't imagine Yansi being allowed anywhere near me, although kidnapping her for the evening was an option. I liked the idea of that.

"Hey," he said, waving his hand in front of my face. "You zoning out on me?"

"Um, no. That's cool. But I don't think I'll bring anyone." I hesitated for a moment, then asked the question that had been bugging me. "So, you and Camille, you guys … you're still … together?"

"Sure, why wouldn't we be?"

"No reason," I muttered, my cheeks heating with embarrassment.

He threw me a knowing look. "You weird about Cheyenne?"

"No," I lied.

But Marcus laughed.

"Look, kid. It was a one-time thing. No harm, no foul. Cheyenne knows that."

I wasn't so sure she did—I'd seen her watching him when we were working together at the Sandbar. I also knew that she had a kid, and Marcus said he liked single moms.

"So you're still going to Papeete with Camille?"

He shrugged. "Yeah, sure," then gave me an amused look. "You're kind of young to think that you have to get serious with a girl. Enjoy life. There's enough miserable people out there—and most of them are married— without you adding to the numbers. Hell, you've got a whole year of high school left—make the most of it. You gotta take what you want from life, because no one is going to give it you. The world doesn't owe you shit. Remember that."

I nodded, because I understood what he meant. And I kind of agreed with him. I couldn't have all the things I wanted: my mom, not having to worry about money—so I'd just have to want other things.

Like surfing.

And Yansi.

And I thought about Sean, and what he had: the designer mom and dad, the car, the house, the clothes, the promise of a good school … but none of that made him happy. Surfing made him happy—and they wouldn't even let him have that now.

We were back at the house before my thoughts spiraled too far into depression. And then I was jolted into the present.

Mr. Alfaro's truck was parked outside.

"Someone you know?" Marcus asked curiously.

I swallowed before I could speak. "Yeah, my girlfriend's dad's."

Then he grinned widely. "Uh oh, someone's been

doing the dirty with the boss's daughter." He laughed as he saw my panicked expression. "Good luck with that one, kid. You're on your own."

He opened up the van and let me pull out my surfboard, smiling to himself as Julia met me at the front door looking anxious. Then Marcus winked and headed to his own room.

"Yansi's dad is here," Julia hissed. "He's been waiting for you in the kitchen."

Shit a brick!

"Okay," I said, trying to find some place of calm inside. But in reality, adrenaline was rushing through my veins faster than a double shot of Red Bull.

Julia looked at me nervously. "I could stay, if you want. I should have been at work by now, but I think I should stay..."

I thought about it for a moment then shook my head. "No, I'll be okay."

She patted my arm. "Well, if you're sure. But call my cell if … if you need me."

I was taken by surprise when she gave me a quick hug, then she picked up her purse and hurried out.

I took a deep breath and walked into the kitchen.

Yansi's dad was sitting at the table, a cup of coffee in his hands. I wished I'd asked Julia how long he'd been there.

"Hola, Senor Alfaro," I said warily.

His eyes studied me up and down as he slowly got to his feet.

"In your house, we will speak English."

I shoved my hands in the pockets of my boardshorts and nodded at him.

"Sit," he said, as he sank back into the chair.

I was kind of annoyed that he was ordering me around in my own home, but I figured calling him on that right now would only piss him off. And I was real curious to know what he was going to say.

I pulled out a chair and sat facing him, waiting for him to speak.

"Thank you for bringing Anayansi home last night. Her mother was very worried about her."

Definitely not expecting that.

"Um, okay."

He nodded but didn't say anything else, and I wondered if it was supposed to be my turn or something.

We sat staring at each other while he chewed over his words some more.

"I do not approve of her having a boyfriend when she is so young. She should concentrate on school, on getting a good education. But she is very strong willed for a girl." He paused. "She is like her mother."

A brief smile slipped out, but as Mr. Alfaro wasn't smiling, I quickly hid it.

"Anayansi tells me that the boy who was taken to hospital had nothing to do with you. I wanted to look you in the eye when I asked you the truth of this."

"I didn't give Sean any drugs," I said hotly. "I'm not a drug dealer!"

His eyes flickered, but he didn't move.

"Did you know he was taking drugs?"

Oh shit. My stomach lurched, and I took a deep breath. "Yes."

"But you did not stop him."

My face reddened with shame. "No, I didn't."

"Do you take drugs?"

This time it was a question, not a statement.

"Not since I started dating Yansi," I replied, almost truthfully. "She doesn't like it." I didn't really count smoking weed.

He seemed to be considering that answer.

"Her mother tells me that you drink alcohol."

Oh fuck—I'd forgotten that Yansi had told Mrs. Alfaro about Erin.

"Sometimes," I admitted

"If I give you permission to see my daughter…"
What the fuck? "Then you will promise me—no more drugs
and no more drinking. None. You will give me your
word."

My mouth fell open.

"There will be no dates on a school night," he
continued, "unless it is a school activity, such as a football
game."

Suddenly, I was planning on being the Minutemen's
biggest fan. Yep, I was gonna be interested in basketball
and soccer and fucking lacrosse, if there was a school
team.

"Okay," I coughed out.

"You will respect my daughter."

"I will. I do respect her."

He carried on.

"You may see her during the summer. Sundays are
family days, but you may join us at our home. We worship
at the Church of Our Saviour. Service starts at 8AM."

Oh shit. The old bastard was really going to make me
work for it.

As I met his gaze, I thought I saw a hint of humor
for the first time, but I didn't want to crack any dumb
jokes if he was going to let me see Yansi.

He stood up and held out his hand.

"We have a deal?"

Stunned, I stood up as well, shaking hands with
Anayansi's father. *You wouldn't be doing that if you knew what
I'd done last night*, I couldn't help thinking.

He gave me one more penetrating stare that made me
look away first, then he pulled out his wallet.

"I must pay you for a new skateboard," he said. "I
understand from my daughter that it was a good one."

I shoved my hands in my pockets again and looked
away. "No, thanks." Then I remembered I needed to be
polite, so I looked straight at him. "No thank you, sir."

He seemed puzzled. "I was wrong, and I wish to

replace the one that was damaged," he explained.

I folded my arms across my chest and stared right back. "My mom gave me that skateboard."

"Ah," he said quietly, putting his wallet away. "I understand."

He glanced at the ceiling, as if struggling to come to a decision, and I thought he was going to leave. But then he spoke again.

"If you wish, I still need an assistant." His mustache twitched. "The pay is ten dollars an hour."

I looked at him and nodded. "Deal," I said, and held out my hand again.

"Deal," he agreed.

Chapter 11

After that mind-fuck of a visit from Yansi's dad, I sent her a quick text message. He hadn't told me that she'd got her phone back, but I was hoping she had. I was relieved when she replied immediately.

> * OMG! You are my get-out-of-jail-free card!
> And you're working for Papi again!
> #miraclesdohappen. ILY x *

My smile was super wide, and I even offered to go and hang with her while she was babysitting her brother and sisters. Unfortunately she was visiting an aunt during the day so we wouldn't be able to see each other.

I was kind of pissed we couldn't spend the day together because after that I'd be back at work, but at least we had tomorrow evening. I'd take what I could get—my new philosophy.

I lounged around the house for a while, watched some TV, even cleaned out the shit under my bed. It occurred to me that I didn't want Yansi to see my porn stash, like ever, so I boxed it up and shoved it in the garage. I'd borrow Julia's car to haul it to the garbage dump later.

Then I decided to tackle the backyard. Mom wanted it to look nice even though she hated yard work, but it hadn't been touched in months.

I mowed the patch of scrubby grass first, then pulled weeds out of the tiny patio area and finished by cleaning off the grill.

"What are you doing?"

Julia's voice interrupted me from happy, mindless non-thoughts.

I gave her a look that said, *Really? Any more dumb questions?*

"Um, I just … it looks good, Nicky." She stood with one hand on her hip, squinting at me like she wasn't quite sure who I was. "How'd it go with Yansi's dad? Was he mad about last night?"

I shook my head. "He came to offer me my job back."

Her expression was stunned, and I couldn't help grinning at her.

"Wow! Seriously? That's amazing … although I'm guessing he didn't know what you two were up to while she was here!"

I felt my cheeks reddening, so I looked away from her, concentrating on the grill.

Her voice had softened when she spoke again. "So, Mr. Alfaro believed you … about Sean?"

"Yansi told him he was wrong and that it was nothing to do with me. He believed her."

"Well, okay then." She hesitated. "Have you heard from Sean? How's he doing?"

I sighed. "Not so good. I mean, he's okay, but he's grounded and they've taken his cell."

"He ought to be grounded," Julia snapped, sounding more like herself. "That was a dumb thing to do—he could have killed himself."

I didn't reply because I knew she was right.

239

"Do you want a drink?" Julia asked abruptly. "No beer though."

I smiled as I looked up at her. "Soda's fine."

I wiped my hands on a rag, and put the grill back together as Julia stepped out onto the deck with the soda.

"Seriously," she said. "What brought on all this?" and she waved her arm at the backyard.

I shrugged. "Mom liked it kept nice."

Julia gave a small smile and sat down next to me on the deck. "Yeah, she did."

We sat in silence for a moment, and for once it didn't feel strained or awkward; I wasn't waiting for her to go postal on me. It felt good.

"So, dinner with Camille and Marcus: that'll be interesting," she said.

I shrugged, noncommittal, not really agreeing that 'interesting' was the word. "I guess."

"Are you inviting Yansi?"

"Nah. Well, I wanted to, but she's busy. I'll see her tomorrow after work."

Julia raised her eyebrows. "Her parents are okay with that?"

I nodded, trying not to smile too much, but Julia caught it.

"Things are really good with her, aren't they?"

"Yeah," I admitted finally.

"Ah, young love!" she laughed.

"Shut up," I muttered, but I didn't really mean it, because it was true.

Then she sighed and looked down.

"I'm sorry about what I said that time … about a foster home … and about your dad. I didn't mean it. I was just worried about you, and worried that I couldn't do it … you know, replace Mom. And I shouldn't have tried. I was just so scared that suddenly I had this huge responsibility. But the last few weeks, you've seemed different … like you found your direction or something. I know I'm not making much sense. I'm just saying … you're my brother, Nicky, and whatever happens, I love you."

"Yeah," I said softly. "Me, too."

Then she sat up straight. "But if you ever pull any stunts like Sean, I'm so gonna kick your ass!"

I smiled.

Julia could be a complete pain, but she wasn't all bad.

I went back to work the next day. Not much had changed: Mr. Alfaro was as silent as ever. But he let me ride inside the truck, and he paid me a bonus because one of his clients asked us to drive over to take care of her uncle's place, and that meant we worked overtime.

I got to see Yansi, too. She invited me for dinner that night. The twins were really happy to see me, using me like a jungle gym, and even Mateo looked pleased, although it would have taken the threat of torture for him to admit it. But Mrs. Alfaro kept throwing me death glares, and I still wasn't allowed to be alone with Yansi in her room.

After a few more murderous stares, Mrs. Alfaro took me aside and said that if I ever hurt her daughter again, she'd do something to me. I don't know what that was exactly because she started speaking really quickly and waving her arms around. Whatever it was, it sounded bad. I made my promise and got the hell out of there.

Yansi threw me a sympathetic look, but I could tell she thought I deserved it, too. I probably did.

The rest of the week, I got a couple more early morning surfs in with Marcus. He didn't mention the evening Camille had cooked us all dinner. It had been a bit weird, mostly because I knew about Cheyenne and suspected that there were others. But Camille had been full on, talking about Tahiti and what they'd do when they got there.

And then the next day, I saw Marcus swapping phone numbers with a couple of girls we met on the beach after an evening surf. I felt bad for Camille, but it was none of my business.

When Friday rolled around, I finally got a text from Sean just as I was leaving for work.

He was being sent to his grandparents for the rest of high school—leaving on Monday. He had the weekend to say goodbye to everyone.

It felt like another part of my life was being ripped away. And if I felt like that, how much worse was it for Sean?

We arranged to go for a morning surf the next day. I tried calling him when I got in that evening, but there was no reply on his cell. I wondered if that meant they'd taken it away from him again, but early on Saturday morning, he showed up at my house.

I loaded my board onto his roof rack and secured the straps.

Sean looked like crap. He hadn't shaved for a week and he had black rings under his eyes as if he hadn't been sleeping much. If anything, he looked worse than the last time I'd seen him.

"Hey, man," I said, as I slid into the passenger seat, trying to make a dent in the thick tension filling the car.

He nodded. "Hey, Nick."

"Rough break about going to your grandparents. I can't believe they're doing that."

He sighed. "Yeah, but now..." he bit his lip, changing his mind about whatever he was going to say. "You know what, I just want to forget about it. I had to fuckin' beg them to let me have today. I want to enjoy it."

"I'm going to miss you, bro."

His lips turned down. "Yeah. Me, too."

We drove to the pier in silence, then unloaded the

boards and paddled out.

The swell was a gentle three to four feet. Nothing special. Nothing special at all, except that this was our last surf. Who knew how long it would be before we were back in the ocean together.

We caught a few waves, but I could tell that Sean's heart wasn't really in it. So we sat on our boards beyond the line-up and stared out toward the horizon, not speaking, not doing anything, just watching the sun rise higher. Just sitting.

Just being.

The horizon was soft today, the edges blurring into the ocean like unfinished thoughts, so you couldn't tell what was sea and what was sky.

Eventually, Sean spoke.

"When your mom died, you were out here for a couple of hours before school and every afternoon until it got dark, even when there was no surf. I thought you'd gone kind of crazy."

I was still staring at the pink tinged waves as the sun rose higher when I replied.

"It was the only place I could stand to be. I don't know why."

"I didn't get it then, but I do now."

I glanced at him curiously.

"Yeah?"

He nodded.

"I think … maybe because everything else seems kind of small out here." He paused. "Sorry, that sounds like I'm dissing your mom—I'm not."

"No, I get it. It just goes on. However crappy you're feeling, the ocean just keeps moving and…"

"…everything else is insignificant."

I nodded slowly. "Something like that."

"It'll be here long after we're dust. Centuries, millennia from now, the ocean will still be here."

"Yeah, I guess."

Sean looked at me. "That's what I mean. What we do doesn't make any difference."

"I don't know. Maybe it does, maybe it doesn't. You've just gotta live the best life you can, right?"

He sighed. "The best life? What the fuck is that?" Then he laughed bitterly. "You know what tourists always say, about how lucky we are living here? Yeah, right—it's just another lousy day in Paradise."

I looked across at him, but he was still staring at the horizon.

"But being here," he went on, "it helps, you know? It's the only ... the only place I feel like I can breathe. Everyone expects something from me: my parents want a straight-A kid, a brainiac who's gonna run for Senate, or cure cancer or something. And ... other people ... all want a piece. And they all keep taking little bites and I feel like there's nothing left of me." He paused. "But out here ... I'm okay out here because it doesn't matter. It's all just so much bullshit, but everywhere else..."

He didn't finish the sentence. He needed to talk so it was my job to listen. I could do that. Because I was shit at offering advice, but I could listen.

"Everywhere else is pointless."

We bobbed up and down on the water, shivering slightly because we hadn't been moving around, but the gentle motion with the waves breaking behind us, it was restful, calm, when everything back on land was a shitstorm of crazy.

"I was thinking about our surf trip," he said, out of the blue.

"Yeah?"

He smiled sadly. "It would have been awesome."

"Yeah, it still will be. We weren't going to go until after graduation anyway." His tone confused me, but I rambled on. "I can't do a whole year away," I reminded him. "But I'll save up as much as I can. Three or four months, for sure—maybe more."

I just hoped Yansi would understand.

He tried to smile. "Yeah. In Bali, you can live on a dollar a day. Marcus told me that."

"Sounds good," I sighed. "Wish I could do that here because ... but hey, I got a pay raise."

"Yeah? How much?"

"Ten bucks an hour."

"Fuck me, you're Donald Trump."

"Nah. I've got my own hair."

The jokes were forced and kind of lame, but it was something.

The swell was dropping again and the beach was beginning to fill up, so we caught a wave back in, sharing the ride.

Yansi was meeting us, along with her girlfriends. Rob had said he'd come for a morning surf, but he hadn't showed yet, which meant he was probably sleeping off another hangover. I didn't mind that bit—I was glad it was just me and Sean.

Yansi was waiting on the beach, and I was already grinning like a crazy person when she was fifty feet away.

Sean rolled his eyes and muttered, "Pussy whipped," but I knew he didn't mean it. Much.

I kissed her thoroughly until she pushed on my chest.

"You're all cold and wet, and you're getting me all wet," she grumbled.

I raised my eyebrows. "Not seeing a problem with that—let's go back to my place."

She bit her lip. "We can't just ditch our friends."

I sighed, knowing she was right. It was Sean's last weekend. His last day.

"Another time," she whispered, smiling shyly at me. Then she turned to Sean. "Hi, Sean. How are you?"

"Peachy keen with a cherry on top," he deadpanned.

Yansi looked taken aback, and I threw Sean a warning look. It wasn't her fault that he was being sent away.

He shrugged and went to sit with Jonno and his friends who'd just arrived.

"He is *so* rude," Yansi complained.

"Yeah, but cut him some slack," I said.

"I always do," she huffed, crossing her arms across her chest.

I pulled her into another hug. "Come on, Yans. He's got one lousy day, then he's being sent away. It's gotta suck being him right now."

"You're too nice," she sighed, her body loosening.

"I can be not nice later," I whispered, kissing her neck.

She giggled then squirmed. "You're tickling me!"

I kissed her again then let her go.

"Anyway," she said, "he's just pissed because I'm here."

"What? That's not true."

"It so is," she contradicted, her voice irritated. "He wants his 'best friend' all to himself. He can't stand me being around."

I disagreed with her, even though secretly I thought she was probably right.

"Come on," I begged. "Give him a break."

"Fine," she huffed out. "But you owe me for this, Nick-y!"

She ran away laughing. I would have chased her right away, but damn if her ass didn't look amazing as she ran. I gave her a head start then caught her in my arms and threatened to toss her into the water.

I paused when I saw Lacey talking to Sean. Although 'talking' might have been an understatement. They were yelling at each other, and Lacey looked like she was crying, too.

"What do you think that's about?" Yansi asked me.

"I don't know. Maybe she's upset that he's going away."

We watched them for a while before I grabbed hold

of Yansi's hand and pulled her back toward the others.

"Wait! I want to see what happens!" she yelped.

"It's not our business. If he wants to tell us, he will."

"What have you got against good gossip?" she joked.

I frowned at her. "I've been the target of 'good gossip'," I snapped, "and it's totally shitty."

She was silent for a moment, then wrapped her arms around my neck. "I know. I'm sorry, okay?"

"Yeah," I sighed, leaning down so my nose was against her cheek.

Her fingers toyed with the hair at the nape of my neck, then she pushed away and pointed with her chin over my shoulder.

"She's coming back, but Sean's heading in the direction of the pier. I think you'd better go talk to him, he looks really upset."

Sighing, I dropped my arms and turned around. Yansi was right; Lacey was wiping under her eyes with a finger, still managing to smear her mascara. Sean was heading into the crowds. If I let him out of my sight, I'd lose him.

"I'll be back later," I called, breaking into a jog.

It didn't take me long to catch up to him.

"Sean! Hey, are you okay?"

He didn't even look at me. "I don't wanna talk."

"But…"

"I said go fuck yourself, Nick!" he yelled, suddenly.

I stopped walking.

"You are being such a prick! What's with you?"

I'd had enough of putting up with Sean's shit.

He looked over my shoulder, somewhere behind me, before squatting down on the sand and picking at a hole in his boardshorts.

"Lacey's pregnant."

I stared, wondering if Sean was joking. He didn't look like he was joking; in fact he looked kind of sick.

"Oh fuck!"

He tried to smile. "That's what I said."

"Is ... is it yours?"

He shrugged. "She says so."

"And you believe her?"

He sighed. "Yeah, I guess. You know we've been ... hanging out a lot. Smoking, ya know. I'm not sure I always wrapped it…"

"Shit, man!"

"Yeah."

With a lurch, Erin and the night where I couldn't remember much at all came into my mind, and I thought, *This, right now—this could be me.*

"At least my parents can't blame *you* for this fuck up," Sean laughed dully.

Then he dropped his head into his hands.

"I'm so fucked," he murmured. "It's like a massive wake-up call, and the world just punched me in the face."

I sat down next to him.

"What ... what's she going to do?"

He studied his hands, pawing through the sand before replying.

"She was trying to contact me all week, but when you told her I didn't have my cell ... she came over to the house last night. With her parents. The shit really hit the fan. Like even more than it had already. Shit, I thought my dad was going to have a fuckin' stroke. Her parents were mad and talking all kinds of shit. Lacey was crying. Mom was just ... I don't know ... being all icy and polite, serving drinks like she was at a fuckin' Bridge party."

He shook his head.

"I just kind of sat there, wondering how the hell I fucked up my life so badly."

He took a deep breath.

"Lacey just told me that she wanted to get an abortion but her parents want her to keep it, so I think ... I think I'm going to be a father."

I tried to find something to say, but no words came

to me. Nothing. I was a crap friend.

"How come they let you out today?" I asked at last.

He snorted with disgust. "They didn't. But I got tired of being grounded, so I just took my keys out of dad's desk and got my car. They've probably sent out a fucking search party by now. First stop, your house."

He sighed.

"They'll figure out I came to the beach sooner or later. Mom and Dad won't come—but don't be surprised if they send Patrick." He chewed on his thumbnail. "He wasn't too bad. Maybe it's because he's always gotten a lot of tail. Maybe he's been there."

He shook his head.

"I don't want it," he said tiredly. "I don't even like Lacey. It was just sex. That's all it was supposed to be." He tried to smile, but it wasn't working. "I get now why Marcus likes single moms—they're not going to forget their birth control pills. They've already fucked up once, so they're not going to do it again."

I felt kind of sick when he said that. Was that what he thought of Mom? That she fucked up twice?

But he hadn't finished.

"And now because of one fuck-up … my life is over."

I thought of Mom, and Julia, and me.

"You fucked up, but your life isn't over, bro. It's…"

"Yeah, it is. I'll have to drop out of school, get a job. I won't be going away to college now, that's for fucking sure."

"Your parents will want you to graduate?" I said, my voice uncertain. I knew his dad was kind of hard core.

"Dad's saying I have to take responsibility. He was pretty   mad—well,   that's   a   massive   fuckin' understatement."

I tried to think of something useful to say. I mean, Sean's dad drove a Benz, they weren't exactly poor. I couldn't believe he'd let Sean drop out just to prove a freakin' point. But then again, what did I know about what dads did and didn't do?

"Yeah, but people have babies and still go to school," I argued. "It'll just be … harder for you. But there are subsidies and stuff, money you can look for. I'll help you, man."

His smile was strained when he glanced up at me.

"Thanks, Nick. Can I stay at your place for a few nights? It's pretty crazy at home."

"Yeah, of course you can—as long as you need. But I thought you were going to your grandparents?"

He shook his head. "I was, but that's kind of on hold for now."

"Will they let you stay at my house?"

He shook his head again. "I don't care. I'm done playing by their rules. They'd have to fuckin' lock me in my room or something. I'm not going back there. Ever." Then he looked up. "You need to clear it with Julia?"

"No, she'll be fine." *I hoped.* "I'll talk to her."

"Cool." He nodded slowly. "You got any weed? I need to get wasted."

"Um, no. But I think Ben left some beers in the fridge, so later we could…"

"Nah, I need something more than that, and I need it fuckin' right now." He poked at the hole in his shorts, absently making it larger. "I gotta go home, pick up some shit before Mom and Dad realize that I left. I'll be at your place in a couple of hours. 'Kay?"

"Yeah, sure. Whatever you need."

His head dropped into his hands, and his voice cracked as he spoke.

"What the fuck am I gonna do?"

I shook my head slowly.

"I have no idea."

"Come on, man! You're my best friend. Help me out here!"

His voice was desperate, his eyes wide and panicked.

"It's not like they're saying you've got to marry her or anything," I reasoned.

He shook his head.

"No, but ... her parents are Catholic. It's what they're pushing for ... Mom and Dad say I have to take responsibility. I told you that."

"Yeah, you kinda do. I mean, it's a kid and everything, but..."

"You think I don't know that!" he shouted.

"Yeah, but..."

He squeezed his eyes shut and I was shocked to see tears leaking down his face. He scrubbed them away furiously.

"I don't want to marry Lacey. I don't even like her. We hook up. That's it."

"So don't marry her," I said decisively. "They can't force you."

He looked up, a shadow of hope on his face.

"You think?"

"No way, man. But you are going to have to help provide for the kid. Pay money, I guess."

The fleeting look of hope vanished.

"How the fuck am I going to do that?"

I shrugged. "Get a job."

"Like you," he sneered. "Shoveling shit for $7 an hour.

My face flushed red. "It's lawn maintenance, and it's $10 an hour. What's wrong with that?"

"Because I want to get out of this fucking town!" he yelled. "I'm not like you! I want more than just to earn minimum wage for the rest of my life!"

"What's that supposed to mean?" I bit out, ice shooting through my body.

He shrugged, but wouldn't meet my eyes. "You're small-town, Nick. You always have been. You don't want to go anywhere else..."

"That's not true!"

"Yeah, it is. But I want to go away to college. I want to surf Pipelines and Hanalei and see the sunset on Oahu. Anything! You just want to stay here."

"It's all I can afford!" I yelled at him, my hands clenching into fists. "I don't have rich parents who'll pay for me to sit on my ass all summer and get girls pregnant!"

His mouth dropped open in surprise, then his eyes narrowed.

"Fuck you, Nick."

And he scrambled to his feet and strode away.

My whole body was vibrating with anger, and I badly wanted to hit something. Instead I flung myself back on the sand and threw my arm over my eyes.

I couldn't believe Sean had been such a prick, but at the same time I was stunned. Having a fight with Sean was like seeing the sky turn green: it wasn't supposed to happen. We never fought. Well, not since he broke my Beast Hunter Transformer back in third grade.

I knew it wasn't really me he was mad at. He was scared and pissed, but hell! We were friends, weren't we? And all this time he was looking down on me like I was some sort of loser?

"Nick?" Yansi's voice was tentative. "Are you okay?"

I sat up reluctantly.

"Not really."

"You guys were shouting," she said softly.

"Yeah."

"Anything I can help with?"

I gave her a small smile. "You always help."

And wasn't that the damn truth.

"Is … is Sean okay?"

I shook my head. "He's really fucked."

She threaded her fingers through mine. "Do you want to tell me about it?"

I huffed out a breath. "Sean's in a whole shitload of trouble. I don't think he'll talk his way out of this one."

"Okay," she said quietly, ignoring my evasion.

It wasn't that I didn't want to tell her. Hell, there was no one else I'd rather talk to about it, but I didn't know if that was cool with Sean.

"We kind of had a fight," I added lamely.

Her face twisted in a grimace.

"Yeah, so I saw. I think everyone saw." Then she looked up. "Is Lacey pregnant?"

My eyes widened. "How did you know?"

She shrugged. "You're fighting with your best friend. She's upset, he's upset—everyone knows those guys only hook up for sex. It made sense."

She was right, but that was my girl—real smart.

"What's he going to do?"

"I don't know. His parents are telling him to drop out and get a job."

"Wow! I can't believe that!"

"I know. They think he needs to learn some kind of lesson, but shit—you'd think they'd at least want him to graduate high school."

Yansi shook her head. "I don't think they'll go through with the threat. I mean, I've never met his parents, but I've seen the car Sean drives—they won't want a minimum wage kid."

I winced, her words hitting home.

"They'll probably just let him think that for a few days to shake him up."

"Really?"

"Probably, at least I hope so."

I hoped she was right too, and now she'd said it, it seemed the most likely thing to happen. But then again, she hadn't met his parents.

I didn't tell her what he'd said about me being small-town, because a part of me that I didn't want to admit to thought he might be right.

Yansi stroked my arm and leaned against me.

"So, what were you guys fighting about? I get that he'd be upset, but why was he yelling at you?"

"It just kind of blew up…"

She looked at me shrewdly. "Because…?"

"I said he needed to be responsible for the kid." I looked down. "Because, ya know, I know what it's like if your dad isn't a dad, just a sperm donor."

"Oh," she said softly, then wrapped her arms around me tightly.

"I didn't mean give up school or anything, but it wouldn't kill him to get a freakin' job, would it?"

She was quiet for a moment.

"It's not your fault that he got himself into this mess, Nick."

"I know … but I feel like I was kicking him while he's down."

"Give him some time to cool off. He'll be fine."

I shook my head. "I don't know. I've never seen him like this—not in all the time I've known him. I'm going to see if I can find him."

"I'll come with you."

I called Sean's cell about twenty times, but it kept going to voicemail. I sent him texts, too, but he didn't get back to me, and nobody had seen him since we'd had our fight.

Eventually, we went back to my place in case he'd gone there. But Julia hadn't seen him either. She believed, like Yansi, that he'd calm down in his own time, but she agreed to let me borrow her car. So me and Yansi drove around: north on Ridgeway, south on Atlantic Avenue, looking for his car. Finally, we drove over to Sean's house. I didn't think he'd go there, but we'd tried everywhere else.

"You'd better let me knock on the door," Yansi said. "They're more likely to talk to me. I'll just say I'm a friend from school."

She was only gone a few minutes while I sat in the car sending yet another text to Sean. But when she came back, she looked really pissed.

"Oh my God! I just met his mother. What a bitch!

No wonder Sean is such a screw up!"

"Why, what did she say to you?"

"Well, first off, she thought I was Mexican and looking for a job cleaning. She even asked if I had a Green Card! Then when I told her I was a friend of Sean's from school. She said, and I quote, 'I find that highly unlikely'. And then she closed the door in my face!"

I was really angry and ready to go and tell Mrs. Wallis what I thought of her.

"Leave it," Yansi sniffed. "She's not worth it. And it's more important that we find Sean."

In the end I had to agree.

We drove around to all the usual places for a second time, but again no one had seen him. By then it was late afternoon and I had to give up because I was due at work in half an hour. So I drove Yansi back to her house first, then went home to change.

But when I got there, Sean was sitting on my doorstep.

"Fuck, man! I've been looking for you all over!"

"Yeah, I saw your messages. I just needed some space, you know?"

I sat down next to him. "Yeah, I guess. Um, I even went to see your mom. Well, Yansi did, but she wouldn't tell us anything."

He gave a small smile. "Yeah, I heard that, too. Mom left a message on my phone. Another one."

We sat in silence for several minutes.

I was relieved he was okay, but was kind of annoyed that I'd spent the afternoon driving all over the place looking for him. Gas wasn't cheap, and I'd done a lot of miles today. But he had enough people pissed at him already, so I kept my mouth shut.

"Look, I've got to get ready for work, but you can stay here. Julia's cool."

He shook his head. "Nah, that's okay. I'm gonna go hang at the beach for a while." His breath came out in a gust. "I thought I could hide from my parents, from my life, but I can't.

"I'll come with you. I'll call in sick to work."

"Appreciate it, bro, but I know you need the money. And … about before … that was out of line. I was being a dick. I'm sorry."

I shook my head. "No worries. We're good. Are you going to stay here now, or do you think they'll still send you to North Carolina?"

His gazed dropped to the ground and he toed a weed growing out of the cracked concrete.

"No, I made a decision about that. I was dreaming if I thought they'd let me stay with you. Hell, you know my old man—he'd cut off the money and force me back. And I can't ignore this—gotta fuckin' face it. Right? I won't be leaving Cocoa Beach now," he stated.

I was confused by his tone. "Did your mom say that? That's a good thing though, right? I mean, you'll be here. I'll help you with stuff. Yansi, too. I know you guys don't get along so well, but she's really great with kids…"

He frowned. "I can't believe there's going to be a kid out there with my name on it. Who the fuck would want me for a father? Another life I can screw up."

"Come on, man, it won't be that bad. You can teach the little dude to surf. You'll be a great dad."

His eyes were watery and he held out his hand before pulling me into a guy hug. "I love you, bro. You always got my back. Now get the fuck out of here before you turn me into a freakin' chick!"

I laughed and shook my head. "Whatever, asshole!"

He smiled. "Dawn surf tomorrow? My last moment of freedom?"

"I'll be there."

"Promise me, man," he said, suddenly serious.

"I said so, didn't I?"

He smiled. "Okay." And he turned to leave. Then he stopped as he was getting into his car. "Julia let me in earlier, so I've left you something on your bed. Call it a goodbye present."

"I thought you said you weren't leaving?" I yelled after him.

He didn't answer, just waved and was gone.

I ran upstairs to see what he'd left me.

Lying on my bed was his Z-Racer Cruiser. Hand-crafted from a 10-layer veneer construction, laser etched logos, sanded wheels wells, 60mm 97A wheels, five sandblasted trucks, Z-Flex Abec 7 Bearings. Also known as two-hundred-and-fifty dollars worth of skateboard.

A note was taped to the deck.

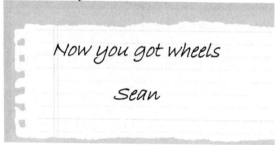

I read the note again, smiling. I hadn't accepted a new board from Mr. Alfaro, but this—hell, yeah! I knew it was Sean's way of apologizing for before.

I sent him a quick text message, but he didn't reply.

I hurried to take a shower before heading to work. At least now I had a skateboard, I wouldn't be late.

But as I was pulling on my jeans, I heard voices yelling in the hall. Well, one voice. Camille.

"You are not serious about anything, Marcus. Except surfing. It is like a drug to you. Or ... surfing is the problem, but it is also the solution. For you. It is like you are ... playing at a relationship. Sometimes I think this."

"Why are you here, Cam?"

"I saw that girl leaving your room."

Uh oh.

257

Marcus' voice was calm when he replied.

"I didn't know you were going to be here."

"It was a surprise. To me as well, I think now."

"It didn't mean anything, babe."

"I would have given you my life! I don't understand why you have done this. You have killed our future. You are just a … pig!"

And then there was a lot of screaming in French.

I heard the front door slam, and everything went quiet. So I ventured downstairs and nearly tripped over Camille sitting on the bottom step.

From the look on her face she knew that I'd heard everything. I didn't know what to say to her. We stared at each other for a few seconds.

"Are you okay?" I asked quietly.

She didn't answer immediately, just looked at me calmly, although her eyes were glistening with tears.

"You could be just like him, Nick. I see it in you. Yes, it's there. But maybe there's more, I don't know. I think you could be more. He could have been more, but chose to be alone."

I stood uncomfortably, waiting for her to leave. She stared at the front door, but I wasn't sure she was really seeing it. Then she turned to look at me again.

"He never wanted to be ordinary—whatever that is. Marcus, I mean. He wanted to be a musician. Did you know that? He said he did, but I couldn't see it. I tried, I did."

She smiled sadly and looked down.

"I got stupidly cross with him because he insisted he is an artist, and yet the music is never his top priority. I don't know, but an artist to me is someone who loves it so much they just have to do it. He does it after surfing, screwing and smoking, and it makes me want to smack his face."

She shook her head.

"He is addicted to this life, this part-time life. Yes,

addicted. He says it's because surfing is the only time he gets peace from the noise in his head, and the pressures of society and other people. He can be out there for nine hours at a time and still doesn't understand why he has no money, and why he never gets to finish any music. So there is an element of stupidity and denial."

She looked up to meet my eyes.

"He doesn't have any roots."

"Not everyone has large families or people who care about them," I said carefully.

I'm not sure she even heard me.

"So, why am I telling you this? Because I see it in you, Nick, this addiction."

I was confused and beginning to feel angry. Who the fuck did she think she was to talk to me like this? She was just pissed and taking it out on me. But no, I wasn't really so dumb. I knew she was telling me something real—and it scared the fuck out of me. Because she was right, because I felt it, too.

Marcus kept life simple and did things the way he wanted. No one relying on him, no one expecting anything from him. I could see that it made him free. It also made him alone. But as he always said—it was his life.

Camille stood up slowly. "I think he wanted me to find him with that woman. So he didn't have to make a choice."

She straightened her skirt and swept a hand through her hair.

"Goodbye, Nick."

And she walked out.

I listened to the front door slam behind her, and sat down heavily.

Chapter 12

When I woke up on Sunday, I was tired from working late at the Sandbar, muscles sore from six hours of standing washing dishes. So I wasn't in a great mood. Sean had left me a text, reminding me that I'd promised to meet him at the pier for a dawn surf. I wasn't happy about it, and I'd tried to text him back, but he wasn't returning my messages or answering my calls, so I had no choice but to go.

I was just glad we weren't fighting anymore. I rode the Z-Flex to work the night before, and it had been awesome. A really smooth ride. I guess I owed Sean. Mofo knew it, too.

The only good thing about getting up so early for a dawn surf is that cold water is a fast way to shake you awake. Hard to be half asleep when salt water is shooting through your body.

I saw Sean's car as soon as I arrived at the pier. It was parked at a crazy angle in the lot at the top of the dunes. Surely the dude couldn't be wasted at this time in the morning? But after the last couple of days he'd had, I guess I couldn't blame him.

Not much surprised me about Sean anymore—because I'd stopped knowing what to expect. Nothing was familiar. It was all changing. We were changing.

It made me pissed that he might have been driving while he was drunk. I hoped not. And he really needed to give up the weed. It was making him a little crazy, and with everything that was going on, he was even more unpredictable than usual.

I walked down to the shore and dumped my skateboard and backpack under the pier, laying my thruster on top, then searching the waves for a sign of him. I squinted into the gray light, the rising sun slowly turning the tops of the waves pink. I breathed in the clean scent of salty air, enjoying the coolness after another humid night of trying to sleep. I searched the line-up, and wondered where the hell he was.

Then I spotted his board half hidden behind a small dune. As I got closer, I could see that it was lying in two pieces. Damn. That was a nice board, too—Quiksilver Pro—about eight hundred dollars worth of shortboard. He must have caught a bad wave and snapped it on the beach break. But it was odd, because the leash was still wrapped around the tail, something we all did to stop it dragging in the sand when you were carrying it. But why bother when it was already broken?

And where the hell was he?

Maybe Sean was taking a leak somewhere in the dunes.

I called his name loudly.

"Sean! Where are you, you crazy fucker?"

But the only reply were the seagulls wheeling overhead.

Damn it! He'd probably gotten wasted again and was sleeping it off somewhere in the dunes.

I searched the beach and wandered along a short distance until I found his backpack, but still no sign of him.

And then…

You know that moment when you feel something is wrong and you have no clue what it could be, but you just *know?* A sensation like iced water was being pumped into my veins began to chill me, and I started to jog across the dunes, calling his name, searching, searching.

And then I saw him, and relief washed through me.

But only for a second. He was lying face down by the shore, and the falling tide was tugging at his boardshorts, his feet moving lazily as if he was dreaming about swimming.

Face down.

I ran faster, calling his name, waiting for him to sit up and laugh his ass off.

But he didn't. And I ran.

I ran towards him and maybe I was calling his name, I don't know.

How did this happen? The surf was small today— kids stuff. How? HOW? Sean could have nailed these waves with his eyes closed.

I slid on my knees next to him and grabbed him by his shoulders, rolling him over.

His eyes were open and I knew, I just knew.

I felt for a pulse, trying to see through the haze of tears, but his skin was cold, and I knew. I didn't want to admit it, but I knew.

And I was on my knees in the wet sand and hugging his cold body against my chest and begging him to wake up, and begging and pleading and promising to be a better friend, promising I'd save him this time if only he would just wake up.

The CPR skills I'd learned came back to me, igniting my brain, making promises I wanted to believe. So I laid him on his back. *Breathe, Sean, breathe,* I begged. *Find the place on his chest, pump eight times, breathe, pump eight times, breathe. Just fucking breathe!*

Again and again, I pumped his heart and breathed air

into his lungs. I kept pumping and I heard a crack as I broke a rib, but I kept pumping his heart because I didn't know what else to do.

When my arms were burning, and sweat was running off my body, my own ragged breath roaring in my ears, I stopped.

We stayed there, I don't know how long. Me crying and begging, him silent and cold.

I stopped.

And nobody came.

I sat there, my body cooling in the morning breeze. But not as cold as his body. Getting colder.

And when I was done and all cried out, I dragged his body up the beach. He was heavy, so heavy, and I pulled and dragged until my frozen limbs were burning again.

And I realized something, why he was so heavy.

The pockets of his boardshorts were full of stones. Pebbles from the beach. All sizes, round and smooth. His pockets were weighted down with stones.

And I knew. I just knew.

He'd walked into the ocean with his pockets full of stones.

Now I knew why he'd insisted that I came to the beach this morning; I knew why he'd made me promise; I knew why he'd texted to make sure I was going to be there.

Because he wanted me to find him at the beach, because I was his best friend and this was the last thing I'd ever do for him, for his family, for his brothers. The last act of friendship in this life.

So I reached into his pockets and I pulled out those pebbles one by one. One by one. One by one, until I had a small pile, a memorial in stone. And then I threw them into the ocean, one by one, one by one, one by one.

Because Sean was a stupid fucker and a dickhead and an asshole, but he didn't want his family to know that he couldn't stand to be who he was anymore—to live his life anymore. But he'd let me know. Just me. His friend. His best friend.

And then I walked to where I'd left my backpack. I walked, because running wouldn't make any difference now. It was too late. I was too late.

I pulled out my phone and I made the call.

Then I sat in the sand next to his body.

"What the fuck were you thinking, man? I thought we were friends? Why couldn't you tell me? You should have told me what you were thinking? You could have come live with me and Julia. We'd have figured something out. You didn't have to fucking kill yourself. Christ, Sean, I would have helped you. I would have. Why didn't you let me help you? You stupid, thoughtless, fucking prick! You were my brother!"

They sent an ambulance. Too late. Much too late.

The sirens shrieked through the morning air, heads turned and people stared, but I didn't turn to look at them. A crowd was forming by the pier, and I didn't turn around.

I didn't turn around when voices called to me or when someone pulled me away.

And I didn't take my eyes from Sean until he was gone, in a body bag, in the coroner's van: they took him away.

And then there were police. And questions, questions. More questions. And the police officer's eyes were tired, and I didn't know if it was because it was the end of his shift, or because now he had to tell a family that their son, their brother was dead.

And when they let me go, after all their questions had been answered again and again, I went home.

Julia went to pieces when she saw me at the door with a police officer.

And because I didn't have any more words, he had to explain to her what had happened—or what they thought had happened.

She hugged me and cried and hugged me again. And

Ben was there, saying over and over, "I can't believe it. I can't fuckin' believe it."

No. Neither could I.

It sucks being pissed at someone who's dead.

They've got a name for people like me—I'm a suicide loss survivor. I guess they have a name for everything.

Except that nobody knew it. I looked it up online: shock, numbness, detachment, confusion, irritability, guilt. Yep, checked those boxes. I couldn't talk to anyone, so I pushed everyone away.

Every time Julia asked, I said I was fine.

Every time Yansi called, I didn't answer. I just texted back later that I was okay. Another lie. I knew I was hurting her—at least in some distant, out-of-focus way, I was aware—but I couldn't lie to her face. She'd know. She'd see it in my eyes. So I stayed away.

The police called it an accidental drowning, but I knew there was nothing accidental about it. I knew. Their first guess was that Sean was drunk or high, so they did an autopsy. I hated that, but what did it matter now? Sean was gone, and what was left was just an empty case of flesh and bones. Even so, I hated to think of it. So I didn't. I kept my brain disengaged, and I went through the motions of living. The coward's way out.

I think everyone was surprised that the autopsy results showed he'd only had a couple of beers. To them it made the 'drowning' all the more tragic, but it was a fucking knife in the heart to me. My best friend had filled his pockets with stones, and walked into the sea sober, and he knew what he was doing, and he wanted it, and he'd done it in the middle of the night, just a few hours after leaving me, hours before I found him.

And he'd planned it all.

Everything changed that day. Sean had been desperate for so long ... we all knew ... I knew, but somehow I'd just stopped seeing. He was crazy Sean, mad bastard Sean, party animal—angry, sad and lost Sean.

But because he'd had his surfboard with him it was filed away as an 'accidental drowning'. I never said anything, not to his family, not to my family, not to our friends. I never said anything at all, because even if I was a coward, I wasn't a liar.

Julia and Ben came to the funeral.

Marcus didn't. You see, summer was nearly over and he was moving on, chasing the next wave, the next woman, the next high.

"Sorry, man," he said. "But I didn't really know him that well."

Jonno was there at the funeral, Frank too, standing with a group of our surfer friends, uncomfortable in shirts and ties, avoiding the blurred eyes of Sean's family, his mother weak and inconsolable.

For the second time that summer, Yansi held my hand while someone I loved was laid to rest: stupid fucking phrase.

We have come here today to remember before God our brother Sean; to give thanks for his life; to commend him to God our merciful redeemer and judge; to commit his body to the ground, and to comfort one another in our grief.

And his mom cried.

We have but a short time to live. Like a flower we blossom and then wither.

And his father cried.

We have entrusted our brother Sean to God's mercy, and we now commit his body to the ground: earth to earth, ashes to ashes, dust to dust.

I looked up and saw Camille standing by herself. She nodded to me and looked like she wanted to say something, but then she shook her head and walked away.

What did they think, these people standing around a hole in the ground, filled with dust and dreams? Were they remembering, wondering? A boy, a man, a kid who surfed? The joker, the laugher, the lover, the sinner ... the suicide? No, that was just me. Just me.

And when we got to the end of the service, his family threw flowers into the grave.

And I threw a pebble.

I threw a pebble.

Lacey wasn't there. I heard after that her family had taken her away.

Yansi didn't let go of my hand the whole time. She kept looking at me, staring at me, willing me to speak, to say something. But I couldn't, because the huge lie burned every word that I tried to force out of my mouth.

I felt like I was watching everything through a thick pane of one-way glass, like I was observing grief from a distance. Again.

Mr. and Mrs. Wallis didn't speak to me at the funeral, but Aidan came across and hugged me, his face broken and lined. Even Patrick murmured a greeting, and Dylan shook my hand and said 'thank you'.

Thank you for coming? Thank you for standing at the side of my dead brother's coffin? Thank you for finding his body? Thank you for watching him fuck his life up and do nothing to stop him?

Yeah. You're welcome.

They had a gathering at Sean's house after. I didn't want to go. Julia said I should, but I couldn't see the point. Ben said I shouldn't go if I didn't want to. They started yelling at each other, so I said I'd go, just to shut them up. Because that's what you do, isn't it? For your family, for your friends—you do things you don't want to do. Or maybe you do what you're supposed to do, to fit in, to be like them, not stand out.

I stood in Sean's dining room, staring at the plates piled with food. Mrs. Wallis had hired caterers. That seemed wrong, somehow. But judging another person's way of grieving is like trying to wear their shoes.

She'd hired waiters, too. They looked like us in their black pants and white shirts. Only their black bow ties marked them out as *the staff*.

"Should I get you some food?"

Yansi tugged at my hand.

"Nick, should I get you some food?" she repeated.

I shook my head and walked away, leaving her standing in the middle of the room. Tears hung like diamonds in her eyes, but she didn't cry, and I didn't try to comfort her. There was nothing left inside me for that.

So I walked away.

I watched the people here, eating, talking, laughing, joking, remembering. Sean, the class clown: that was the one they seemed to remember the most.

I watched his parents, moving with measured steps around the room, wearing their pain like a winter coat in summer: a word here, a half-smile there; his brothers, silent and serious.

Did they ever wonder? In their quietest hour? In their darkest thoughts? Did they think of the strange coincidence that their son, their brother, who'd knocked up a girl, and believed them when they said he'd have to drop out of school, did they ever wonder how desperate he really was? It was safer to blame the ocean. Easier. But did they wonder?

Finally, it was over, and I was allowed to leave and try to breathe again. When we arrived back home, Marcus was gone. All his things had been packed up and the room was empty.

It was like ... I don't know ... as if ... as if I'd been as seduced by him as Camille and all those other women. By the way he lived, by the way he moved on, leaving a memory, like the scent of cinnamon rolls at the edge of a dream. A footprint in the sand, washed away by the tide, just like all the people who'd wanted to call him their friend.

I realized something ... that I'd never really known him. He only showed you what he wanted you to see. Julia said that was a shell person because there wasn't anything else there. Maybe she was right. I don't know. He must have had his reasons. He didn't get connected—like he always said, whatever I chose to do, it was my life.

Or death.

I didn't blame Marcus for moving on, not really. Shit had got real, and Marcus spent his life avoiding that. Sean had been drowning for a long time, I just never saw it. So if anyone was to blame, it was me.

But I didn't want to be like Marcus either. Not anymore. I didn't want to be the man who left people behind.

So yeah, life is black and white, but there's a whole load of colors in between.

I don't want to be the bastard asshole that leaves people because life is shitty and difficult and all the colors that aren't black and white.

Julia stared at the empty room.

"That didn't take long. Oh well. I'd better put another ad on Craigslist. I think I'll ask for a girl this time." Ben raised his eyebrows, and Julia muttered, "Or maybe not."

"I'm going for a surf," I said.

Julia frowned. "But you're going to drive Yansi home first?"

Before I could reply, Yansi said, "That's okay thanks, Julia. I'll wait here for him."

"What for?"

The room fell silent and everyone stared at me.

"Nick, that's a bit rude," Julia said quietly.

Ben tugged on her arm, pulling her toward the kitchen.

"Let them work it out," he said as he closed the door, leaving us alone.

Yansi stared at me. She was trying to look angry, but

her lip was trembling. Just what I didn't need—more fucking emotion.

"I'll drive you home," I said.

But before I could pick up Julia's keys from the table, Yansi grabbed them and threw them out of the open window.

"What the fuck did you do that for?" I snapped.

"God, Nick! Just *talk* to me, please!" she cried out.

"I've got nothing to say."

She grabbed my arm. "Stop it! This isn't you!"

I shook her off. "Jesus, Yansi! Call your dad, or get Julia to give you a ride. Just leave me the fuck alone!"

I stormed off up the stairs to my room, furious and frustrated when I heard her following me.

She slammed the door shut, so we were trapped in my room. I felt caged and tried to move her out of the way, but she gripped my arms and wouldn't let go.

"It's not your fault!" she began, her lips trembling.

"Get the fuck off me!" I shouted.

"No! You have to listen to me! It wasn't your fault!"

"Get off!"

I tore her arms free and tried to push past her, but she grabbed hold of the door handle and wouldn't move.

"It wasn't your fault!" she screamed. "It was just a stupid accident!"

Something broke inside me, and I yelled back.

"It wasn't a fucking accident!"

She gasped and her eyes went wide. "What?"

"I've got to go," I begged her, running my hands through my hair, tugging at the roots.

"Nick, what? What do you mean it wasn't an accident? Tell me!"

Defeated and desperate, I slumped onto the bed. "It just wasn't," I choked out. "It wasn't an accident."

She sat next to me, her eyes huge and unhappy. "What do you mean?"

"I mean, Sean killed himself. He wanted to die."

I couldn't control it anymore as the words ripped out of me.

"What? But…? How … how do you know? Did he leave you a note?"

"No," I said, my voice cracking. "He filled his pockets with stones and then he walked into the ocean."

Her face froze in shock.

"But … I don't understand. The police said it was accidental…"

She clasped her hand over her mouth, and I knew she understood.

"He was so fuckin' scared—about being a father, about everything. He just wanted out. He told me that. I thought … I thought he meant just check out for a while, you know? Not … not *this!*"

I closed my eyes in despair—thinking about the last few times we'd talked, remembering everything he'd said.

"That's why he wanted me to meet him that morning," I whispered. "He wanted me to find him. Just me."

Yansi pressed her arms around my neck as I began to cry.

"Oh my God," she gasped over and over again. "Oh God, Nick. I'm so sorry, baby. No wonder…"

"I keep thinking, what if he changed his mind? What if he was struggling to breathe and…"

I couldn't finish the sentence, but Yansi's hands were around me, pulling me in closer, holding me tighter.

She held me for a long time, until there was nothing left, not even tears. Then she pushed me gently, so I was lying on the bed, and she curled into my side, still holding me.

"Why didn't you tell me before?" she asked, her voice shaky.

I shrugged, not meeting her eyes.

"Nick?"

I sighed and stared at the ceiling. "Because he didn't

want anyone to know and … because of the Catholic thing … about suicide."

"Oh," she said softly. There was a long pause. "I'll pray for his soul."

There was an even longer pause before I replied.

"Okay."

I felt her hand grip my fingers, and I turned my head to look at her.

"You're not going to tell anyone, are you," she said, and it wasn't a question.

"No," I shook my head. "It's not what he wanted."

"Are you sure?"

"Yeah, I'm sure."

And I was. And sometimes I hated Sean for laying that on me, but I guess I understood, too. He didn't hate his family; all he'd ever wanted was their approval. I knew that now.

"Okay," Yansi said softly.

We lay there as the light faded and the shadows crept across the floor, the Earth spinning into the future, the day dying.

I don't know how long we'd been lying there—I think Yansi had been sleeping. My eyes were dry from staring at the ceiling, but I didn't want to move because that would make everything real.

I heard voices outside, then footsteps on the stairs. There was a light tap on the door.

"Nicky?"

Julia's voice was hesitant.

"Yeah?"

I sat up, my eyes sore, my body sluggish, and my brain too exhausted to function.

"Can you come to the door?" she whispered.

I stood up and pulled the door open.

"Oh," she said when she saw me, and I knew she was taking in my rumpled clothes and the black tie still knotted around my neck. "Sorry," she said quietly, "but Yansi's dad is here. I didn't know what to tell him…"

"We fell asleep. What time is it?"

"After ten."

"Shit, I didn't realize. Is he mad?"

"It's hard to tell," she admitted, and that forced a small smile onto my face.

"Yeah, he's kind of hard to read."

Then Yansi's voice sounded from the bed. "Is Papi here?"

"Yes, honey," Julia said apologetically. "He's waiting for you in the kitchen."

Yansi nodded. "Okay, I'm coming."

We walked down the stairs hand in hand. When I saw Mr. Alfaro, I could tell immediately that he was angry, but his face softened as he saw us.

"Your mother has been worried about you," he said to Yansi.

"I know, Papi. I'm sorry. But I needed to be here."

He nodded slowly, then stretched out his hand to my shoulder.

"We are sorry for your loss," he said.

Then he wrapped his arm around Yansi, nodded at Julia, and turned to leave.

Yansi paused just before she reached the door, and she smiled. Her lips moved, sending me a silent message.

I love you.

And that made it a little bit okay.

Chapter 13

"You know what? Sean would have hated that fucking funeral!"

It was four days before school started and I was still ranting. Yansi was watching me patiently, as she'd done for the last two weeks. Well, almost patiently. She'd heard the same thing several times now, but it was an itch I couldn't scratch and it got to me.

I knew he'd have really hated the pretentious crap at the gathering afterwards. Suit jackets and fucking ties—he hated all of that. That was what his mom and dad wanted; it wasn't what he would have wanted. And that's what bugged me—even now, Sean didn't get to have it done *his* way.

Yansi smothered her yawn. I guess being the supportive girlfriend came with an expiration date. I could tell I was nearing it. It wasn't that she didn't care, but I kept on going over the same old ground, never making any progress.

"So what *would* he have liked?" she challenged me. "You said the only things he ever really enjoyed were surfing and screwing. Maybe you should plan a mass orgy on the beach—check two boxes off at once."

"Yeah," I grinned at her. "That sounds like a plan. I'm up for it."

"You're always up for it," she whispered, a warm breath across my cheek that made me shiver.

It was true. We hadn't had a chance to have sex again. I was allowed to see Yansi, but she was still banned from being at my house alone with me; at her house, we never got any private time at all. We were working on it. But damn, it left me feeling horny as hell.

But it made me feel ashamed, too. Not because of the sex, but because I was ashamed of being happy; ashamed for feeling anything positive now that Sean was gone. Well, flashes of feeling good, but at other times, all I wanted was to be alone—foul tempered, exploding without warning.

I knew it made no sense, and I knew that Sean would call me on it and say I was being a whiny pussy. And Mom … she would have just wanted me to be happy. But how could I be happy when I'd lost both of them? Sometimes I forgot, and then I could allow myself to feel the good stuff. It was confusing.

Yansi's question made me think: what *would* Sean have liked? And then the answer came to me.

"We could have a paddle-out," I said, although it sounded more like a question, with my voice curving up at the end.

It was a surfers' tradition, I guess you could say, to honor a fallen comrade. Everyone took a board and paddled out on a calm day, forming a circle on the ocean—maybe bring flowers or say a few words. I hadn't figured that part out yet, but I thought it was something Sean would have liked. Guy always did enjoy being the center of attention.

"Oh! That's a great idea!" agreed Yansi, a huge grin lighting her face. "He'd really like that." Then she kissed me quickly, because we were at her house again, and

Beatriz and Pilau were sitting on the floor in front of us watching TV. "See! I knew you were more than just a pretty face—that's brilliant!"

I relaxed into a smile, and it was okay—it felt like it was allowed.

With school starting in four days, I didn't have much time to pull things together. The first thing I had to do was speak to his parents. I wasn't looking forward to that.

I'd finished working for Mr. Alfaro, although he asked me if I'd be interested in working Saturdays when school started. The Sandbar were cutting my hours now it was the end of the season, so I'd need the money. I said yes.

We'd come to an agreement, I guess. He still didn't talk much, but he trusted me to get on with the work, and the slow, easy rhythm of the day suited me. And Yansi liked the way it hardened and sculpted my body, and as she was running her hands across my chest at the time, I wasn't dumb enough to pass up the opportunity to keep her interested.

I told Julia about the paddle-out first.

Her eyes got glassy and she hugged me hard enough to break a rib.

"I'll come, too," she said.

I was stunned. Julia hated going in the water because she said it made her hair frizz out or some shit.

"But you'll have to lend me one of your biggest surfboards—one that's got really good buoyancy, please."

"Sure thing, sis," I grinned at her.

She smiled back, but her lips turned down again. "We could take some flowers for Mom, too," she said quietly.

"Yeah," I nodded. "And she kinda loved Sean."

Julia laughed sadly. "Yes, she did. Although she said once that if she'd been his mom, she'd have tanned his hide for some of the stunts you two pulled together."

"You're talking about the saran wrap in the staff restrooms stunt, aren't you—back in ninth grade? We'd planned to do the whole school, but we got caught before we'd finished."

Julia raised her eyebrows and shook her head, but she was smiling again. "That was one of the times, yeah."

Sean's parents were surprised to see me, and even more surprised when I put my suggestion or request or whatever the fuck it was to them.

I was just glad that they weren't yelling at me. I thought they might have.

"Will anyone come?" asked Mr. Wallis.

I blinked, not having expected that question.

"Well, yeah," I said, kind of stunned that he'd asked that. "Sean was real popular."

Mrs. Wallis gasped, and put her hand to her chest. "He was? Sean was popular?"

"Yeah," I said quietly. "He was always laughing— always joking around, you know? He was kind of a goofball, but he made people happy."

She swallowed several times, then looked at her husband with an odd expression halfway between smiling and tears.

"Oh," she said softly. "That's good."

"Yeah, he was a good guy." I took a deep breath. "He was my best friend."

Mr. Wallis clapped me on the shoulder. "Thank you for doing this. I think … I think Sean would have liked it."

On the way out of their house, I ran into Patrick. When I told him the plan, he immediately said he'd tell his brothers and see if they could fly back for it. Then he looked at me and frowned.

"The house is so quiet without that little prick. Who knew I'd miss him so much?" He shook his head. "And

I'm so fucking mad at him for drowning in three foot waves. It really sucks."

"Yeah," I said, "I know."

Paddle-out day was set for Sunday at sunset.

Word had spread quickly and it looked like most of the high school was going to be there, along with some of the teachers, all the guys who surfed, plus friends of Sean's brothers and his family, and, well, just about everyone we knew.

We were doing it Hawaiian style because Sean would have thought that was cool. Julia asked the local florist if they could make some leis for any of our friends who might want them, and then started crying again because the lady said she'd make them at cost. I guess death brings out the best in some people. That's a joke. Well, it would have made Sean laugh.

Yansi said she'd taken care of getting some leis for us.

Then she scared the fuck out of me because she said, "Have you decided what you're going to say?"

"Huh?"

"Nick, you're organizing this—people will expect you to say a few words."

"You're shitting me!"

She wrapped her arms around my neck and pulled me in for a hug, ignoring her brother's disapproving glare.

"You were his best friend," she said, trying to calm me down. "Just say whatever you think he'd like."

"Such as? I don't know what you're supposed to say at these kind of things."

"Just say something about him. You know, his good points. Some funny stuff. Anything that comes to mind."

"He'd laugh his fuckin' ass off," I muttered.

"You'll think of something," she said soothingly.

If that was supposed to be comforting, it wasn't. I'd just sort of figured that we'd paddle out, form a circle, someone would say a few words, and we'd throw the flowers into the water. It never occurred to me that I'd be expected to say anything.

I couldn't sleep that night. I lay in bed listening to the sound of the waves lapping against the beach, quiet, peaceful. When it was like this, it was hard to believe that the surf could rise into monsters higher than a two-story house and come breathing salty smoke, thundering onto the sand.

It was even harder to believe that the beach where I'd grown up and lived and fallen in love, that it was the same place Sean had died. I didn't know how to feel about that.

I thought again about the two things that he'd really enjoyed in life. I couldn't say anything about fucking, even though Sean would have gotten a laugh out of that, so I'd have to speak about surfing.

And then I remembered something we'd read in English class once. I think it was the only time I saw Sean pay attention.

I got up and padded down to the kitchen, then fired up our cranky laptop. I surfed a few sites before I found what I wanted. Then I printed it out and took it upstairs with me.

I must have slept after that, because when I woke up the sun was bright and the air was sticky and humid, and even though school was starting back the next day, it was hotter than fuck and nothing like Fall—it felt like everything was ending, because summer break was over, but maybe it was just a beginning. I knew I was a different person now, for lots of reasons: Mom, Sean, Yansi, and maybe just being older, and my eyes wide open. I had now and I had tomorrow and I had a future—whatever that was going to be—and I was okay with that.

Julia spent the day doing school work and filling out forms and all the shit that went with her job as a teacher assistant. I did a couple of loads of laundry, and then Julia shoved some money in my hand and told me to do the grocery shopping. Plus she gave me an extra $10 to go crazy, providing I got everything on the list first.

Yansi came over after an early supper, carrying two beautiful garlands. One was made up of purple and white flowers, the other red and yellow.

"Papi made these leis for you," she said quietly.

"Wow, that's … that's great. Thank him for me?"

She smiled and brushed a soft kiss over my lips.

"I think he'd like it if you thanked him yourself."

I nodded. "Okay."

By 7 o'clock, my stomach was tied in knots, and I was almost shaking with nerves at the thought of speaking in front of a bunch of people.

Yansi kept rubbing circles on my back, soothing me as I was a wild animal about to bolt.

And I really wanted to.

Instead, I passed her my smallest shortboard, and pulled out a longboard for Julia and another for myself. Ben had resurrected a surfboard he'd used when he was still in high school, and Julia frowned at him when he started brushing cobwebs off it in the middle of the kitchen.

We secured all the boards to the roof rack of Ben's car and headed down to the pier.

Yansi looped the lei around her neck and Julia carried the other one; the scent of the flowers filled the car.

As we got closer to the pier, the crowds were thicker and I nearly puked my guts out when I saw the number of people who were gathered underneath the pier, as well as the small knot standing at the end by the fisherman's hut.

"Jeez," Ben breathed, "there must be 500 or 600 people here."

"More than that," Julia stated.

Yansi grabbed my hand. "You'll be fine," she whispered.

I nodded automatically, even though I felt anything but fine. I checked again that I'd got my ziplock bag around my waist with the paper that I'd printed out last night folded inside.

"I think we'd better park here," Ben said. "We'll never get any closer by car. Looks like we're walking the rest of the way."

We unloaded the boards and dumped our clothes in the car. Seeing Yansi's body in her cute yellow bikini was a welcome distraction. Even so, my mouth was like a freakin' desert, and I wasn't sure I'd be able to get any words out at all.

We started walking down to where everyone was waiting. It was the weirdest feeling as the crowds parted to let us through. I saw Sean's brothers right away, and Aidan came across, pulling me into a tight hug.

"Thanks for organizing this, man," he said. "It means a lot to Mom and Dad." He pointed to the end of the pier. "They're waiting up there. They were stunned when they saw the number of people who turned out."

"Yeah, me too," I croaked. "Sean would have been stoked."

He smiled sadly. "Yeah. I can't believe he fucking drowned in three feet waves. I taught him better than that. I thought I did…"

I looked away, but Aidan didn't seem to notice.

"I guess we'd better get going," he said.

Yansi came up and took my hand.

"You can do it," she whispered.

I took a deep breath and walked down to the water's edge, feeling the cooler sand beneath my feet. When the water was at waist height, I slid onto my board and started paddling.

Yansi, Julia and Ben were on one side of me, with Aidan, Patrick and Dylan on the other.

When we reached near the end of the pier, we started to form a loose circle. It took over 10 minutes for everyone to paddle out.

We sat there, a quiet murmur wrapping around the splashes as the last few found their places. There were so many people, we had to form two circles rather than just one.

Finally, when everyone was situated, we all joined hands. The murmuring fell away and Yansi looked at me and smiled.

"You're on," she whispered.

I had to let go of her hand to pull the piece of paper out of my ziplock, nearly dropping the darn thing into the sea. There was a ripple of laughter as I almost overbalanced.

I cleared my throat several times, and then spoke.

"Sean was a giant pain in the ass."

Everyone laughed, and it made me even more nervous. I looked across to Yansi and she smiled at me encouragingly.

"I'm not sure Sean ever read a book, a whole book all the way through," I stated, as more laughter rippled out, "but I think he'd have liked these words by Jack London. He wrote them back in 1911…

> " 'The whole method of surf-riding and surf-fighting, I learned, is one of non-resistance. Dodge the blow that is struck at you. Dive through the wave that is trying to slap you in the face. Sink down, feet first, deep under the surface, and let the big smoker that is trying to smash you go by far overhead. Never be rigid. Relax. Yield yourself to the waters that are ripping and tearing at you. When the undertow catches you and drags you seaward along the bottom, don't struggle against it. If you do, you are liable to be drowned, for it is stronger than you. Yield yourself to that undertow. Swim with it, not against it, and you will find the pressure removed. And, swimming with it, fooling

it so that it does not hold you, swim upward at the same time'."

My voice faltered and I had to take a deep breath before I could continue.

" *'It will be no trouble at all to reach the surface'.*"

There was silence among the crowd of people, just the soft slap of water against our boards. I swallowed the lump in my throat as I folded the piece of paper.

"I never thought I'd be doing this," I said, my cracked voice carrying across the water as the sun dipped toward the river in the west, and the sky darkened around us. "I never thought I'd be saying goodbye to Sean. I thought he'd always be there. And I didn't get to say goodbye, so I'm going to say it now. Sean, buddy, thank you for everything you have ever done for me. For being there for me, for listening to what I say, for making sure I'm okay. I'll never forget you till my last breath. I love you, man."

Yansi gripped my hand, tears trickling down her cheeks.

She passed me the lei that she'd worn, and I threw it into the center of the circle. Julia did the same, and I knew that was for Mom. Everyone tossed in leis or small bouquets, and from the pier, flowers rained down from all the people who hadn't been able to paddle out with us.

In our own way we each said goodbye.

Yansi squeezed my hand.

"You did great, baby. I love you."

I nodded, but I couldn't speak. I'd said enough words today.

I didn't get much choice though, because dozens of people stopped to talk to me as I walked back up the beach. Each one had a story they wanted to share about Sean. Some were laughing quietly, several of the girls were crying (which I couldn't help thinking Sean would have liked a lot), and most of the adults said something, like it was a darn shame and such a waste. I had to agree with that.

Sean's mom and dad came down onto the sand from where they'd been watching on the pier, and I saw them wiping their eyes several times. I was glad they'd come; I was glad they'd finally learned that Sean was a good guy who was liked, loved, by a lot of people—even if it was too late.

His dad shook my hand. "Thank you," he said.

It looked like he was trying to say more, but in the end he put his arm around Sean's mom and they walked away, their heads bowed.

It took me an hour to get back to the car, but Julia and Ben were waiting for me.

Julia pulled me into a tight hug.

"Mom would have been so proud of you," she said. "I am, too."

It was dark by the time we drove home and unloaded the boards. The sky had turned purple, and stars were filling the night with diamond points of light.

A small piece of the weight that I'd be carrying fell away. *You should have been here, Sean. You shouldn't have given in.*

I guess I'd never really understand the decision he made; I hoped I never felt that desperate, that level of despair. Then Yansi's hand curled around mine, and the world was a little bit right again.

"Can you come in for a while?" I begged, not willing to let her go yet.

She smiled, although her face was touched with sadness.

"Of course. Mami and Papi aren't expecting me for a couple of hours."

We walked upstairs hand in hand, and it seemed completely natural when we kicked off our flip-flops and lay on my bed, our bodies wrapped around each other.

"You did good today," Yansi said, her voice soft. "I think Sean would have liked it. I can't believe how many people showed up. I was watching his mom and dad. I think it really helped them. Did it help you?" she asked, stroking my shoulder.

"I don't know if anything helps, but yeah, it felt right to say goodbye."

Her arm moved around to my back, and even that feather light touch was enough to start my body getting worked up.

I knew she could feel me getting hard, and I started to move her hand away; it seemed kind of disrespectful when we'd just come from Sean's memorial. And then I heard his voice in my head.

Don't be a douche, man! She's hot for it. You want to nail that while you can!

The thought made me smile.

"What?" asked Yansi, her hand resting under my t-shirt just below my shoulder blade.

"I was thinking what Sean would say if he could see us right now."

Yansi scrunched up her nose. "Oh God, what a thought!" and she giggled. "But he'd probably be telling us to go for it, too."

I laughed a little. "Yeah, I think he would have approved."

She paused for a moment, then her face pressed against my chest. "What are you waiting for?" she asked, her voice lower now and totally fucking sexy.

That was all the permission I needed.

Yansi slid my t-shirt across my body, and I sat up, tugging it over my head. Her fingers trailed promises along my chest and stomach as I lay back down, a shiver making my whole body tremble, my eyelids fluttering closed, resting my hands above my head, surrendering to her, to love, to life, to tomorrow and the day after, and the next day and the next and the next.

Give me a lifetime of feeling this. Give me now and then and soon and when, and give me a future, give me life, give me hope.

My thoughts trail away and all I'm left with is sensation and touch and taste and her. All around me her, *and no one ever told me it would feel this good.*

My breath stutters in my chest as her warm lips kiss their way down my body, pausing to bite and tease my nipples, until my breath is ragged and sharp.

Her waist feels small and soft as my work-roughened hands drag across her skin, her breasts cool at the surface from the damp bikini, hot underneath as her blood rushes and trembles, turning her sweet caramel nipples to dark chocolate. Her t-shirt goes up and off, and her bikini top goes down and away, and I lean up on my elbows to touch and taste and make love to my girl.

I'm making love. Because we can and we want it and we need it; it heals us and fills us and saves us; a little crazy and a lot in love, because we can, because it's us and the world still spins and the tide still falls, and the universe around us is too large and too dark, the stars pinned against the blackness, tiny points of light and hope. And that's us, holding back the dark from this room, holding it away with arms of love because it's so fucking fine, and blood throbs in my veins, and beats through my heart, and it's her and hope and being here and living for now.

And we fight a little and struggle a little and laugh a lot as our clothes fall away, and it's just us and skin and sheets and the misty future which is a lot like hope.

And the heated center of me is my heart and my dick, and she takes both, or I give them, or we meet half way, because she gave her heart to me, too. And her center shimmers and ripples above me, and she slides down my shaft, her soft moans shooting through my brain and across my skin and my cock pulsing inside her.

A slow trickle of sweat runs down her neck, pooling in the hollow of her collar bone and I trace it with my finger as her eyes full of fire and love and questions and answers gaze down at me as our bodies rock together.

"I love you too much, cariño," she whispers, the words a soft moan.

And our bodies move together, heated in the night, blood boiling and rising, promises made and given, and love and sex and here and now, and her cries mingle with my tears, and she brushes them away with her fingers, my lips turning upward in a smile.

"I love you more than that," I reply, because it's true and it's cheesy and it's us and it makes her smile and makes me laugh, and we laugh for joy because we're here and we're alive and we have now and this moment, and we'll take tomorrow, and the day after, and the next day and the next and the next.

So, on the day I said goodbye to my friend, I got to make love to my beautiful girlfriend, too. Like I said, I think Sean would have approved.

Epilogue

School started up the next day.

It was strange—I kept expecting to see him or hear him or find him leaning against my locker.

It hurt so bad when I remembered that would never happen again.

Sometimes I felt like giving up, but I didn't. I studied hard enough to get mostly Bs—and an A in Spanish—and I thought about going to college.

Every Saturday, I worked with Mr. Alfaro, and I kept my job bussing tables and washing dishes at the Sandbar one or two evenings a week, saving my money, planning ahead.

Every now and then I heard someone mention Marcus—last heard of in Bali, or maybe it was Fiji. Nobody talked about Sean, not his name anyway, just 'that kid who drowned'.

I never corrected them. I never said anything at all. After a while, no one remembered that he'd been my best friend. Except me.

I surfed alone and I didn't hang out at the pier anymore. I missed it, and I didn't.

Yansi and I were good, mostly. A year later, we graduated together, wearing the dumb graduation gowns and our Cocoa Beach High School medals.

No one thought we'd still be together after all this time, high school sweethearts and shit. We did break up once, but after a couple of weeks neither of us could stand being apart any longer.

Now we're going away to college together. Like Marcus, as it turned out. Guy had a degree in Marine Biology. He never said.

Julia and Ben got engaged. They're still not married. They're waiting. What are they waiting for? *Don't wait for life*, that's what I want to tell them; that's what I've learned. But I don't. Because maybe you have to learn that for yourself.

Maybe Julia's way is right for Julia. I don't understand her, but that's okay, because I don't need to understand her to love my sister. I had to learn that, too. But it's okay. We're okay.

Rob is taking a year to go traveling: Europe, surfing Indonesia, other places.

I didn't want to go. It was something I'd planned to do with Sean, so it just doesn't feel right to go with anyone else.

But I have another reason—I'm afraid that if I start traveling I'll never stop. And I know that will have a cost—not just me, but Yansi and my sister, too. And I know it, because a part of me *is* like him, like Marcus. Camille was right about that, but she was wrong too, because I can choose. I can make that choice *not* to be like him.

I choose to live in the world with the people that I love. And I still have a life to live—I just don't know what that's going to be. Not yet. But I'm hopeful.

I've gotten a little further with my dream of being a shaper and selling my own surfboard designs. Yansi talked me into studying Business at college so I'd have a better chance of making that dream come true. She's good at that—making me see that I could really do things, do more than just dream.

I feel Yansi's grip tighten and her thumb rubs over the back of my hand as I stare down at the grave. It's covered with grass now, smooth, vivid green grass. I guess even cemeteries have sprinkler systems.

The flowers we left are long gone, but someone still comes here—his mother, his brothers, maybe his dad. Someone comes, but the people who loved him, we all remember.

So I stare down and the memories rush back. Good, good times.

Bad times.

Worse times.

And I remember.

Sean Wallis

September 25th 1997 to July 22nd 2014
Son, brother, friend

Taken too soon

"Are you ready?" Yansi asks.

My car is parked at the front of the cemetery, packed, ready for us to go, new lives, college students, on the other side of the country.

It'll be some road trip to Southern California. But I had to be near the ocean. And I owe it to Sean not to be small-town either.

I look up and smile at her. I smile.

"Yeah, I'm ready."

Because summer is over and it's time to go.
And you've got to grow up some time.
Right?

POEM FOR SEAN

Sea Fever

I must go down to the seas again, to the lonely sea and the sky,
And all I ask is a tall ship and a star to steer her by,
And the wheel's kick and the wind's song and the white sail's
shaking,
And a grey mist on the sea's face and a grey dawn breaking.

I must go down to the seas again, for the call of the running tide
Is a wild call and a clear call that may not be denied;
And all I ask is a windy day with the white clouds flying,
And the flung spray and the blown spume, and the sea-gulls
crying.

I must go down to the seas again, to the vagrant gypsy life,
To the gull's way and the whale's way where the wind's like a
whetted knife;
And all I ask is a merry yarn from a laughing fellow-rover,
And quiet sleep and a sweet dream when the long trick's over.

John Masefield (1878-1967)

ABOUT THE AUTHOR

"Love all, trust a few, do wrong to none"—this is one of my favourite sayings. Oh, and 'Be Nice!' That's another. Or maybe, 'Where's the chocolate?'

I get asked where my ideas come from—they come from everywhere. From walks with my dog on the beach, from listening to conversations in pubs and shops, where I lurk unnoticed with my notebook. And of course, ideas come from things I've seen or read, places I've been and people I meet.

My little Jack Russell named 'Pip' is nearly 12 years old as I write this. She brings me so much joy, and many of my ideas come when I'm taking her for walks on the beach. Her calm, unconditional friendship is very special—as all dog owners know and understand. That's why this book is dec

Reviews

Reviews are love! Honestly, they are! But it also helps other people to make an informed decision before buying my book.

So I'd really appreciate if you took a few seconds to do just that at the following link www.amazon.com.

Thank you!

Don't forget to claim your free book!

My acclaimed novella *Playing in the Rain* was featured in Huffington Post's list of Top Ugly Cry Reads!

You'll receive it for **free** when you sign up to my **newsletter**. Easy peasy!

You'll also get a chapter each month of my serialized novel A BAD START about US Marine Jackson Connor and war correspondent MJ 'Maggie' Buckman, **exclusive** to **VIP newsletter readers** and completely **free**.

Sign up at **www.janeharveyberrick.com**

When I'm not in my writing cave, I can be found at the beach, watching surfers.

I love hearing from readers, so please do get in touch.

www.twitter.com/jharveyberrick
www.facebook.com/jane.harveyberrick
www.instagram.com/jharveyberrick
www.pinterest.com/jharveyberrick

Printed in Great Britain
by Amazon